SIGNAL FAILURES

Signal Failures is set against a background of Union Workhouses. The Act of 1834 that established them was passed with the intention that the inmates' lives should be less congenial than any but the most deprived existence on the outside. In physical terms this was quite difficult as absolute destitution was endured by many on the streets. The inmates were dehumanised; husbands were separated from wives, and all but the youngest children were taken from their mothers. The uniform was a badge of shame, those wearing it were despised and the institutions were universally feared by the respectable citizenry.

There was, however, education for workhouse children in district schools, and often they entered the world of employment better educated than those who'd scraped by on the outside. Whilst the workhouse was not a prison, and adults could leave at any time, provided they returned the uniform and took their dependants with them, a separate system was set up to cope with delinquent children. Entry was controlled by magistrates and, unlike the district schools which were financed locally, the reformatory schools were under the control of the Inspector of Prisons and financed by central government.

Much information has been gleaned from the works of Peter Higginbotham, who has written extensively on the subject of Union Workhouses and their inmates. His research and insights inform *Signal Failures*. Any mistakes are the author's responsibility. In the interest of the narrative it is suggested that the two types of school could be run as one. This was not the case in reality, though in time the distinction became blurred in the public's mind and changes were made to the reformatories in an attempt to correct this.

This book is a work of fiction and, other than certain public figures that are alluded to in passing, the characters and events in *Signal Failures* are entirely products of the author's imagination.

SIGNAL FAILURES

David J Boulton

Matador
9 Priory Business Park,
Wistow Road, Kibworth Beauchamp,
Leicestershire. LE8 0RX
Tel: 0116 279 2299
Email: books@troubador.co.uk
Web: www.troubador.co.uk/matador
Twitter: @matadorbooks

ISBN 978 1838590 062

British Library Cataloguing in Publication Data.
A catalogue record for this book is available from the British Library.

Printed and bound in Great Britain by 4edge Limited
Typeset in 11pt Adobe Garamond Pro by Troubador Publishing Ltd, Leicester, UK

Matador is an imprint of Troubador Publishing Ltd

Also by the same author

Sam Spray Series

Fatal Connections
Echoes Down the Line

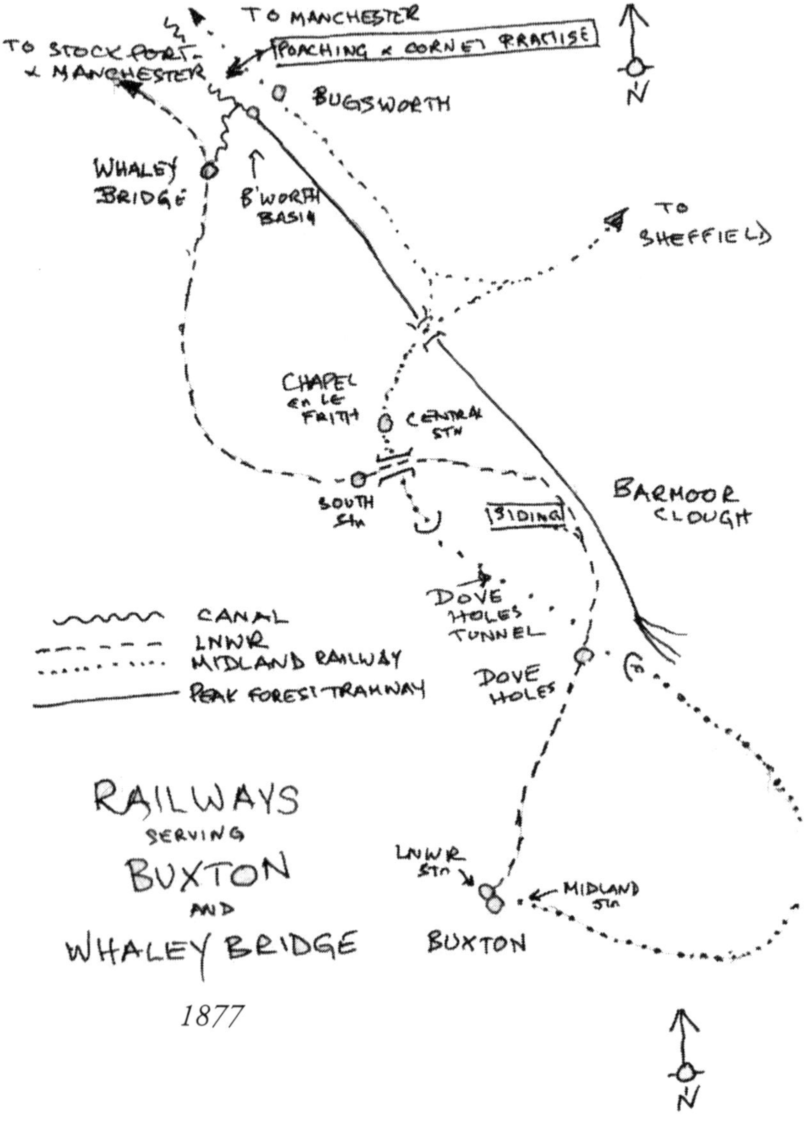

TO MANCHESTER

POACHING & CORNET PRACTISE

TO STOCKPORT & MANCHESTER

BUGSWORTH

N

WHALEY BRIDGE

B'WORTH BASIN

TO SHEFFIELD

CHAPEL en LE FRITH

CENTRAL STN

SOUTH Stn

BARMOOR CLOUGH

SIDING

DOVE HOLES TUNNEL

DOVE HOLES

CANAL

LNWR

MIDLAND RAILWAY

PEAK FOREST TRAMWAY

LNWR Stn

MIDLAND Stn

BUXTON

N

RAILWAYS SERVING BUXTON AND WHALEY BRIDGE

1877

PROLOGUE

THE LITTLE PACKET HAD PASSED THROUGH MANY HANDS, not all of them kind. Making the journey to its present resting place was a miracle of sorts; not that the house of God had done much to help.

Inside, the knobbly collection of beads gathered around a crucifix and formed an unappetising brown lump. Mrs Pincher stretched them out and mused sadly on their residual power so long after the Church had washed its hands of the rosary's owner. It had lain alongside an envelope which, over the years, had become dented and creased by its unforgiving companion. It was addressed to a regimental headquarters somewhere in the Far East.

Written in a neat, educated hand, in ink that had faded with the years, it fascinated Mrs Pincher. She wondered how long it had lain in the packet with the rosary, and why it had never been posted. Most of her charges arrived with nothing and the orphanage expected little else. The children were born into destitution and would mostly perish there despite her best efforts. Perhaps it was the price of postage to such a faraway place. There must have been money at some stage – it cost to acquire a hand such as had written that address, she mused.

Emmeline Pincher's stern, unflinching manner was, she felt, a necessary adjunct to her life's journey. After all, she represented the official view that the poor who could not support themselves were, by definition, undeserving, and their issue were no better. Her own descent to their level was an ever-present threat, should she lose her position. Her harshness was her protection.

But… but inside there was a void, and a yearning to fill it with something softer. Somehow the child that had been abandoned with the packet had crept into the emotional vacuum that was the matron's heart, and was making itself a home of sorts.

PART 1

ONE

Monday Morning, 30th April 1877

THE FIRST MAIL DELIVERY OF THE DAY WAS TIMED TO arrive before the occupants of the office. In the makeshift accommodation that housed the recently established Manchester branch of the London & North-Western Railway Constabulary, there was no box to collect letters as they arrived. Scattered on the floor, they proved an obstruction to opening the door, and Sergeant Spray had to squeeze his arm through a narrow gap and scrabble around to clear it.

By the time he'd gained entry to his newly acquired domain he was holding much of the day's post in his hand. He wasn't entirely comfortable with his new duties and dealing with correspondence on a daily basis was his least favourite chore. Under the old regime it had been Superintendent Wayland's responsibility but now, in charge of an outpost further north in Stockport, Spray was getting his share.

The incongruity of calling this new establishment the 'Manchester office' and then locating it in a town six miles to the south of the city was not lost on Sam Spray, but it was a matter of suitable accommodation. Not that the poky room that he'd been given on Edgeley Station had much to commend it. The smell of damp paper and mouse urine lingered despite the spoiled documents and their attendant droppings being removed weeks before.

The previous spring had all but overwhelmed the habitually unruffled detective. Everything had changed in the wake of a single unconsidered action. By his own estimation, it had been a failure. To have saved only one life when two were at risk had haunted him despite the obvious desire of the girl to put an end to herself and her innocent child. He had lunged forward to drag them from the parapet, only to find himself with a baby in his arms whilst her mother fell to her death in the raging torrent that was the River Goyt in flood.

Even as he berated himself for his failure, the warmth of the child snuggled beneath his greatcoat had given him a sensuous pleasure. By the time he'd arrived back at 37 Mill End and handed the little girl to his friend and widowed landlady, Mrs Elizabeth Oldroyd, he'd been captivated by the infant with her sweet baby smell, notwithstanding a dirty nappy. He was a changed man.

Not that the new man had appeared on the instant. There were less agreeable matters to settle first. Even as he was reporting to the town constable what had happened, and helping with the downstream search for the unfortunate girl's body, he was nursing a memory of the baby's warmth as she had nestled against his chest.

When he finally returned, cold and wet from the river, he'd first gone to gaze at the infant, now peacefully asleep, having been changed and given some pap by Lizzie. The two adults had stood quietly, and in the silence both had made the same resolve.

In an attempt to keep alive his detective skills, Sam tried to reason from their envelopes which of each day's letters were most important. He deemed the flimsy brown one, with *Royal Mail, Official* but no stamp in the top right corner, the least important and put it to the bottom of the pile. There'd been ongoing correspondence about deliveries to his new office occasioned by the 'Manchester' in the unit's name and its location in Stockport.

"Morning, Sergeant." Constable Archer, still living at home with his family, was allowed a little latitude to fit in with the morning train service from Crewe.

"Morning, Constable." The two had become friends as well as colleagues, and later would lapse into greater familiarity, but their first greeting of the day paid lip service to their superior officer's sensibilities. "Be with you in a minute." Sam slit open the last of the day's mail. "This won't take long."

The contents certainly had a connection with redirected mail, but not quite as the sergeant expected. Covered in addresses, each crossed out as the ageing letter had made its uncertain way around the British Empire, there had been no room to insert another destination by the time it had reached Manchester, hence the official envelope. Deciphering each stage in its journey would take some time, such was the confusion of tangled words. Sam went straight for the contents.

Afterwards he couldn't remember at what stage his embarrassment had begun to be felt, but by the time he'd finished and unravelled the full name of the intended recipient, he knew he should never have opened it.

Peover
12th May 1827

Dear Charlie,
Each day since sending you away I have cried for you. It was the most difficult thing I have ever had to do, but it seemed right for both of us at the time, what with the marvellous opportunity of your posting to India, and our family's objections. Faith is such a cruel master and it is even more cruel now I cannot hide my condition.

I did not know I was with child when we parted, so at least I was spared the agony of whether or not to tell you. Now, facing destitution, I will have another life to consider.

I intend to call her Charlotte if it is a girl baby and Charles if it is a boy. Even if you care no more for me, please think of your own flesh and blood.

In forlorn hope and love,
Beatrice

It had been addressed, all those years ago, to Ensign Charles Wayland, 1st Bengal Lancers, Regimental Headquarters, Delhi, India, but the first postal stamping on the outside was dated November 1875. Most difficult of all to decipher was a tiny postscript on the back of the envelope, the ink faded and overwritten:

Charles Appleton, b. 1st August.

"I can't, Sam, I just can't." Lizzie had kicked the snow from her feet and was taking off her coat in the hall. "They could barely speak to me."

The shawl, greying now, had seen much service over the years, initially having kept the infant Lizzie warm. Her mother had crocheted it whilst she was expecting, and then later it had been draped around the ailing woman's shoulders during her final bedridden months. It was as a memento of her mother that Lizzie had cherished it and now, resting against Sam's chest, it was taking on a new life wrapped around a baby girl.

"'Take it to the orphanage,' she said: that was the baby's great-aunt, but they were all the same, the whole of Mary's family," said Lizzie.

The baby whimpered, and for a moment Lizzie's indignation waned. Emotion of an altogether different quality welled up as she gazed at Sam nursing the little girl.

"It's to do with the suicide, and there being no father. The woman couldn't quite say the words, but she mumbled something about 'it being born in unforgivable sin'. She called this innocent scrap of life, 'it'!"

"Then she'd better have a name. Do you think we should call her after her mother?" Sam cuddled the child closer as he spoke.

Later, thinking back, Lizzie could hear the word 'we' changing things forever. At the time she had done no more than agree and go off to the kitchen, intent on making tea.

Sam sighed as he refolded the letter and replaced it in its envelope. If only he could go back to that untroubled age, only minutes past, when his biggest problem was remembering whether it was his or William's turn to make the tea.

He put the much-travelled and overwritten envelope back in the official Royal Mail one, but there matters came to rest.

"You look like you've been struck by lightning." William was busying himself with the tea. It was the one perk that came with the new arrangements: the fire. It drew well, with a swinging hook for the kettle and, best of all, a porter on early turn would light it before the policemen arrived for work. "Anything I can help you with?"

"This child needs more than a name, Lizzie; little Mary needs a home."

Silence… tentative on Sam's part, patient on Lizzie's. Neither a passive patience, nor a calculating one: perhaps optimistic would be the most accurate description.

"Loving parents mean more than anything to a child. I was luckier than you in that respect, Sam."

"I can't bear to think of her growing up without love." That had been Sam's lot in an orphanage and it had left scars.

The baby, stirring, made a gurgling noise, and would have continued to sleep, but Sam picked her up.

As the warmth of the infant's body seeped through his shirt it unlocked his reserve at last.

"Do you think we should make a home for her; you and I together?"

The moment had come, Lizzie knew it, and she also knew it would be fatal to giggle at the tortuous manner of the proposal, but it was a struggle.

As it was, Sam, wrapped up in his complicated emotions, heard only what he needed to.

"You mean we should...?"

"Yes, Lizzie, that is what I mean. We should marry and..." At last it was out. "And be together. Will you say yes?"

At the moment of their coming together it seemed to them both that the world was a beautiful place, full of new delights to be explored. Lizzie's acceptance had pierced the carapace behind which Sam hid his feelings, and seeing him emerge, like a moth from the cocoon, gave her the freedom to reveal her inner self. This period of mutual exposure, in all its rawness, lasted long enough for the formation of an indissoluble bond, so that when, inevitably, the complications of the real world reasserted themselves, they faced the future as one.

They had to wrestle with the matter of where they should marry.

"Father would like it to be in the chapel, but the minister hasn't spoken to me since..." They hadn't yet spoken of Lizzie's previous foray into matrimony.

"You decide, I'll agree."

TWO

Monday Afternoon, 30th April 1877

IT WAS NO GOOD, THE RESPONSIBILITY WAS HIS; IT WAS HE who'd opened the superintendent's letter. Inadvertent it may have been, but there was no denying he'd intruded into a most private corner of his senior officer's life. There was no help to be had from William. Sam was on his own.

"No thanks, William; it's something for the Whale. I'll take it to him later."

If the other man was surprised at the special journey, he didn't let on.

The last day of February was a Monday, and had started like every other. A trudge through the streets of Crewe to work, in a cold wind that reminded William that winter wasn't over yet.

"Can we have a quiet word?"

He and Sam had found themselves side by side as they neared the office on the station platform and Sam had something on his mind "Better show our faces first though."

There was nothing unusual in this, although William noted an unlikely spring in his sergeant's step. Later, though, when the conversation resumed, things were different.

"See here, William… Look, do you think you could…? You'd be just the man… I need a favour…"

"Yes, Sam, what do you want?"

"It's like this… We're getting married."

It was almost irresistible. What, you and me? William suppressed the riposte. "You mean you and Lizzie? Sam, that's wonderful. It makes me almost as happy as the two of you must be."

"We thought it for the best, Lizzie and I. Little Mary needs a respectable upbringing."

"Is that all you have to say about it? You've made the most important decision of your life so that orphan grows up respectable? Sam Spray, you're a fool." Later, William wondered at his presumption. "You and Lizzie were made for each other; you have been ever since you met. Have you any idea what it's been like watching you torture yourselves for the last year? You're marrying because you're in love, and the baby's lucky to be caught up in it."

"Oh, you see it like that? Perhaps you won't want to help me out, then. It doesn't matter, I suppose."

"Help out with what?"

"I need a best man. I thought perhaps…?"

It had taken quite a while to organise, despite there being no more than a handful of people on the list.

The first problem was where. Sam hadn't seen the need to attend church since his military service, when church parade had been obligatory. Even then he'd had no idea of what it all meant; the Quaker meetings of his childhood, simple and tranquil, were no preparation for the goings-on in an Anglican service.

Lizzie's family were Chapel, but their Wesleyan Nonconformism had not been to the taste of Albert Oldroyd and she had been married for the first time at St James's, Taxal, under the auspices of the Established Church. Then there was the Romish interest. Mary Thomas's family may have washed their hands of the child but there was no denying little Mary's connection. Providing a home for the infant had, after all, been the catalyst for the forthcoming celebration.

Lizzie rather wished Sam had an opinion: the responsibility weighed heavy. In the end relief had been found in New Mills and its register office. "It can't offend anybody," she reasoned. Then, as an afterthought, "Or possibly it'll upset everybody."

The spring morning didn't do anything for Sam's state of mind. It was cold, and in other moods he would have found the crisp, sunny weather invigorating. Not today. Perhaps he wasn't fit to take the kind of decisions that had led him into his current predicament? He'd always told himself he could hold his head high if he confronted the world square on. To this end he'd seen virtue in looking into every murky corner and beneath every suspicious stone that came his way.

If only… if only he'd been less eager, more circumspect, more professional about the letter before he'd opened it. With the whole thing still sealed in its flimsy, official Royal Mail packet it might have made today's journey alone, with no more than a covering note: *Sir, I think this requires your personal attention.* Sam could even now have been back in his office dealing with some comfortingly mundane problem of missing parcels. If only...

When *hadn't been difficult. The register office had offered a date and it had been accepted without more ado.*

Who *had turned into a quagmire.*

"Father can give me away, and you know William will stand by you, Sam." Both invitations would be accepted with alacrity. "It'll be simple with just the four of us. I'm sure Elsie will look after the baby. We should be back in under an hour."

In the office on Crewe Station, Constable Archer had been unable to contain himself, and before a day had passed it was known that the sergeant was to be wed. An embarrassed Sam endured encouraging words and slaps on the back aplenty. He never found out who had told the Whale, but the next morning there was a summons to the superintendent's office.

"I understand congratulations are in order, Sergeant. Mrs Oldroyd's the lady in question, I gather. A very sound choice if I'm any judge."

Sam had wondered if his superior officer had ever had cause to make any such judgement.

"Now, when is it to be?"

Elsie was happy to look after the baby, but had wondered if "it would be nice if little Mary was there?"

If Mary was to be there then so was Elsie, and if Elsie came then so would her husband, Fred... It went on until there were upwards of twenty-five people to be accommodated. Mary's family had all but ruled themselves out, but Sam and Lizzie had agreed to invite the baby's uncle.

Sam willed himself to open the carriage door and alight at Crewe. He ordered his legs to take him to Superintendent Wayland's office and, reluctantly, they did so.

"Morning, Sarge. Don't see much of you round these parts now." The desk constable went on cheerily, "Going well is it, with the little 'un an' all?"

Sam could only grunt. Afterwards it occurred to him that he'd left the man with an unduly bleak view of the state of his marriage.

"Come in."

This is it, thought Sam, *there's no turning back*. He pushed open his superior officer's door.

"Sergeant, this is a surprise; a pleasant one I may add, we haven't met since…"

It had been the walking that caused the biggest problem. Old Mr Bennett might just have made the distance; back in that moment of simplicity when only four people were to be present, Lizzie had been sure he could. But the superintendent would need transporting between New Mills and Whaley Bridge.

By the time Sam had left the Whale's office with his senior officer's congratulations ringing in his ears, it had been plain that an invitation to the wedding was expected. How to tell Lizzie that her plans were wrecked had exercised Sam's mind all the way to Whaley Bridge, but by the time he arrived Lizzie already had problems of her own.

In the end her philanthropy had provided a solution. "We could use the Reading Room, Sam. The gala tea was a great success in there. No one will mind, I'm sure."

The cost of the wedding had been immaterial when only four people were to be involved, but by now it was becoming a problem.

"We can't expect the Whale to ride in a farm cart, Sam. We'll have to do something better than that."

Nothing could be found in Whaley Bridge, but in the end a wagonette was hired from Bugsworth. Lizzie had been on the point of justifying the expense with 'you only get married once' but thought better of it. The matter of her first marriage still hadn't been discussed. As it was the vehicle would be put to good use, taking her and her father to New Mills, then collecting Superintendent Wayland from the station, and finally bringing the newlyweds and the two older men back to the Reading Room.

It had become clear to Jimmy that he must do his bit. He'd not been told in so many words what was going off, but there'd been bits of information to be collected and tucked away for later.

The first item had been a bombshell.

"Someone done 'emself in." This from a boy throwing snowballs. "Last night, it were. Next door went out lookin' fer t' body in river."

Jimmy, on his way to take Benjy out before school, found time to throw a snowball back.

"That Sergeant Spray o' yourn, he were there." Another snowball accompanied the remark.

Jimmy, head held high, pretended to ignore both and hurried on. He was pleased to have his connection with the constabulary recognised, but there was work to be done.

"Mornin', missus." He'd popped his head round the door. A reply from the kitchen was lost in the cry of a baby. He'd ventured in through the scullery.

The voice tried again. "You're early, Jimmy."

Was there something up? Now the baby had quietened down, Mrs Oldroyd sounded a bit funny.

"I haven't taken Benjy yet." He'd look in again before school.

"Very good." Was that a sob? Certainly a break in her voice.

"You all right, missus?" The lad had reached the kitchen door. Inside, things were in disarray and the baby was crying again. "Bab's not very 'appy. Want anythin' done?"

By this time the tears were running. "No thank you, Jimmy, there's nothing you can do about Mary... She's gone."

"The body in t' river..." Sudden realisation. "It's the bab's ma... an' you've still got the little 'un."

After that he'd heard his ma talking about some disagreement with Mary's family, and then he'd heard the sergeant and Missus Oldroyd saying 'how many there'd be'. The parts all came together to make a whole picture when he saw the notice:

The Reading Room will be closed for a private function from 1pm, Thursday 29th March.

So that was it; they were getting wed, Mrs Oldroyd and the sergeant. Now he knew. It all made sense.

Wednesday 28th March was a dull, damp day. No sun reached Whaley Bridge until mid afternoon, and even then it was no more than a watery gleam. Not that anyone had noticed at 37 Mill End. Inside it was all bustle and rush. Elsie Maida was there helping, mainly with Mary. It was, after all, she who'd helped bring the little mite into this world. The bride-to-be was busying herself with preparations for the reception.

"I don't know how it's come to this, Elsie." Lizzie had her hands in a mixing bowl. "I've never cooked a hare before."

The hare in question had arrived in the meat safe two days earlier.

"Summat a bit different, missus," he'd said. "It were a right chase; Benjy ain't had a hare before."

"Thank you, Jimmy, I'll see to it." She was being told more than she wanted to hear.

"We started out with four people and a walk to New Mills; now look at us, Elsie."

A voice from the scullery. "I'll just leave the cake out here."

Even with her friends helping, Lizzie was at her wits' end.

A sweepstake had been held in the Crewe office of the Railway Constabulary. The two winners set about polishing their buttons.

"You must have a ceremonial guard, Sergeant." Superintendent Wayland, having secured an invitation for himself, had extended it to include two officers who would stand to attention as the newlyweds emerged from the ceremony. "It's the least we can do for you."

All Sam could see was two more mouths to feed.

The Whale had the day all mapped out. "If we catch the 9.10 for London Road, there's a train out from Manchester that'll get us to New Mills in time."

Sam, closeted in the Whale's office, felt like a piece of driftwood at the mercy of the elements.

"You'll tell this wagonette thing what time we're arriving?"

"Sir."

"I'll see to the tickets, first class all the way for us. Rail passes to Manchester for the rest, then I'll get them second class to New Mills. You happy with that, Sergeant?"

And that was how they'd arrived: five men with freshly washed necks, their uniforms brushed and buttons gleaming. They stood to attention as their senior officer clambered unsteadily into a modest wagonette waiting on the station forecourt.

Four people sat in the front row, separated into pairs by the central aisle. All rose as the registrar entered. With Lizzie's father and William flanking the bride and groom, the essentials were in place. Behind them a less official role was being played out. Sam, raised in an orphanage, had no relations present, but Superintendent Wayland was remedying the situation. He'd assumed the status of groom's family and had busied himself shaking hands and directing people to their seats.

Afterwards Sam could remember nothing of the ceremony. He was handing his new wife from the wagonette when the real world finally caught his attention. A boy – or more properly now, a young man – standing outside the Reading Room, put a cornet to his lips.

Jimmy had found the fanfare in an old trunk where the town band kept its sheet music. Practising down by the canal, he reckoned he'd mastered it, and now was the moment of truth. It had lasted just long enough for the bride and groom to walk past, followed by the first few guests. A big man with a limp had smiled at him, and his mother said she didn't realise he played solo; and then it was over.

"...since your wedding. Topping affair. Haven't enjoyed myself so much for years. Fine woman, your wife. You're a lucky man, Sergeant. Luck well deserved, I might say. That child... your wife's much taken with it; saw her nursing...?"

"She's called Mary, sir, and she's ours... my wife's and mine." Sam paused. "That is to say, she's ours now. Her mother died, a late casualty of the Fenian business."

The truth dawned slowly on Superintendent Wayland. "You mean... you mean Slade's misbehaviour... She's that man's bast…" Just in time, on the lip of the abyss, he realised what he was saying. "That man's baby?"

"That's right, sir; Slade raped Mary's mother, and although my wife took the girl in, she couldn't face the world as a fallen woman. She killed herself. Mrs Spray and I are resolved to give the baby a home."

There was nothing else for him to do. The hare had gone into a sort of meat loaf, he'd seen it cooling in the scullery; and he'd played his cornet. Jimmy was at a loose end.

He'd just set off for home when he heard his name.

"Jimmy, hold on." William had run after him. "Jimmy, Lizzie – that is, Mrs Oldroyd… that is, Mrs Spray – sent me to ask if you'd like to come in?"

Would he just. "Yes please, Mr Archer." At that moment he'd wanted it more than anything in the world.

The Reading Room had been laid out with the spread on an oblong table in the centre and the guests seated around it. A smaller overspill was separate, and it was there that Jimmy had been placed in the company of two uniformed constables. No one was eating, and whatever was being drunk hadn't reached the smaller table.

Mr Bennett was on his feet saying a few words. "… proudest day of my life… fine young man…"

Jimmy didn't quite understand that bit. Sergeant Spray was definitely old.

"…wonderful daughter… mother would have been so happy…" With rhetoric almost exhausted, the old man was making a run for the toast.

Lizzie, seeing the problem at Jimmy's table, slipped from her seat at the centre of things and took glasses of ale across to the two constables. "Come with me," she whispered to the lad. As her father raised his glass she resumed her seat just in time, and Jimmy, standing behind her chair, was able to toast the happy couple in lemonade.

As the chatter started and competed with the rattle of plates, Jimmy felt exposed and set off for the small table in the corner.

"Here, take these." Lizzie, calling him back, gave him two plates laden with food. In pride of place in the centre of each one was a slice of meatloaf. "Give them to the other two and come back for yours."

"Bloody good vittles, considerin'." The constables, both from the Cheshire Plain, were not usually inclined to rate the wild uplands of the Peak. "Wonder what's in this?"

The man who spoke was collecting up the last of his slice. Jimmy didn't enlighten him.

"That bab, d'ye think it's the sergeant's?" By now the new Mrs Spray had relieved Elsie of the baby and was feeding it pap.

"Bit strait-laced, he is. Hadn't got 'im down fer fatherin' a bastard." The conversation continued, ignoring Jimmy.

"P'raps she's brought another man's brat to the party?"

"Don't see Spray standin' fer that."

Jimmy had been all ears. "That's not right." Indignation got the better of him.

"And what do you know about anything, nipper?" One of the constables glared.

"That's Mary's bab. The missus and Mr Spray got married to look after it 'cause Mary drowned in t' river."

Any further explanation as to why the marriage had taken place had been interrupted by a loud banging. Jimmy watched as the big man with a limp got to his feet.

"A most satisfactory celebration, Sergeant."

"Sir."

"I hope you enjoyed it as much as your guests?"

Sam, for whom getting married had been not only a new experience, but a baffling one, couldn't remember much. "I'm glad you all had a good time."

"Happy with my announcement? Bit much springing it on you like that, but the opportunity was too good to miss."

"As you say, sir" Whatever he'd anticipated, Sam hadn't expected promotion to be added to his newly acquired responsibilities of a wife and someone else's child.

"Now, tell me why you're here."

"I've come to offer my resignation, sir."

PART 2

THREE

Monday Evening, 30th April 1877

AFTER THE THUNDERBOLT; SILENCE. SUPERINTENDENT Wayland's usual response when words failed him, 'Carry on, Sergeant', was hardly appropriate. It was so... so... He settled on ungrateful.

Since the wedding, he'd basked in an unfamiliar glow. The applause that greeted his announcement of the bridegroom's promotion had been most gratifying even if the boy's fanfare had been a bit over the top. And then, the guilt that he felt at receiving high praise from his superiors that rightly belonged to Spray had been relieved. These things he appreciated, but self-awareness eluded him.

He was quite unable to understand that the warmth and acceptance extended toward him during the celebration mattered more than anything else. In the absence of relatives, he'd been the nearest thing the bridegroom had to a family, and it was the betrayal of that connection that hurt the most.

"What d'ye mean, Sergeant; resign? You'll remain in post and that's an order."

"Perhaps you should look at this, sir." The official Royal Mail envelope was passed across the table. "It arrived this morning and I opened it."

"Good God, man, that's what you're paid for."

"If you look inside, sir…?"

The much-travelled envelope was laid on the desk. Wayland reached for his pince-nez and peered at the tangle of addresses. Spray leant forward and put his finger on its centre.

"That's the original destination, sir."

Wayland mouthed the words silently.

Ensign Charles Wayland
1st Bengal Lancers
Regimental Headquarters
Delhi
India

"That's me, but it's a mighty long time ago, Sergeant."

"But look at the earliest franking, sir; less than two years ago."

"Curious. What d'ye make of it?"

"I really think you'd better look in the envelope, sir. It would be best if I wait outside."

"No it bloody well wouldn't. Sit there."

Travelling homeward, he was a much happier Sam Spray than the one who had headed south earlier in the day. He even managed a cheery "Good day t' you, sir" for the man in the seat opposite. The greeting was acknowledged with a nod, causing the other passenger's black silk topper to glint in the low afternoon sun.

Sam had plenty to think about. He'd sat, mute, opposite the Whale as his senior officer read and reread the letter. There were periods of silence in which the air of authority, usually to be found on the superintendent's face, waned, and on one occasion Sam thought he might have seen a tear. He tried to imagine what the older man was going through.

"Very well, Sergeant."

Superintendent Wayland was back in control, of himself and his department. *This is it*, thought Sam; *he's going to accept my resignation.*

"This matter came to light on your watch."

If only it hadn't.

"You'd better investigate it."

"But—"

"I need hardly add… the utmost discretion… I leave it in your hands. My regards to Mrs Spray – that meat loaf she produced at the wedding; superb."

Yes, Sam was certainly happier: he'd still got a job and there'd been no row, but what the devil was he to do with the assignment? What to say to Lizzie? The question had troubled him ever since Stockport.

There'd been time to stick his head round the door of the office before his connection. William was just leaving for home with no more than a "You're back, Sam; will you lock up? I'll see you in the morning" before running for a Crewe train.

From across the tracks Sam watched travellers pouring out of a refreshment room onto the main-line platform. A London-bound train drew in, obscuring his view. When it left, the crowd had disappeared, safely on its way south. A few who'd made the short journey from Manchester were hurrying for the way out, leaving only two passengers in conversation. The more smartly dressed of the two looked familiar, but it was the other man that caught Sam's attention.

Sam and William had occasionally discussed what it was about their calling that gave them away. There was certainly something instantly recognisable about a policeman; young Jimmy had never had any difficulty singling them out. Whatever it was, the man across the tracks had it, but both men had disappeared by the time a goods train had puffed and clanked its way through the station on the slow line. With his diversion gone, Sam returned to the matter of what the Whale meant by discretion.

He was still pondering the issue when the Whaley Bridge train drew in. By now the platform was busy, and as the train slowed to a stand, someone in a hurry emerged from the stairwell of the subway, and Sam allowed him to board first. For the second time that day he found himself sharing his compartment with a man in a shiny topper; this time he was also a man who'd had brief meetings with plain-clothes policemen during a break in his journey. *From? To?*

"Good afternoon, sir, quite a coincidence, wouldn't you say?"

Silk Hat barely acknowledged the greeting and stared at his copy of the *Times*.

"Come down from London, I would hazard? The train I joined earlier was fast to Crewe, then Stockport and Manchester."

Had the *Times* been printed on cheaper paper, Silk Hat's copy would surely have disintegrated, so hard did he stare at the leader page. Sam enquired if he was for the spa waters, but it seemed not so. The train stopped at Hazel Grove, and Silk Hat alighted hurriedly, failing to close the door properly. Intent on saving a porter the trouble, Sam stood up to set things to rights.

Glancing along the platform prior to slamming the door, he caught sight of Silk Hat's rear view heading towards the way out. That might have been the end of it but for… but for what? Afterwards he told himself it was professional curiosity that led him to open the window. Hazel Grove didn't merit a long halt and the guard was giving the right-away when, at the last moment, further along the train, a carriage door opened and Silk Hat regained the train, shutting the door behind him.

"You're late today, Sam."

It still felt strange, letting himself in through his own front door and finding himself at home. He'd never had possessions before and, despite Lizzie's insistence that he was to share everything at Number 37, he wasn't sure he had any now, but he couldn't deny the warmth.

"A busy day, my dear." He took off his coat and gave his wife a peck on the cheek.

That wasn't enough for Lizzie, and she put her arms round his neck. "Sam, you're worried."

How on earth can she see that? he wondered.

"Is it something you can tell me about?"

On and off, he'd been contemplating that question since leaving Crewe. There'd been welcome distractions, and one such had been following Silk Hat to Buxton instead of alighting at Whaley Bridge and arriving home at the usual time. After following him past the nondescript premises of some sort of charity, where he pushed an envelope through the door, Sam had seen him enter the Old Hall Hotel. The silk hat had not been just for effect. It was admitted, with its owner, into the sort of premises that stank of money. The uniformed doorman clearly thought Sam had an insufficiency, and refused him when he attempted to gain entry.

The steep incline of Mill End had become easier to climb. He was fitter for making the effort daily over the last weeks, and he was striding toward Number 37 when he'd made up his mind. It had been a relief to discard the diversions he'd used to avoid the dilemma, and face reality. The Whale had given him imprecise instructions and urged discretion. It was up to him to decide how to proceed.

Seated now, each with a full plate, piping hot and, in Sam's case at least, finding the aroma of Lizzie's cooking irresistible, they ate tea together. Since their wedding it had become the best moment of the day, and both treasured it.

"I've had a trying time, my dear, but perhaps you have too?" At work his daughter slipped into the background, but as soon as he returned home she filled his heart.

"Mary gives no cause for anxiety, Sam, as long as she's fed and talked to and dandled and changed and…" Lizzie stopped, not wishing to appear a scold. "But when she smiles the world lights up."

With the meal over they sat on, companionably, at the table.

"I resigned my post today."

"Oh! Sam…" Not much put Lizzie out of kilter, and it had usually occurred in Sam's absence. He was startled by the look on her face.

"It was refused, but I am left with a perplexing assignment."

As the story came tumbling out, Sam felt relief creeping over him, so that by the end it was almost as if the day had never happened. But not quite…

"What do you think the Whale expects, Lizzie?"

"It's his own flesh and blood, Sam. He needs to know what's become of them because he feels responsible."

FOUR

Tuesday 1st May 1877

IF MUCH OF MONDAY HAD BEEN SPENT IN THE SEARCH FOR distractions, Tuesday left no time for such things. Sam and the regular man on his platform at Edgeley were on nodding terms, but today the porter was standing waiting for the policeman and, as he alighted, stepped forward with a message.

"Beggin' your pardon, sir, but stationmaster says would you go straight to his office? Very perticler, he was, straight there."

"Very well, Mr...?"

The reply was mumbled and Sam didn't catch a name.

"Very well, Mr... thank you. Any idea what it's about?"

"Told me t' say nothin' t' no one, he did." There was a pause in which the porter struggled, and failed. "There's a woman's body, and a bit of blood..." He nodded in the direction of a solitary coach. "In there, an' it'll have to be moved soon, 'cause the Buxton goods is due, and then..."

As they talked, a grubby tank engine, released briefly from the yard, crept cautiously onto the main line and gently buffered up to the coach. By the time it had come to a halt the fireman was down into the six foot and ducking underneath to couple up.

Sam, helpless, watched his evidence being towed away.

"At last, Sergeant." The stationmaster glared at Sam as he entered. "Most inconvenient. I doubt the Buxton service will get back the time all day." Bald and portly, the little man bristled. "You'll have to get rid of it, bad for morale."

"Sir?"

"The body, Sergeant, the body. It's defiling my station, it'll have to go."

"I take it you mean the bloodied body of an unfortunate woman who as we speak is being shunted off the main line to…? Perhaps you can tell me where I may start my investigation?"

Sam had already disobliged the stationmaster. He'd called in at the office and left a note for William so that by the time the stationmaster had unearthed the whereabouts of the detached coach, the investigation was already under way.

"Now then." As instructed, William was interrogating the porter. "Let's just go through what happened here this morning."

"It were the 8.02 departure for Manchester. Always arrives full from Buxton, and when it leaves it's even fuller. There were complaints. The end compartment were locked and them wi'out seats couldn't see why."

"And you? Did you know why?"

"I did after I'd opened it up."

William was shown a standard square-ended key.

"Allus have one of these, standard issue." The porter was relishing the attention. "Blinds were down. Odd, that, but a mercy really; the passengers hadn't seen nothing."

"And inside?"

"It were plain she were dead, soon as I saw her. Blood on the floor and the body there too. Shut the door quick, I did."

"What happened then?"

"I spoke to the guard and then the stationmaster. After that it were bedlam. We had to get the passengers out of the other compartments, and there weren't no seats on the rest of the train."

"What did you do with them all?"

"Put 'em in the refreshment room." He looked at the station clock. "The next train for London Road's due in seventeen minutes, if it ain't been held up."

"You mean they'll all disappear?"

"And good riddance; one of them threatened me."

William squared his shoulders, and by the time he reached the refreshment room door, was up to facing the mob. As he pulled it open a man in a hurry barged out and, so it seemed, seeing the uniform, tipped his hat forward, and in turning away from the policeman, avoided showing his face.

A waft of warm air surprised William as he entered. Across the crowded room feathers were being ruffled as Sam could be seen making his way through the stranded passengers waiting irritably for the next Manchester-bound train.

"Follow that man, see where he goes." Still several tables away, Sam mouthed the words, with little hope of being heard above the hubbub, pointing in the direction William had just come from.

It was not going to be easy. Quite apart from his uniform, William had no idea why, and as he stepped back onto the platform his quarry had disappeared. In either direction he could see only men at work. At the point where a guard's van might be expected to come to rest, men in the uniform of the Royal Mail stood by their loaded trolley.

"Good morning."

Unimpressed by a mere policeman, however civil, one postman grunted and both turned away.

"Did you see a gent in a silk hat come this way a few moments ago?"

Another grunt sounding rather like "No."

"Would you have noticed if such a man had come this way?"

"We've noticed you, haven't we? Now why don't you bugger off and find something useful to do?"

William set off in the opposite direction.

"Thought you lot'd be back. I told him as came before all I knew." A porter was filling in time before the next arrival, sweeping up rubbish. "You've no idea what people throw away, and there's a litter basket just back there."

It was an involuntary act, insignificant in itself, but as William glanced in the direction of the pointing finger, he saw a sign. *Gentlemen.*

"Seen anyone up this end in the last minute or two?"

"Can't rightly say." The porter glared at his broom. "Too busy with this." He looked up. "Suppose someone might have gone for a jimmy riddle... yes, I think they did."

The odds were barely in his favour. William assessed his chances and wasn't impressed. On the one hand, the man in a silk hat hadn't gone straight for the stairs to the exit, he'd have had to pass the postmen, but he had disappeared. He'd hardly have gone into the ladies' waiting room, and from where he was standing, William could see into the general waiting room. So he must have gone into the gents'.

"Open both ways, does it?" They were on an island between two tracks. The refreshment room served both platforms; he'd seen Sam making his way from the other entrance.

"Oh aye, serves both sides, it does."

So Silk Hat could slip through the convenience and out the other side onto the next platform and along to the stairway, unless… unless Sam had gone back to halt his progress? But Sam would be busy trying to get information from the waiting passengers. Then again, did that matter? It only required Silk Hat to think Sam might be on the platform for him to stay hidden.

"This where the engine stops?"

"Depends; depends on how long the train is. Not if it's a short one."

William wondered if the man was just being difficult. "And the next train?"

"The 8.58 departure's fast to Manchester. It's express from London. The engine stops here."

With its arrival imminent, stranded passengers poured out onto the platform and were joined by others arriving in dribs and drabs. It was going to be more difficult than William had imagined. There was little chance that, in his blue uniform and helmet, he would blend into the crowd. Silk Hat, however, had plenty like him to hide among.

William had a plan. True, it depended on things beyond his control, but the first part went better than he could have hoped.

"Can I come aboard?" With the train now in the station, William spoke urgently to a muscular young man who was leaning nonchalantly from his cab window, viewing the busy scene. "It's a bit of urgent police business." He showed his warrant card.

The fireman looked to his mate for agreement. The driver nodded, and William stepped onto the footplate.

"So what's up? Not us, I hope." The driver, seated with his hand on the controls, was listening for the guard's whistle.

"I'm watching for a chap in a silk topper and I don't want to be seen."

The fireman offered his cap. "Here, gi' us yer helmet and put this on." He took up his shovel and, bending down out of sight, tended his fire. "He'll see nowt but yer 'ead over the tender, and you'll be able t' keep watch."

It had all been for nothing, or so it seemed to William. The guard had given the right-away and received a toot from the engine in reply. There was no sign of Silk Hat as the driver moved the regulator over and was rewarded with an exhaust beat from the chimney. The heavy train started to ease forward, and by the second beat William thought it was all over. At that moment a hatless man in a hurry emerged from the gentlemen's convenience and just scrambled into a moving carriage. The defining nature of headgear had been acknowledged in their different ways by hunter and hunted, but the policeman's helmet was tucked away out of sight on the footplate, whilst the other man's silk topper boarded with him, carried beneath his arm.

"'Appen you'll be comin' all the way fer free. Next stop London Road."

William, who'd been congratulating himself on his success, was deflated by the accusation, and reached into his pocket. "I've got a pass for the whole network."

"Not fer my footplate, you ain't." With that settled, the driver turned his attention to the road ahead.

By now the fire was looking after itself. "See here, Mr Policeman, if yer goin' to follow that gent in Manchester you'll stand out a mile." The fireman was resting on his shovel, and William was attempting to return his cap. "If you were to keep it I could say it'd blown off in the wind and get another from the stores. I'd 'ave to pay for it, mind."

"So if I give you the money for a new one, I can walk through the streets in yours?"

No one had seen anything, or if they had they weren't telling a nosy police sergeant. Having been evicted from their perfectly good seats and left several miles short of their destination, the stranded passengers were in no mood for cooperation. Even free cups of tea from the refreshment room urn, ordered by the stationmaster to head off complaints, were insufficient to placate the more indignant.

"This'll be your fault, I'll be bound."

Denying it was futile.

"What were up wi' the carriage? Ours were the only one as stopped."

It had been particularly galling to see the rest of their train resuming its journey. At least one man posited a corpse, but Sam avoided answering. And then they were gone.

Hardly worth the effort, concluded Sam, who'd learnt nothing for his pains. Now for the body.

"Can't tell you. It's been pandemonium this morning." Seated at his desk with a cup of tea to hand, the stationmaster was hardly convincing. Sam was attempting to find the detached carriage.

"I think I should tell you, sir, that a report of this incident will find its way to Euston; the company board is particularly exercised by police matters. Indeed, quite recently my senior officer, Superintendent Wayland, was in conference with Mr Moon..."

With mention of the LNWR's chairman, the atmosphere changed. "Oh, I see. I..."

"So, cooperation..."

"Yes, of course, Sergeant."

A minion was summoned, and in turn came back with a man who knew, and who led Sam to where the carriage was standing. It had been a long trek to the goods yard, and with no platform to bring him level with the door, Sam started to climb the running boards. He was making heavy weather of it.

"You'll need a key, mister."

"Have you got one?" Sam was back at ground level.

"No."

"Bloody well go and get one, and come back with a ladder." As he watched the retreating figure, Sam regretted his irritation. Why did he feel so silly? He lost his equanimity so rarely, but whenever he did he felt the worse for it.

Inside the compartment the smell of putrefaction dominated. With the blinds down and the windows closed, the early-May sun had raised the temperature and the body had started to decay. Lying in a crumpled heap, the young woman looked as if she had been thrown to the floor and left to die. Certainly her knees were drawn up as if in pain, and she lay on her right side.

"You'd best get a litter," Sam called over his shoulder to the two men who'd brought the ladder. "A plank won't do; she's stiff, and curled up."

In the confined space of the carriage floor it was difficult but he wanted to know how it had been done. The thin fabric of her ragged dress was slit from the back toward the left side. Beneath, there was a single incision between her ribs from which had seeped blood. The porter had exaggerated the quantity; the narrow wound had bled remarkably little. Sam attempted to roll the corpse. So far as he could see it was her only wound, with nothing on the right side. He didn't feel the need to explain to himself the two dark stains on the front of her bodice, well away from the fatal stabbing.

"You finished up there, sir?" The two men were back with a canvas sheet stretched between two poles.

Sam felt obliged to treat the body with decorum but it proved difficult as he dragged the unfortunate woman, feet first, into the open doorway of the carriage. After climbing down the ladder he moved it to the side to allow the poles at his end of the litter to be lodged on the lip of the floor. With the other two, their arms held high, at the further end, the canvas was almost level and he endeavoured to drag the cadaver onto it and out into the open air.

It would have worked had he not stumbled, with his ends of the poles held high, after lifting them away from the door. He fell and, with the litter now at a steep angle, found himself beneath the murdered woman. Her dress was torn further than before, laying bare an overfull breast, much at odds with the rest of her underfed torso. To add to the indignity, the hem had ridden up revealing a poverty of undergarments that in life she would never have wanted exposed.

Despite the unseemly disarray, as Sam clambered to his feet he discreetly purloined the train ticket that had fallen from her dislodged shoe.

Trapped in the arrival bay at London Road Station, the footplate was very exposed to the public. The hatless fireman had climbed down into the six foot and ducked underneath to attend to the uncoupling. His mate stood across the other side, gazing out on the people streaming past his cab, and received the occasional "Thank you, my man" or at least a nod of acknowledgement for his trouble. Any well-wisher who cared to look further would have seen a grubby cap, its wearer mostly obscured by the portly driver, and assumed he was the fireman.

The danger was short-lived. William's mark, silk hat now back on his head, hurried on without a glance at the locomotive. Following discreetly was not so easy for a man in a policeman's uniform, whatever his headgear, and William decided for the moment to screw up the cap and tuck it into his pocket. Dignity was restored, and with his helmet back in its proper place he set off in pursuit of his quarry.

With toppers aplenty on the station concourse it was tricky, but his man had a characteristic gait and his hat was of a superior quality not so common amongst the denizens of Manchester. Concealment was easier in the crowd, but it thinned outside and the policeman was more conspicuous as Top Hat looked in vain for a cab. The rank was empty, and to William's relief he set off down the station approach on foot.

William was congratulating himself on avoiding the problem of how to follow a hansom when one came, empty, round the bend from the main road and started to strain at the hill toward the station. Up went an arm and the cabbie saved his horse the climb by turning round near the bottom. He'd be back into Piccadilly in no time with a fare aboard who'd be good for a tip, if the silk topper was anything to go by. William hurried down the hill, if only to see which direction the cab would take; a poor return for his ingenuity so far. But all was not lost.

To get out of the side road and turn toward the centre of the city the cabbie would have to cross the traffic in the nearside and join the stream moving in the opposite direction. Wily he may be, but even an experienced man has to wait for a break in the traffic, and the hansom was held up for half a minute or more. William, seeing its direction of travel, headed out onto the nearside pavement and set off in the direction of Piccadilly Gardens.

He arrived in time to see the cab go trotting past and into Market Street, only to be stopped by an accident; not that it was involved directly, but traffic was at a standstill until a reckless lad, who must have misjudged things whilst dodging across the road, was laid on the pavement, and wheels started turning again. It all took time, and William, hurrying along on foot, not only caught up but could have drawn ahead.

It proved impossible to watch over his shoulder as he walked, not to mention the possibility of being spotted by Silk Hat facing forward in the comfort of his cab, so he hung back until the jam started to sort itself out. Even then, the congestion was such that he had no difficulty in keeping up. The slow pace must have irked Silk Hat because William saw him climb down at a junction and set off along a side road.

Having served him well so far, the busy thoroughfare was no longer his friend, and the policeman found himself stranded on the wrong side of Market Street waiting to cross. He resorted to stepping out into the traffic and flaunting his uniform in a manner that he would have shunned moments before. It was a risky business, and not a popular one.

"Bloody rozzers, we don't need you; traffic's bad enough already." The carter had stopped his heavily laden wagon and would have to get it moving again against the gradient, but he hadn't run William down, and others slowed so that a gap opened up sufficient for his purpose.

But to what purpose, wondered William? Silk Hat had disappeared round the corner, not into a side alley, but a road equally as busy as Market Street. Pressing on was his only option and he set off hotfoot in the hope of catching up. He ignored turnings to right and left, opting to keep to the main drag, dodging round portly matrons and smartly suited gentlemen as he hurried along. Here was not the blighted city of decay and dereliction to which his last visit had introduced him, but a Manchester of wealth, privilege and self-regard.

Occasional glimpses of his quarry led him on for a while. Then Silk Hat disappeared. William kept his eye on the point of last sighting and when he drew level found himself outside a run-down building declaring itself the home of a newspaper. Peering in, he could see Silk Hat's back view as he was escorted deeper into the heart of the place by a liveried attendant.

William followed and approached the doorman as he returned.

"I've a gentleman's notecase, dropped in the street." William reached toward his pocket. "The person who handed it in thought its owner came in here. The gentleman in a silk hat, he said." With his thumb firmly over its LNWR crest, William purported to look inside. "What name did he give?"

A ledger lay open on a small desk, pen and ink to one side. So far William had not had his arrival recorded, but to be allowed further inside, each visitor was noted by name and destination.

"Mr D. Fewster; went for ads."

William looked confused.

"You know, small advertisements all over the front of the paper."

William had a good look at his own wallet. There was no deceit in declaring that a mistake had been made.

FIVE

Wednesday 2nd May 1877

THE REST OF SAM'S DAY HAD BEEN SPENT CHASING around after the coach that had carried the corpse to Stockport. Standing forlorn and out of place in Edgeley Goods Yard, its present position had not been in doubt. Its recent movements were a matter of interest, though. Where had it been before and after the unfortunate woman had boarded for her last ride; perhaps her first ride in her life? To Sam's eye she'd looked destitute, but a valid third-class ticket from Buxton to Chapel-en-le-Frith had fallen out of her shoe. It was issued for travel on the 30th April, but she could hardly be blamed, given what happened, for making her last journey after its expiry.

The body had been stiff by the time he'd examined it at 9.16. Even with his rudimentary knowledge, he knew the victim couldn't have boarded alive and well that morning. He was convinced that she had stepped off a platform and been attacked as she entered the carriage. A good push would have sent her sprawling clear of the door, which was then shut and locked behind her.

"Yer've made a mess of my diagrams, that's fer sure." Sam had finally tracked down the man responsible for passenger stock movements. "That rake'll be running about, one coach short till tomorrow." The man had held the policeman personally responsible. "An' where's the guard goin' to ride? It were his van, tha knows."

"Do you know the movements of the detached vehicle for the last forty-eight hours?"

"Oh aye, I do that." A silence followed.

"Are you prepared to tell me?"

"I will if you want me to." Then further silence, in which Sam grew more exasperated.

"I do want you to tell me."

"Yer should have said that to start with."

"Damnation, man; I did." It had been the second time in the day that Sam had lost his equanimity. Later he wondered whether it was the effect of matrimony, and if other men's experience was the same. For the moment the conversation continued.

"No you didn't, you asked me if I knew about the coach's movements. Then you asked me if I was prepared to tell you. You never asked me to tell you. When you did ask you started swearing."

It had gone past irritation, and was turning to comedy. Sam couldn't suppress a laugh.

"It's not how a policeman should carry on; of that I am sure."

Sam, having been put in his place, was at last treated to some crumbs from his tormentor's table. The coach had been immediately behind the locomotive hauling the Manchester service to Buxton, arriving at 10.30pm. It had been the last service of the day, its counterpart in the opposite direction having departed at 9.25. Always busy, there would have been complaints if the compartment door had been locked during its journey, or so he was told. Sam would have to check on that later, but for the moment he'd assumed the victim had boarded after the train's arrival at Buxton. Or been forced to board? With a valid ticket in her possession, she must have intended to travel on the 30th but had not done so by the time of the last departure of the day.

The LNWR station at Buxton was unusual for a terminus. Passengers found their way in and out through a booking hall halfway along the arrivals platform. Where the station concourse would generally have been found, at the head of a newly arrived train, there was no more than a narrow access to the departure platform opposite. It would have been a dark corner and, at 10.30 of an evening, deserted; except for an engine, patiently waiting for the station shunter to draw away its rake of coaches and allow it to make its last journey of the day to the shed.

The crew would still have been on the footplate, wouldn't they? Sam had pencilled a reminder in his notebook. And what about the guard? If he had a compartment in the coach there'd be mailbags, and mailbags meant men collecting them. No; not such a quiet corner after all: more reminders.

To unearth the office from which the movement of coaching stock was controlled had required a trip to one of the less salubrious corners of the warren that was London Road Station. Unbeknownst to each other, the two policemen had been in Manchester during the day, but by the time Sam, on his way home, had called in at the Stockport office, the only sign of William was a note left on his sergeant's desk.

Man in silk topper named D. Fewster. Visited newspaper office. Behaved suspiciously until London Road. After that behaved normally – must have decided he wasn't being followed.

It had taken William a whole day's work before he could put those twenty-six words together, and Sam wondered if it had all been a waste of time. *Just coincidences and a suspicious mind*, he'd told himself on more than one occasion, and yet... Why would a respectably dressed man behave suspiciously on – Sam had counted him twice dodging his own uniform, and William's once – on three occasions, and make transient contact with a detective in plain clothes, before undertaking some business with a newspaper?

He'd been climbing Old Mill End when he concluded William's exertions had, after all, been worth it. It had been excellent work on the constable's part, Sam had been in no doubt about that from the moment he'd seen the note, so now, as he was letting himself into Number 37, and Lizzie was calling, "Is that you, Sam?" he could bask in the warm embrace of domesticity with a clear conscience.

By the time of his leaving the next morning he'd nursed little Mary twice, once when she woke whilst Lizzie cooked their tea, and then again in the morning. He'd explained to Lizzie that he was travelling to Buxton and could linger over breakfast longer than usual on account of the later train time, and even told her about William's good work in Manchester. What he hadn't mentioned was a young woman, dead of a knife wound, her lifeless body abandoned and locked in a railway compartment.

It was certainly not professional discretion. Sam still didn't know much about married life, but one thing he'd been clear about from the start: no secrets. No, not that; but when he'd arrived the evening before he'd been quite unable to sully the contentment that was his newly acquired family life. Later, perhaps, when he knew a bit more.

And he expected to know a bit more by the end of the day. After reading William's note he'd written one of his own:

> *Go to mortuary at half after two o'clock. Collect report on autopsy of woman found dead in rail carriage earlier today.*
>
> *Will discuss result tomorrow.*

Riding to Buxton in solitude, Sam mused on the increasing movement of passengers at each end of the day. He shared his morning journey to Stockport with a crowd whose numbers increased at every station. He'd come to recognise many and pass the time of day with a few, but Buxton it seemed was much less of an attraction. The coach immediately behind the locomotive suited his purpose perfectly. In the front compartment he'd arrive just where the unfortunate murder victim would have been forced to board two nights earlier. No doubt the noise of a steam engine, just the other side of the end panel of the coach, straining noisily from the Goyt Valley up into the Peak, was a deterrent to many, but he relished its power.

Little Mary was a contented baby. She took her pap eagerly, she smiled and gurgled, and provided her nappy was changed promptly she would, for the most part, settle down to sleep. But she liked routine too, and that had been disrupted by Sam's later departure for Buxton. It was late morning before things were set to rights, and Lizzie, pot of tea brewing, felt able to relax for the first time that day. She was in the middle of pouring when she heard the familiar click of her letter box.

Since taking on the child she'd discovered how tiring motherhood was. Initially she'd thought perhaps it was the consequence of taking on someone else's daughter, but that had been months ago. Now Mary was hers… hers and Sam's. They both felt the same way, she knew; between them they had a child and the little trio were a family. It made no difference, though; Lizzie was still exhausted, and she thought guiltily about leaving the newly delivered mail till later. But old habits die hard and she left the freshly poured cup to collect the post.

Only one letter lay on the mat behind the door, and Lizzie didn't recognise the hand. Bold and confident, it had directed the Royal Mail to deliver to Mrs Albert Oldroyd, 37 Mill End, Whaley Bridge.

She was about to defer the pleasure of her morning tea even further by opening the envelope, but Mary, still unsettled by the change in routine, started to cry, and with Lizzie unable to resist the baby's command, the missive was left on the hallstand and forgotten in the confusion of motherhood.

Sam walked forward toward the end of Buxton arrivals platform. The locomotive had come to rest well short of the buffer stops and was itself a significant length, so that the compartment from which he'd alighted was about thirty yards from the dark corner of his imagination. There was, however, a door set in the back wall of the platform, more or less opposite the engine.

"Good morning."

The driver, head down, attending to some mysterious task low on the footplate, straightened up.

"A decent run from Whaley Bridge, I should say."

"Aye, nowt so bad." The driver held the handle of an enamelled can. "Due for a mash now. We shan't be out of here for a bit."

"Always have to wait a while, do you?"

"Depends."

"On what?

"If it's a short train us can stop further back. We uncouple from the front coach, like 'e's just done." A grimy fireman had appeared down in the six foot, his face just visible from above. "Then draw forward clear of the crossover points, and 'e goes an' tells the bobby."

"And a right walk it is too." This from the fireman, now back on the footplate.

The driver gestured to his mate to get on with making the tea. "Then the bobby sets the road and pulls off the dolly an' we reverse onto the departure line and away."

"How often does it happen like that?"

"You're mighty nosy. S'pose it comes wi' the job if yer a policeman."

"All right, I'm nosy, but can you tell me how often?"

"You're investigatin' summat..." The voice took on a conspiratorial tone. "You tell me what you're after an' I'll tell about the engine movements."

By the time the exchange was complete the driver was more sure than Sam that "a murder on this very spot" had taken place two nights ago. For his part Sam had learnt that only one regular movement allowed the engine to escape, and that was the last train of the day. The rake of carriages stood in the arrivals platform overnight and formed the first train the next morning.

"Where does that go to?" Sam pointed to the door.

"Parcels office, back door. Kept locked except when it's not."

"When it's not?" Here was something to be nosy about, thought Sam.

"We'll… y'know; it's the quickest way to the jakes. I seen the clerk nip in the refreshment room for a wet too."

"Does he lock it behind him?"

"Bloody hell… you're the policeman, not me. How do I know?"

The empty coaching stock was being drawn away as Sam walked toward the way out, and was gone by the time he'd reached the booking hall. He turned into the space that separated the nation's most comfortable railway from its most imperious. The two stations were mirror images facing each other across a busy roadway. The Midland had recently abolished second-class travel and provided upholstered seats for third class. Its pride was only dented by the LNWR, which styled itself as the Premier Railway by virtue of being the biggest joint stock company in the world. Each company's parcels service plied for business opposite each other, and in different circumstances might have had barkers competing for custom. Not in the more restrained world of railways, though.

Sam entered the LNWR office. If there had been any, the customers would have stood with backs to the door, facing a wooden counter. It was shorter than the room was wide, and on the floor at the open end stood a machine for weighing heavier items, leaving space beyond to pass between front and back. Fresh tobacco smoke hung in the air although no one was smoking. The place was empty.

"Anybody about?" Sam called out, and finding a handbell on the counter, gave it a shake.

What emerged from the doorway to the inner sanctum were unintelligible words that nonetheless signalled displeasure. Whatever the shifty young railwayman with a half-smoked cigarette drooping from his lip expected when he emerged, it certainly wasn't a man in uniform with sergeant's stripes on his arm.

"What the devil d'you want?"

"Prompt attention for a start."

It began to dawn on the parcels clerk that this wasn't any old bluebottle, but one that might be a threat. He'd never seen a member of the Railway Constabulary and didn't know quite how far their authority extended, but the man in front of him had an LNWR insignia and a warrant card and… The cigarette was extinguished in short order and shoulders were straightened.

"Sergeant?"

Whatever went on out of sight at the back, there was a marked reluctance to reveal it, but Sam pushed his way past the weighing machine anyway, and found himself in a storeroom. The smoke was thicker there, and he couldn't stop the war coming to mind. That was it! Turkish tobacco; the locals smoked it in the Crimea. Out there it was rough stuff, but the Egyptians had turned it into a gentleman's smoke.

"This allowed on duty, is it?" Sam pretended to waft away the fug. "Get these in Buxton?" A yellow tin printed with *Le Khedive* lay on a bench. It had been for sale in France from the look of it. There was something in small letters about certification by the *Government Français*. "Well?"

He watched as in the ensuing silence the clerk searched for an answer.

"Someone gev me them."

"Oh yes, and who would that be?"

"Chap in t' pub."

"I'll bet there isn't a public house in the town where you can find Egyptian smokes. The Palace Hotel maybe, but they'd never let the likes of you in."

"I… er…"

"You stole them, that's what." Sam pointed toward the parcels that filled the store. "Easy enough. 'Just broke open on the way, sir. If you think there's anything missing you can fill in this form, sir, and we'll see what we can do. Not very hopeful, sir.' Most of the time people give up, I expect. Those that don't, the form gets lost. That's how it is."

"No, Sergeant, no, no. I'd never do that. More'n my job's worth; nothin' goes missing from this office."

"If I believe that, I'm left with you finding Egyptian cigarettes in a Buxton drinking house, and I certainly don't believe that."

"But it's true; well, not inside exactly, outside in an alleyway."

"So you and whoever didn't want to be seen together?"

"He… we… er…"

"So you were being given a little something for your trouble. Question is, what little bit of trouble did you take?" Sam opened the yellow tin and counted. "How many d'ye smoke a day?"

"Seven or eight."

There were fourteen left.

"So you smoked that number yesterday, and it's mid morning now so you've had one or two today, let's say ten. There were twenty-five in the tin; I don't suppose Mr Smokes would have been such a cheapjack as to pay you with an opened tin. I mean to say, fine feller like you wouldn't stand for that, now. Keeping up, are you?

The clerk looked like a rabbit in thrall to a cavorting weasel.

"So you had one to try them out the night before last, just after you'd gone to your *little bit of trouble.* Like to tell me what you did for him?"

In the silence the clerk glanced toward a door at the back of the storeroom.

"Leads out onto the platform, does it, so you and the guard can load parcels straight into his van?"

"Yes, sir, that's it."

"I'll tell you what you did for Mr Smokes; you let him have your keys so he could get in here."

The mixture of fear and surprise on the clerk's face was enough. A croaky "Yes, sir" only confirmed his culpability.

"So how did it work? Mr Smokes came here with his little job, did he?"

"Oh no, sir, never seen him here." The voice was clearer now. "Outside the Railwayman's, then in the alley."

"So you gave him the keys. What time would that be?"

"He had a word when I'd finished, 'bout a quarter after eight. I were on my way for a drink an' he came up to me an' said he could do me a bit o' good if I met 'im later."

"Later?"

"Half after ten."

"Was he alone?"

"Not so sure about that; there were a woman hangin' about but I never saw them speak. She wouldn't have cost much, that's fer sure; right dowdy, she was."

"You familiar with the cost of a woman on the streets of Buxton?"

This time the clerk coloured up in the ensuing silence.

"Bring them in here after hours, do you? Is that what you thought Smokes was doing with your keys?" Another pause. "I'll tell you what he was doing." Sam was heated now. "Smokes was persuading a woman, no doubt the 'dowdy' one you saw, to pass through here, onto the platform and into a compartment of the empty stock." He was shouting now. "Then he stuck a knife through her heart and closed the door on her dead body."

The clerk seemed to have shrivelled, and mouthed the word 'murder', but no sound came out.

Sam, quieter now but menacing, continued. "What he did then was lock the carriage door. How did he do it?"

No answer.

"You could have done it. You'd have a key."

The hapless man pointed to a T-shaped object, its shank squared off toward the end, hanging by the back entrance. "But I didn't do anything, honest."

"Someone did." Sam lifted the key down. It had been painted once, but now had a dull metallic surface. Two days ago a darker mark on the crosspiece might have been red, but now it was just a dirty smear. "I'm keeping this."

"But you can't, I need it for work."

"Tell them at the stores that you've lost it and get another."

"But I'll—"

"I know; you'll have to pay. What I don't know is who Mr Smokes is. But you do, and you're going to tell me."

"But I don't. Smart sort o' man, 'bout your age: acts like you, orderin' people about an' don't expect any answering back."

"The sort of man to have Egyptian cigarettes in his pocket?"

"No, sir, he usual… I thought he'd slip me cash."

Sam noted the mistake, but stored it up for later.

"Thing about him, sir: the whiff. Ain't caught that since I were little."

"What do you mean?"

"Workhouse, sir; Mam couldn't keep us, me an' our kid, so we was left."

For a moment Sam envied the clerk. He too had been reared by strangers, but without ever knowing his mother. The present reasserted itself. "If he's giving out bribes and ordering you about and murdering defenceless women, it's not likely he's seen the inside of a workhouse recently: prison, perhaps."

"I ain't never been in prison."

"You'll be lucky not to end up there by the time this is over." Menace returned to Sam's voice. "You're going to tell me about the other times: the times when you're paid cash."

Not much of a day's work for a young man, *Go to mortuary at half after two o'clock.* True, the post-mortem report might be interesting, but then it would be back to watching out for fare dodgers all morning if he couldn't think of anything better. William had arrived for work as usual only to find the office still locked and the note from Sam.

What was he up to? The two of them had developed a comfortable routine since the Stockport outpost had opened. The Whale had said nothing about where they had to live under the new arrangements, so William continued to live at home over the bakery in Crewe. Sam, newly married, had moved to Whaley Bridge. The distances were much the same but the Whaley service was the more conveniently timed, so up till now Sam had been the first to arrive. Not today.

It occurred to William that if he went early to the mortuary he might glean a bit of extra information. He might, if he were prompt, see the doctor at his work. The family bakery was across the street from the best butcher in Crewe and he'd seen animals slaughtered and cut up often enough: it couldn't be that different and it would be more interesting than chasing unpaid fares.

The previous day he'd travelled north to Manchester on the footplate of a locomotive. Viewing Stockport from above as they'd passed over the Mersey was a revelation. But today, as William descended the station approach, he came to realise the price the town's denizens had to pay for its rail connection. The viaduct, dominating the town, filled the skyline and he was glad to turn south into Wellington Road away from its glowering presence. He was bound for the infirmary and its recently established public mortuary.

Even from the back the attendant was an unprepossessing sight. His stoop and drooping shoulders served to mask the stature of what must once have been a tall man.

"Whad'ye want? We don't allow no gawpers. No respect for the dead, most of 'em." The man was dragging a cadaver from a trolley with precious little of the respect he'd just mentioned. With the supine corpse safely on a ceramic slab, he turned. "Oh, it's the constabulary. You're too early. His Nibs ain't here yet. Then there'll be the report. I told the other bluebottle two of the afternoon." Then, as an afterthought, "An' 'e were a sergeant."

"I thought I'd come and see what's to be found, first hand."

"You sure you're up to it? The bigger you are, the harder you fall." The long, thin face lit up with relish at the prospect.

William was saved a reply by the arrival of the doctor. His ramrod-straight back made him look taller than the attendant. Occupying his face was a magnificent and much-tended moustache.

"Everything ready, Corporal?"

"Sir."

Catching sight of William, he nodded. "Make sure you fall backwards, Constable. Makes things difficult if the living join the dead on the slab."

With no more ado he was helped out of his jacket and, with sleeves rolled, donned a once-white apron and set to work.

The corpse had been covered in a sheet, but this was swept aside to reveal a woman's naked body, lying supine, its pallor tinged with blue in death. William watched, trying to concentrate on the process. The atmosphere of putrefaction seemed less as time passed but the nausea it induced got worse.

"See here, Constable, this was the fatal wound." The moustache obscured William's view as the point of entry was closely scrutinised. "Knew what he was doing, your killer." Then, "Give me a saw, Corporal."

Straightening up, the doctor displayed the instrument with his thumb placed close to its end. "'Bout an inch and a half, wouldn't you say, Constable?"

"You mean the depth of blade, sir?"

"'S right." More muffled now as he leant into his work. A long, thin instrument was being worked delicately into the wound. "Ah; there we are." Now a probe was waved under William's nose with the same thumb about eight inches from its tip. "It'd have to be that long to reach the heart."

"A stout kitchen knife, sir?"

"I suppose so." The doctor sounded disappointed. "You'd think if you were going to end a life you could do it with a bit more style; something made for the job."

"From my experience..." In his attempt to control his dizziness William lapsed into pomposity. "In my experience..." He wavered.

Meanwhile, the doctor was investigating another aspect of his cadaver. "Here, Constable, this might prove of interest to your..." He was preparing to make an incision in a distended breast. It was too much for William. Living across the road from a butcher hadn't prepared him for this after all. He sank to the floor, oblivious to the contribution he was about to be offered concerning the case, and, knees having crumpled, fell sideways.

It was late afternoon before the Stockport office of the LNWR Constabulary was fully staffed. Sam, having extracted what he could from the parcels clerk, had gone for a walk through Buxton. By retracing the route which Silk Hat had followed on Monday evening he identified the door through which the letter had been posted.

William, having been unceremoniously dragged out of the way during the autopsy, had spent some time on the mortuary floor. A splash of cold water brought him to his senses.

"Found that instructive, did you, sir?" As he opened his eyes a lugubrious face peered down at him. "Anything you missed'll be in the report. His Nibs'll write it up when he's done."

Tea was a necessity. The fire had been lit early as usual, but with no one to tend it for much of the day, it was out. Whether they would have it for much longer was doubtful in any case. The railway only provided such luxury in its waiting rooms for the colder months of the year, and May was not considered one of them. Where the coal had come from for their little office neither man had cared to ask. They made their way to the refreshment room where Sam settled himself in a secluded corner. William, as befitted his rank, was deputed to order the tea.

"I suppose you know all about this?" Sam pointed to the autopsy report he was reading. "Saw it first hand; you said you'd gone along early."

"Er… not exactly, Sam, a lot of it passed over my head."

"Quite so." The subject was dropped. "It says there was a single stab wound to the chest, left posterolateral. Round the side towards the back, he must mean."

"I suppose so."

"Then it says the blade had gone between a couple of ribs." Sam, with his right hand inside his uniform, was counting his own to find the space between ribs number five and six. "And long enough for the point to pierce the heart."

"That's what killed her."

"So you were paying attention. Did he explain what 'cardiac tamponade' means?"

"No… If you must know, I fainted."

Sam did his best to suppress a grin. "I think it's something to do with where the blood goes when it leaks from the heart. No matter; it was done by an expert with a knife…"

"I did hear that bit; the doctor said just the same: he was good with a knife."

"Now this is interesting." Reaching for his tea as he read, Sam nearly upset the cup. "He says the woman was lactating when she died. You understand what he means? She was feeding a bab."

The vision of a man in an apron, scalpel poised above a full breast, forced its way into William's mind. Seated, and supping sweet tea, he didn't quite fall off the chair, but it was close.

"You all right, William?" He was recovering by the time Sam looked up. "It says she was quite well nourished, considering."

"Considering what?"

"Considering she was poverty-stricken, and providing milk for a bab at the same time." Sam, taking pity on William, omitted the details concerning the fullness of the breasts and its implications, giving only the conclusion.

"She was feeding quite a young baby, probably six months or less. The question is…"

At last William had something to occupy his mind. "Where's the baby?"

"Quite possibly dead, I'd say." It was Sam's turn to feel squeamish. As he spoke his mind filled with the picture of a girl falling to her death whilst he stood in the snow, holding little Mary. "It's thirty-six hours since the mother died. How long will a baby live without sustenance?" Neither of them knew.

There were other matters to discuss.

"He's hiding something, I'm sure." Sam was reporting on his interview in the parcels office. "I'm sure he'd lent out his key on other occasions, but he wouldn't admit it."

"All he's guilty of so far is a breach of railway regulations."

"You're right, William; unless we can establish who killed the woman and then tie him to the clerk, we're stuck."

"Now, tell me why I was following the respectable Mr Fewster all over Manchester?"

Sam explained about Silk Hat's furtive behaviour after complimenting William on his endeavours the previous day. "Topping bit of work."

"Perhaps he just doesn't like policemen."

"Ah, but it's a bit odd. I'm certain he put something into a letter box on his way through Buxton, and when I went back there the door was locked."

"Empty?"

Sam explained there'd been no response when he knocked but he'd tugged the bell pull and knocked again.

"He ain't 'ere." A child's voice, muffled, from inside. "It's locked an' 'e's got the key."

"Who's 'he'?"

"The porter; who else?"

"What's his name?"

"Don't know. They don't tell us kids nothing."

And that was that. An adult voice had shouted from inside and the child disappeared.

It was becoming commonplace, the moment when the pots were done, little Mary was nestled in Sam's arms, and Lizzie could join the two of them. The fire was an extravagance for May, but she could see how much the austere bachelor had softened in the few months since they'd married, and she was loath to break the dream. But break it she must.

After dinner she'd remembered the letter and spent much of the afternoon considering its contents. She'd even gathered the baby up in her arms and gone to see a friend on account of the complications it would bring.

It needed a reply and Lizzie knew where her conscience was taking her, but how would Sam see it?

"This came today—"

Just then the baby chose to vomit and the uncertain moment was delayed.

"I spoke to Elsie Maida; she's stopped work to look after a new grandchild." Having cleaned the sick from Sam's waistcoat, Lizzie had returned to the letter. She'd watched Sam as he read and was not reassured by the troubled look that crossed his face.

Dear Mrs Oldroyd,

I write on behalf of our little group of ladies.

We are motivated by the highest ideals and seek to follow the example and sustain the Christian work started by Miss Louisa Twining and her Workhouse Visiting Society, now sadly disbanded.

The establishment of a Library & Reading Room to the memory of the late Mrs Kezia Bennett does great credit to Mr Bennett your father, and to yourself. It has been suggested that such a philanthropic act might be associated with a desire to help further in the relief of the deserving poor.

I have been asked to put it to you that you might care to apply to join us in our endeavours. As a respectable widow of independent means you are ideally suited to our purpose.

Yours sincerely…

"She'd be happy to have Mary for a few hours." Did that sound as if she was rushing things? Lizzie regretted having spoken and was taken aback by his reply.

"I'm investigating the murder of a young woman." Her poverty and destitution hung in the air. "It's probable that she's seen the inside of a workhouse, and may even have been living in one at the time of her death."

Lizzie sat quietly, unsure of where this was going.

"I learnt today that she was… 'lactating' was the word in the doctor's report. She'd had a baby recently, of which there was no sign, even though she'd been suckling until shortly before she was killed."

"The poor woman. What do you think happened?"

"The baby died? The doctor told William there's measles about."

"But where's the little body?" Lizzie glanced at the infant

asleep in Sam's arms to reassure herself. "What if it died a while ago and the mother's been wet-nursing?"

"Of course you must do as you please about the visiting, my dear." Sam looked at the envelope. "I suppose they're concerned with Chapel Union Workhouse." The letter had been posted in Chapel-en-le-Frith. "But I'm not sure it's wise."

Lizzie was disappointed and it showed. It must have been her crestfallen look that prompted Sam to go further.

"The victim had a rail ticket for Chapel with her when she died. Whatever's gone on, it seems the workhouse there might be involved."

"But, Sam, I'd be able to look round and ask a few questions."

"But it might be dangerous." The idea had obviously occurred to Sam already. "The wife of a policeman…"

"Look at the letter; they don't know I'm married to you."

"It doesn't say much for their detective work, I agree."

"And if they find out I could say I was trying to save embarrassment." Lizzie's grey eyes gleamed with enthusiasm.

"And anyone with a guilty conscience wouldn't believe it for a second." He was weakening. "Lizzie, my dear, I couldn't bear for you to think I would… would use you. It goes against all…"

"Don't be silly, Sam. I'm not being used, I'm volunteering."

SIX

Thursday 3rd May 1877

JIMMY HAD MADE A NEW FRIEND, OR, MORE ACCURATELY, Benjy had found a new friend and made the introduction.

With the days getting longer, budding musician and lurcher had started going out as soon as it was light. They'd find their way to a place between the cut and a railway line where the dog hunted rabbits and Jimmy settled down to practise. His music had become a serious matter. Leaving third cornet parts behind months ago, he now had his eye on first cornet. Not lead player; it wasn't only talent but tact that put that out of his reach. His father held the position for now, but joining him in the first section was attainable. So he found a place by the canal where only the passing boat traffic could hear. If they didn't like it they passed on soon enough, and when it rained there was a derelict hovel nearby that kept the worst weather at bay.

This Thursday it was fine and it was left to Benjy to check all was well with their refuge. To start, a rabbit distracted him and it was quite a few minutes before he poked his shiny black nose through the doorway. Fear swept over him as he did so; not his own, but that of the ragged child sheltering inside. The boy cowered as Benjy, tail wagging, sniffed around his huddled body.

The last stray boy he'd come across by the canal had given him food and stroked his head. Not this one, though. Benjy sat on his haunches and looked hopeful but to no avail, so he gave the pinched face a lick and settled down with his head resting on the boy's chilled body. Still no food, but the smell of fear began to subside.

Notes from the first cornet part of *Valentine's Gallop* had been played several times over before they'd been hit square and lined up in the right order. By then it was time for a break. Benjy started at Jimmy's whistle but was in a quandary. Some instinct told him he was needed in the shed; on the other hand, breakfast summoned. He stuck his head through the doorway and barked: then another whistle and more barking.

Benjy almost never barked. The arrangement Jimmy had with Mrs Oldroyd – Mrs Spray, as she had become – would hardly have lasted if he did, particularly in the last months with a baby in the house. As it was things had settled to a comfortable routine with the dog kennelled in her shed, and Jimmy free to come and go as he pleased. Indeed, he'd taken to keeping his instrument with its sheet music there, and had come to feel quite proprietorial.

But today… There must be something wrong! Jimmy set off running. By now the sun was up and, dazzled by its brightness, he could see nothing inside the hovel until his eyes adjusted to the gloom. The boy, startled by the barking, had retreated as far from the door as he could and stood, eyes wide with apprehension, as Jimmy entered.

"What are you doing here?" Even as he spoke Jimmy regretted his tone. The frightened boy had raised an arm as if to fend off a blow. "I'm Jimmy Allcroft; what's your name?"

"Can't say." Less fearful now at the more emollient tone, but no answer to the question.

"How long you been here?"

"A time."

"Bit sharp first thing. You cold?" Seeing better in the dark now, "You look it. Come outside, there's a bit o' sun."

"Can't, might get seen."

"Oh." Realisation struck. "You're runnin'."

The silence that followed was answer enough.

"Tell you what; wait here while I get something."

Even if the boy had wanted to run he couldn't. There was a dog between him and the door. Jimmy returned carrying a black case with a bulge at one end. Its interior, once carefully sculpted and covered in plum velvet, had provided a protective nest for a trumpet. It didn't suit the deeper, stubbier shape of a cornet and had been discarded, leaving space for extras packed around the horn.

"Here; you ain't 'ad no snap." Jimmy unwrapped a bit of greaseproof and handed over a piece of boiled ham. Benjy sat watching as his breakfast disappeared down the runaway's throat. "Better have this too." It was Jimmy's turn to watch his meal disappear.

The food seemed to fill out the boy, so that afterwards he seemed stronger in mind and body.

"So what y' runnin' for?"

It was too soon. Suspicion reasserted itself and the boy refused to answer.

"Well, tell me y' name."

After a pause, "Mikey" emerged as a mumble.

"Right, Mikey, Benjy and I got to go now. If you promise not to run with it I'll give y' a lend of my coat."

The letter had been signed *P. Peachment (Miss)*, so, after her own address and the date, that was how Lizzie started her reply. The discussion on Wednesday evening had only strengthened her resolve. She was determined to accept, but had conceded Sam's point and agreed to settle the matter of her marital status at the outset.

Dear Miss Peachment,
I thank you for your letter of the 2nd inst.

Your kind remarks concerning the little project undertaken by my father and myself are most gratifying. As is the invitation to apply to engage with your charitable endeavours.

Lizzie had resolved to make no mention of her new husband's occupation. Whether Sam was aware of this intention was not entirely clear, but she quieted her misgivings with the thought that he would have made a point of it if he'd considered it important. She confined herself to the following:

There is perhaps one matter to which I should draw your attention. Since opening the Reading Room & Library last year I have been fortunate enough to have been joined in matrimony to Mr Samuel Spray.

Likewise, it seemed to Lizzie that mention of little Mary would lead to unnecessary complications and serve no useful purpose. She continued:

> *Unless you feel my newly acquired marital status is an impediment, I would be grateful if you would consider my acceptance into your group.*

If she was to be of any help to Sam she felt the sooner she started with her good work the better, and finished with:

> *I would be happy to make your acquaintance, and that of the other ladies in the group, at your earliest convenience, the better to understand what my duties might be.*
>
> *I look forward to the pleasure of meeting you.*
>
> *Yours sincerely,*
> *E. Spray (Mrs)*

At less than 150 words it was modest in length, but the letter had taken all morning and much of the afternoon to write. True, Mary had made demands on her time, but something else had impeded the writing.

Elizabeth Bennett had been born the daughter of a guard on the railway. Marriage to a clerk represented social advancement, although Albert Oldroyd had treated the divide by ignoring it. Whatever failings there might have been in her first marriage there was no discord on that issue. In widowhood Lizzie had resolved the anomalies of her position as houseowner, proprietor of a small business and centre of a social group that could never aspire to either, with grace and humility. Inheriting money from her brother-in-law had certainly brought her a huge problem but that was nothing to do with social standing.

Now, for the first time, she was to be tested on the issue and this response was the first hurdle.

By the time her reply was ready to post, Lizzie could hear Jimmy in the yard.

"Yes, missus?" He had come to the scullery door when she'd called.

"Could you run an errand for me and take this to…" Lizzie had a better idea. She'd been trapped in the house all day and needed some fresh air. "No; would you mind staying for a minute and listening out for the baby? I'll go for the post."

It hadn't been in his plan, to hang around after school, but needs must. Benjy seemed pleased to get his tea before going for a run out. *He won't like it when we get back*, thought Jimmy. He'd brought some scraps from home, and Mrs Oldr… no, Mrs Spray, always left something out as well. He told himself that it was an easy mistake. The scraggy offcuts on a tin plate sat next to a pan with the remains of last night's Irish stew. Under the lid there was at least another meal for two. But whose meal? Jimmy borrowed a tin mug and took a scoop from the pan out to the shed with the scraps.

"I'm back, Jimmy." Lizzie called from the hallway. "Did you find what I'd left out for Benjy?"

Jimmy would need his coat before going home, and he was running late. The tin mug didn't help, and there was something else.

“Please, missus, you got any old sacks I could have? Don’t matter about holes.” He was round the back of the bakery. The man himself was away to his tea by this time, leaving his wife to manage. Bakers start early. Jimmy was at school with their son.

“Hello, Jimmy, what d’ye want old sacks for?”

“Mek a bed fer my dog.”

“Here; the mice ’ave been at these, will they do?”

He couldn’t run with an armful of hessian and the cold stew in his hand. No time for practice tonight. Jimmy hurried as best he could. He hadn’t considered the possibility earlier of Mikey taking off with his coat, but as he and the dog neared the hovel he did wonder. In the event, Benjy raced ahead and was trying to get his head scratched by Mikey as he arrived.

“’Ere, cop this. Best I could do. Cold stew is still stew, and better ’an no stew.”

Without speaking the boy wolfed down the food, watched by a pair of mournful eyes. The dog was ever hopeful.

“I need my coat, I’ll be in trouble else. These’ll keep out the cold.” Jimmy handed over the sacks.

So far Mikey had barely said a word. He stared at the floor and finally came up with, “What y’ do it for?”

“’Ad a bit of trouble my sen. Someone ’elped.” Jimmy remembered Constable Archer rescuing him at London Road ticket barrier. “I’ll see what I can do in the mornin’.”

“I’m afraid we’re a bit short tonight.” Lizzie was preparing their tea whilst Sam sat by the fire in the parlour. “There’s less of this stew than I thought. I’ll have to boil up some more potatoes to go with it.”

With little Mary snuggled in his arms Sam wasn't really listening. He was trying to reconcile his lately found contentment with his working day in Buxton. He and William had spent much of their time in graveyards, and they hadn't been prepared for the diversity they met there.

"Ain't got no time fer gab. Anyway, 't ain't seemly whilst I'm digging." The voice came from six feet down, and the grave was clearly for an adult. What they were after was something smaller.

"Ain't buried no little 'uns fer months." This from an old man, gnarled and bent, who looked happy to rest on his shovel.

"No, Sergeant. Not at St John's." The sexton was adamant. "There have been no graves dug for minors for several months."

"What about newborns put in an adult's coffin?"

The sexton looked shocked at the suggestion. "Really, Sergeant!"

"He didn't actually deny it, William." The two detectives were making their way to the premises of Dickens & Nephew. "It happens and it's cheap. I'm pretty sure an undertaker will do it just as he's screwing down the lid. We'll see what Mr Akers has to say."

It had started well the last time Sam and the undertaker had met. To Akers' amazement he and the Whale had rousted the coroner out on a Saturday at the outset of the Tarp affair. Not only that; before it was over the man had resigned amid rumours of corruption. Later Akers had slumped over a table in his favourite public house, leaving such a narrow gap between sober professional discretion and alcoholic stupor that Sam had found extracting information hard work.

"Ah, Sergeant… such a pleasure… and you've brought a constable too."

Archer was introduced.

"Not another murder, I hope." The gleam in Akers' eye suggested the opposite.

"We are concerned with the identity of a woman, lately deceased. It seems likely that she gave birth shortly before her own death. We thought that if the infant is also dead you might have heard something."

"Here in Buxton, you mean?"

"It's one line of enquiry, yes."

"You've tried the graveyards?"

"We've been round the churches."

"There's a private chapel up at Colonel Sturgis's, out towards Harpur Hill; the Hall." Akers paused, biting his lip. "Something in the paper a month or two back…"

"A bit out of reach for our cadaver." Sam was thinking of the wretched woman lying dead in a rail compartment. "I don't suppose there's a burial ground anyway."

"Oh there is, for the family, like… That's it – an announcement of a private funeral; Mrs Sturgis died whilst the colonel was away in Africa."

Not what we're looking for, thought Sam as they left. Not that they'd found anything that *was* what they were looking for, as William pointed out.

"Bit of an empty day, Sam."

Sam was about to agree but startled William by stopping dead in his tracks and saying, "Let's go in here."

They were outside an oak-panelled door with a polished knocker and a spotless step. As Sam grasped the heavy scroll of brass and declared their presence, William read the list of qualifications engraved into the gleaming plate on the wall.

"Sergeant Spray, this is a surprise – a pleasant one, I may add, and with a colleague too."

Introductions were made and the two visitors found themselves in the room where Sam and the doctor had last met.

"You've not been much in Buxton of late, or at least, not so it appeared in the public press? I read about your exploits in the Tarp affair in the *Derbyshire Times.*" He turned to William. "No doubt you were involved too, Constable? Most creditable, yes… er, most… What can I do for you today, gentlemen?"

Sam explained. "And we're sure she died here. There must be an infant, most probably a dead infant, and Buxton seems the place to start looking."

There was a silence in which the doctor attempted but failed to remain impassive. Clearly he was a man troubled by indecision.

"There was a small outbreak of scarlatina in Buxton a short while ago. To my knowledge not many children died." There was another silence. "Professional discretion prevents me from going into details, but such diseases are no respecter of status. The quality suffer equally with the teeming masses."

And that was it. The conversation survived a few minutes more before the two detectives were escorted politely to the door and found themselves on the street.

"Pleasant enough for a sawbones," was William's view. "Not much help, though."

Sam strode off, leaving William to follow. As they walked, they climbed. Buxton's reputation as the highest town in the country didn't mean it was at the top of anything. Then the route deceived and sent them downhill before turning toward Harpur Hill and they resumed their climb. Nothing was said, but by the time they reached the Hall both men were happy to rest on the wall opposite its imposing gates.

"You see, William, clever fellows, like our sawbones back there, don't always talk straight. What he told us, by not actually saying it, was that a child of the gentry died recently. I don't suppose he was talking about the Cavendish family; however hard he polishes his doorknocker they'll be having London physicians at Chatsworth. No; what he's talking about is the local gentry. We know there's a private cemetery here so we'd better take a look."

The wrought iron was impressive enough but the gates provided no security, being unlocked. The unmistakable outline of a chapel stood amid some stunted yews just off the drive.

William's tentative "Wouldn't be much of a detour…" was cut short as Sam set off for the graveyard. Still some distance from the house, and hidden by the old trees, they investigated gravestones. The Sturgis family traced their line through two centuries. One General Wilbert Sturgis had departed this life in 1868 and lay beside the mortal remains of Eleonora, his wife who predeceased him by twenty-one years. *The parents of the colonel presently serving in Africa*, thought Sam. Of the headstones, there was only one more recent, but of greater interest to the two detectives was the nearby pile of earth. William spotted it first.

"No time yet for a stone, Sam; and too big for a baby."

The earth had been turned up long enough for the wind to have dried it out and a paler crust had formed on the surface of the dark loam. Flowers had been laid on top, but the daffodils had been there some time and lent an uncared-for air to the grave… except. Except that at one end a small area of the surface had been disturbed and on the darker, moister soil lay a nosegay of white scented flowers, small but fresh enough to have been picked that morning.

"What d'ye make of them, William?"

Neither man cared much about flowers, but after a few weeks of marriage Sam had often enough seen Lizzie throw out wilted bunches. She would certainly have disposed of the daffodils by now, and quite possibly replaced them with the white ones.

"Been there a while, those yellow ones, don't you reckon?"

"You mean, whoever put them there doesn't care enough to change them."

"What about the others?"

William wasn't much impressed by the little bunch and said so. He also said he didn't think there was much point in making further enquiries. Nonetheless he found himself walking round the rear of the house whilst Sam knocked politely on the imposing front door.

"The likes of you go round the back." There was an air of permanence about the woman's disapproving look. In Sam's judgement it wasn't just reserved for policemen. "What d'ye want wi' us? We're respectable folk here."

"I'm Sergeant Spray," Sam said, proffering his warrant card, "and I'm investigating the murder of a young woman."

"We haven't had any murders here, Sergeant, and if we had the master would insist on an investigation by an officer of a higher rank than sergeant."

"But he's in Africa subduing the natives, so you'll have to put up with me."

"Well, really!"

"My apologies," the woman was dressed in black bombazine, "I should have offered my condolences at the outset. Mrs Sturgis died recently, I believe."

"That is a family matter, of no consequence to you."

"I heard there has been scarlatina about. These must be worrying times."

It was only Sam's foot that prevented the door being shut in his face.

"Here, you can't do that, you haven't the right."

"Has a child died in this house in the last week or so?"

The question proved too much for the woman and, lunging, she unbalanced Sam. In an attempt to stop himself falling he withdrew his foot from the threshold and the door slammed shut.

William returned, having fared even less well than Sam. "Door locked, couldn't get an answer."

Walking together, away from the Hall, there didn't seem much to say, but to William's surprise they found themselves returning to the graveyard.

"There's something here that I'm missing." Sam stood staring at the white posy. "They're not snowdrops, I'm sure of that, but they mean something."

Back on the road they were making good progress downhill. The wild moorland gave way to something softer and they came level with a garden. Humble it may have been, but it sported an air of purpose on account of the labour that had gone into the digging of it. Everywhere the soil was turned and much of it planted. Here and there the cultivated rows were separated by patches of established plants, many of which were already in flower. Close to the gate was a particularly striking show.

"Good afternoon to you, sir." Sam addressed the posterior of a man bending to his work.

The response was unpromising. The gardener, when he finally stood, was straight as a ramrod and he glared at his questioner. A scar across one grizzled cheek gave him a lopsided look; the face of a man with three score and ten behind him, and yet…

"I got work t' do; an' I don't hold wi' coppers neither. Had enough of bein' ordered around for one lifetime."

"We were admiring your garden. You do well to keep it up…" 'At your age' was left unsaid.

"Been at it man and boy fer nigh on sixty year, 'cept when I weren't."

"I'd hazard you were in India."

Whilst not softening, the old man's glare turned to interest. "How d'ye come t' that?"

"The sun does something to the skin, and there wasn't too much of that in the Crimea, so maybe further east?"

"You in the Crimea?" After Sam's nod, he looked across to William. "Not 'im. He ain't been nowhere."

With that settled the two old soldiers, reconciled now, totally ignored the youngster.

"What'll y' be after? In my experience men in uniforms like yourn allus want summat."

"I want to ask about those flowers." Sam pointed to the mass of white blooms by the gate.

"Why'm you askin' 'bout they?"

"I saw some the same less than an hour ago; a little posy on a grave without a stone."

The old man glanced uphill, back along the policemen's route. "You been up there, 'ave you? Ain't been the same since the young master took charge."

Sam did a little sum. The colonel must be at least forty, probably older.

"The old general, now, 'e were a real gentleman. It were 'im what took me out the garden and then set me back there after India. Head gardener at the Hall, I was, till the general died."

"So you don't think much to Colonel Sturgis?"

"He's all right, I s'pose. Lets me 'ave this cottage. It's his woman… was his woman. Mrs Sturgis, she were all right till she died, then this other one moved in."

"He married again?"

Reluctantly, the gardener agreed.

"So that's the grave of the second Mrs Sturgis back there without any stone?"

A young voice calling from the cottage interrupted Sam's questioning. "Gramps, you must come in now, it's time fer yer tea." Although taken aback at the sight of two policemen, she continued. "Whatever it is, it'll have to wait."

Gramps turned back to the visitors and looked skywards in mock exasperation. "Worse than a sergeant major, she is, but she will have her way. You'd best come in."

Inside was cramped. In its day the cottage would have sheltered a whole family, but now it housed only a young woman and her grandfather. The two of them had spread themselves, so the men in uniform seemed to fill the place to bursting.

"If you stay there I'll see to a brew when I've settled him."

'Settling him' consisted of placing a plate, overfull with a Barnsley chop and boiled potatoes, on the table. Perhaps the granddaughter ate hers separately, thought Sam.

Later, the tea things cleared and each with a mug, they returned to the matter of flowers.

"They'm lily of the valley, them white ones. Smell strong; if y' like that sort o' thing."

Sam had been troubled for much of the afternoon; something that floated close to consciousness, but never quite getting there. 'Smell strong' cleared the way for understanding. The old man continued grumbling.

"It's her what likes 'em. They get all over a garden if ye don't keep at 'em. I'd have had rid 'cept fer the fuss it'd cause."

"Gramps, you wouldn't! Gran loved them when she was still with us."

"S'pose. Anyways, you seem to be doin' it for me, the number you takes up there." He gave a nod in the direction of the Hall. "Takes some every time she goes there fer work." Gramps spoke in mock confidentiality to the two men. "Thinks I don't notice."

"So it's you that put the little posy on Mrs Sturgis's grave?"

"Not hers…" The girl's vehemence startled her audience. "The…"

"The baby's?" The question came from Sam unbidden.

"How do you know? That woman told me to say nothing to anyone…"

Sam assumed he'd already met 'that woman' at the door to the Hall. Confusion reigned.

"You've spoken to Mrs…" She faltered. "Can't talk 'bout that either."

"The woman who left last Monday?"

The girl was mute, but Sam read her look as agreement.

"It was after the baby died." This time a statement; Sam was surer of himself now. "The grave was opened and the baby placed in its mother's. Did she kill the baby, the woman who left?"

"No, no, no, she was feeding it…" Too late now for secrecy; the words tumbled out, "giving it suck. She came when Mrs Sturgis got ill. That man arranged it."

"That man?"

"I dunno; never really seen him. He came and took her away after, though, I know that much. The baby died of a fever… wi' spots an all. Afterward that woman said the wet nurse had to go. Me and Betsy Piggin were the ones who loved little Ellie. We called her that 'cause no one else would give her a name. Got it from the graveyard."

The policemen had found what they came for, but Sam had one more question. "How long since was the colonel sent to Africa?"

It was the old man who answered. "'Bout eighteen months."

SEVEN

Friday 4th May 1877

"I've replied to Miss Peachment."

Sam looked at her quizzically.

"The workhouse visiting lady. I decided to tell her we're married. I don't want to be Mrs Oldroyd in anyone's eyes. I'm married to you."

"If you think that's for the best, my dear." Sam had thought so from the start but didn't say it. Whatever Lizzie's reasoning, the acknowledgement pleased him.

"I didn't mention Mary or your position."

"Oh."

"The other was a matter of putting her right over a misunderstanding. You being a policeman and our taking in little Mary hasn't arisen. Were it to do so I should be entirely open."

All perfectly reasonable, thought Sam; even so, he resolved to send William to Chapel Workhouse and keep the name Spray out of it.

"I think we've established the identity of our murder victim." Sam described his day. "I was puffing by the time we'd climbed up to the Hall. You're feeding me too well."

They both laughed at his ignorance of flowers, and were sad at the death of a child.

"So you see, Lizzie, you were ahead of me, about the wet-nursing. I should have listened last night when you suggested it. That's what she was doing up at the Hall until the baby died."

"How do you think you find a wet nurse, Sam?"

He didn't know, but he hoped William would find out the next morning.

"What do you want?"

The two men eyed each other warily. The policeman with his uniform and warrant card derived advantage from status, but the other was on his own territory, and that too carried weight. With a Board of Guardians, and five hundred inmates, not to mention the paid staff, the Union Workhouse was a substantial institution and he controlled its entrance.

"I'm investigating a murder."

"We ain't got no dead today. I'd know, I 'ave to keep the register. I strikes 'em out when they pass over."

"Have you got Betsy Piggin on that list?"

"Nope."

"You seem very sure; hadn't you better look?"

"I know about Betsy Piggin, she ran when it happened. Left a brat. They're not supposed to do that."

"What happened?"

"No better 'an she oughter be, that one. Calls 'erself Mrs but I ain't never seen no Mr Piggin, and she comes 'ere bold as brass wi' a boy and another on the way."

"Perhaps Mr Piggin went off and left her to it."

"Perhaps. Anyways, the baby was lost. They don't thrive 'ere, them women loses most on 'em."

"When was that?"

The date wasn't forthcoming but between the two of them they decided it was about six and ten weeks ago.

"Tell you what," the porter dredged a nugget from the back of his mind, "it were about a time that busybody came nosing round. Mind you, he keeps on coming so that ain't much 'elp."

"How often does he come?"

"Now an' again. Usually when 'e wants summat."

"What does he want?"

"Supposed to inspect the school."

"You have a schoolroom here?" William was learning fast. The workhouse was not a topic often discussed amongst the respectable.

"Ooh, aye... did 'ave, but the bigger ones 'ave been sent to Buxton; just."

"So why does he come here now?" At the time William didn't know why he was pursuing the subject of the school inspector. As he probed deeper the porter had become increasingly evasive, and later William decided it was this that had spurred him on.

"Dunno." Deceit hovered over the answer.

"Where's Betsy Piggin's boy? Was he sent off to Buxton?"

"Aye, wi' the rest."

"That would be after she left?"

"You ask too many questions, Mr Policeman, and seeing as you're off your patch I don't have to answer."

The man had finally noticed the LNWR insignia on his uniform, thought William.

"Show me Mrs Piggin's quarters." William, trying to assert authority with an order, came a cropper.

"Can't do that. She were still lyin' in."

William was mystified.

"Don't allow men in wi' all they loose wimmin giving birth. Only man let in there's the doctor, and he don't come any too often."

They stood just outside a cubbyhole in which the porter spent much of his day. The doorbell jangled, demanding the man's attention, and in the confined space they shuffled past each other so that he could get to the door. William found himself alone in the little room, and as the new caller was attended to he looked about him. He'd already got used to the all-pervading smell of boiled cabbage and unwashed bodies that enveloped the place, but inside the porter's den the smell of sweaty feet was overwhelming.

There was only room for one chair and, seated, he could hardly avoid examining the porter's desk. On it was an unappealing selection of items, dominated by a register lying open. William wondered if his own name would ultimately be entered, but probably not as against each entry was a description such as 'paup.', 'common p.', 'orphan' and such. It was a register of admissions and discharges, the abbreviation 'dd' attaching to many of the children.

Tucked beneath its battered leather binding, amongst the dust and crumbs, not to mention the odd mouse turd, lay a sheet torn from a newspaper. It was the front page of the *Manchester Evening News* from some weeks back and would not have merited a second look, but for one thing.

"'Ere, what you a-doin'? This is my place, ye're not allowed." The visitor had been disposed of.

"Just keeping out of your way."

"Yer can keep out of my way by leavin'. I ain't got no more time fer ye."

The ledger, lying as it had before William had looked beneath, obscured the page of small advertisements, and the desk appeared undisturbed.

Alone in the constabulary office, Sam contemplated the day ahead. He was sure about what he'd done, but even so he didn't like compromises, and the complexities of married life had forced one on him today. He and William should have gone together. In all likelihood the murdered woman had been a resident at the Chapel Spike, and other than that they had precious little to go on. But whatever else he had to protect his family, and it was in Lizzie's interest that the name Spray was kept out of the investigation.

In the past he'd always been clear about what was right and what was wrong, but that was a matter of knowing. Now he was being driven by feelings, and he'd become increasingly aware of how much more powerful than merely knowing they could be. And then there was the Whale.

As he considered the propriety of devoting constabulary time to such a personal matter, not that he had any idea of where to start, there was a knock at the door.

"Please, sir." Outside stood a boy of perhaps fifteen years, cap in hand, neckerchief knotted rakishly to one side and an air of purpose about him. "Please, sir, are you the rail company rozzer?"

Sam, pleased to have his problems displaced by the possibility of action, took no offence at this description. "I'm Sergeant Spray of the LNWR Constabulary, yes."

"I been sent for yer, 'cause of what I found."

"And what was that?"

"A dead 'un, in the clough up by Barmoor."

"You mean a dead body?"

"'S right. Bit of a toff from his clothes… well, he would've been if he'd been wearin' them."

"You mean he's naked?"

"Well, he ain't got 'is breeks on. They was rolled up by 'im."

"Where's Barmoor? "

"Yer know, Barmoor Clough, up near Dove 'Oles. 'S where your railway meets up wi' us."

"You mean the tramway; little wagons with horses?"

"And a plane wi' the heavy ones goin' downhill, pullin' t' others up." The lad had a sense of pride, and he wasn't going let Sam belittle his place of work. "You've got a siding there, it goes off just as the two lines separate, and runs alongside us fer a bit an' then into a disused quarry."

"What's your name, young man?"

"Me? I'm George, they calls me Nipper George 'cause that's what I am. Nippers is boys what look fer the 'osses. I got a team o' five."

Sam had seen the antiquated tramway from the train window on his journeys to Buxton, and thought it a relic of the past, but here was a boy telling him a different story.

"We sends stone and such down t' Buggie Basin."

Of course; Sam remembered seeing the tramway terminus at Bugsworth with the bodies of the wagons being tipped so that their loads of limestone ended up in the boats.

"Why have you come here? Wouldn't it have been nearer to find a constable in Buxton?"

"Your lot gotta big name. Anyroad, 'tis on your ground."

"Are you sure?"

He ignored the uncertainty on Nipper's face. It was enough that he was getting out of the office.

Sam hoped he wouldn't have to have a showdown with the guard. Nipper had arrived on the footplate of a locomotive, his wagoner having flagged it down as it picked its way through the clough. Whatever the passengers thought of coming to a screeching halt in the middle of nowhere, the driver had been happy enough to take the lad to Stockport, so he'd arrived without a ticket. Now, riding in the splendour of third class, he was depending on Sam to fix things if there were any questions on the return journey.

In the event the guard was nowhere to be seen, and Nipper arrived at Dove Holes without a stain on his character. During the journey he had regaled Sam with the wonders of a cab ride.

"That fire's right hot, an 'e kept shovin' more on." Clearly the boy was impressed by the extravagant use of coal. Back home things must have been more frugal.

Some way after Chapel he'd waved a hand at a grimy mill in the clough. "Th'owd feller works there an' we lives close by."

Stockport Edgeley Station too had been a revelation. "Bigger'n Dove 'Oles, innit?" Nipper could walk to Dove Holes. There and Chapel, in the opposite direction, were as far as he'd ever been from home.

Sam couldn't think of a way of stopping the train in Barmoor Clough so they travelled on to Dove Holes. He set about impressing the station official with his warrant card and travel pass whilst Nipper made himself scarce.

With the porter out of sight the two travellers set off back along the track. Soon, more open country gave way to a ravine.

"See, this is where the clough starts." Sam might as well have been on one of Mr Cook's guided tours. "There, look!" He was being led out of a short tunnel. "That's the tramway, and your siding's along there." This was said with a mixture of resentment and triumph. "My gaffer says we had to move our track to let your lot in, and then y' took the trade." Nipper was walking in front but Sam could imagine the scowl on his face. "Then the seam failed."

By now they had entered the narrow defile with its rusty track.

"Right, Mr Policeman, here he is."

The body, lying in a crumpled heap, had been there for some time. With his trousers in a bundle beside him, his bare legs had been gnawed at by a hungry animal. His eye sockets were empty and decomposition had set in. Weeks rather than days, thought Sam.

"'Spect it's the crows." Nipper gave his opinion, unmoved by the gory sight. "I seen dead sheep on the moor wi' their eyes pecked out. They'll do it when the animal's alive and just cast."

Sam asked what he meant by 'cast', and had to endure a pitying look from the boy.

"You lot don't know much." After a pause to rub it in, he relented. "Sheep, usually a yow wi' a full fleece, gets on her back an' can't get on 'er feet. Farmer loses her and her lambs if she ain't righted."

The corpse hadn't suffered that fate, thought Sam. The blow that had crushed the side of his skull would have killed instantly. All the other mutilation must have happened after death. He knelt down by the remains and pulled aside the coat. One of its outside pockets was ripped open, as if in a frenzy, but from inside the garment Sam was able to extract a money case and pocketbook intact. Whatever had happened to him, it wasn't done to rob.

"Why did you come here in the first place?"

From where they stood it was just possible to see past a lever, standing up from its ground frame in rusty solitude. It operated the points that allowed access to the disused siding from the main line. Beyond ran the tramway, the track itself lower and out of Sam's line of sight, but its position marked by a stack of rusty metal.

"Wheel broke. 'S allus 'appenin'. They gets hot an' cracks. My wagoner and a mate were fixin' a new one from the pile." The lad pointed to what Sam had assumed was scrap. "I were seeing to th' 'osses, but they were quiet enough so I came here fer…" Quite what he'd come for he couldn't bring himself to say, but it must have required more privacy than a jimmy riddle. Sam didn't press the matter.

"Have you had to stop for repairs here before?"

"Can't ever remember. It's the curves where the wheels get hot. That out there's straight." He waved a hand in the direction of a team of horses plodding, one by one, across the narrow field of vision which was as much as they could see of the world outside. Following came a line of wagons creaking under their loads of limestone.

Any further along the siding and they would be out of sight. It afforded absolute privacy, so why, thought Sam, had the man died so near the main line?

"You'd best be off; your gaffer will be wanting you back."

"Nah. He said come back t'morrer. Mind you, they'll dock me a day's pay." Nipper treated this with a philosophical shrug. "Might as well come wi' you."

"Right, let's go and see what's along here."

They walked deeper into the cutting. Its steep sides gave way further on to a wider space with the old quarry face towering around them. A simple buffer stop prevented the now non-existent traffic from falling off the end of the track. Sam had walked in the cess, but it hadn't been easy. Weeds hid the unevenness of a track bed in a state of disrepair. Nipper fared better, having found a stride that suited him on the sleepers, staying between the rails.

It nagged at Sam, but what *it* was he couldn't quite say until the youngster let out an expletive quite inappropriate for a lad of his age.

"Will yer look at this?" He was trying to dislodge the mess from his boot. Fresher on the inside than its crusted exterior, it had been lying on the track for a while. "That's nivver sheep. Them's usually black and lumpy, like rabbits', only bigger."

Sam could only agree. What Nipper had put his foot in was evidence of human bodily function. He looked around and found more in varying stages of decomposition. It all lay along a short length in the middle of the track.

All of a sudden *it* came into focus. Unused by quarry traffic, the siding should have been completely derelict, but it wasn't. Old and rusty the rails may have been, but not quite rusty enough. He'd examine the lever frame more carefully on the way back, but he was certain it would be greased and easily moved when he tried it. Something was shunted into the siding from time to time, and it had a lavatory. An on-train convenience, no better than a privy over a cesspit, despite its ceramic bowl, dropped its effluent straight onto the track.

What to do?

Jimmy knew he shouldn't be pinching food from Mrs Oldroyd… no, Spray. She were all right, he thought, even if he didn't always remember her new name. If he upset her he'd be… in trouble, yes; failing her, yes; but failing himself as well. He prided himself on getting things right and getting them done too.

Just now, what needed doing was Mikey. The boy would die if he wasn't fed and watered and kept warm. Well, he'd done what he could with the sacks, and he'd found a bit of food for yesterday; what about today?

It had needed planning; mainly the purloining of a bit of greaseproof the night before.

"I'll have mine hard, please, Ma."

"But you like them soft, Jimmy." His mother always sent the family out with a good breakfast. "Never mind, I'll do 'em wi' yer dad's."

As the eldest it was Jimmy's job to help. With limited space Ma was at the frying pan, and Jimmy held plates out to be filled and then, turning, delivered them first to his dad and then the rest. Since they were an odd number there was always a single plate, usually his Ma's. Today he contrived to deliver the one on its own to himself, and with his free hand deposit one of his fried eggs and a piece of bacon into the greaseproof.

"I'm off to see to Benjy." This was his regular morning routine and Jimmy left without comment from the rest.

They might have been surprised to see him run up Mill End, and Mrs Spray might have wondered why he didn't pop his head round the door and wish her "G' mornin', missus", if she hadn't been distracted by a crying baby.

He hurried on, Benjy having to trot to keep up, even in the town, but Mikey was hidden further away than Jimmy usually had time for in the morning and he didn't want to be late for school again. It'd be a thrashing this time.

As before, Benjy arrived first at the hovel, and this time he didn't have to beg for attention. Mikey looked up apprehensively when Jimmy entered, as if he might not be entitled to the morsel of affection bestowed on him by the dog.

"Here, 'tis the best I can do."

Gratitude shone out of the waif's eyes, but 'thank you' was beyond him as he wolfed down the food. He still looked blue and cold, but brighter than yesterday.

"I'll be back later." And Jimmy was off.

After school, he had time, but nothing more. He didn't get dinner in the middle of the day, and tea was late in the Allcroft household on account of his dad's job. Nothing had been left out for Benjy either. Mrs Spray must have more on her mind, thought Jimmy. With something on her mind she might be more amenable to a plan that he'd been weighing up all day. He still had doubts, but when he brought the dog back it might be the ideal moment to try it. Meanwhile, he'd have to do the best he could.

"Got any stale bread ye can't sell?" The bakery was closed and he'd returned to the back door.

"Oh, it's you again. Did those sacks do fer ye dog all right? I don't think there are any more I can let you have."

"They did just fine, missus, ta."

"So it's yesterday's loaves yer after? I didn't know your ma kept chickens."

The woman had her back turned, and Jimmy was able to mumble a reply that didn't quite amount to a lie.

"There's nothing fer free; this is today's but it'll be a halfpenny in the morning."

Jimmy put a hand to his pocket and did his best to look crestfallen.

"Oh go on then, you'd best have it, but I'll not mek a habit of it. He'll…" She glanced up at the ceiling above the shop. "He'll want to know where the profit's going."

So that was it: bread that would be stale by morning.

If Jimmy felt he'd failed, the boy in the hovel didn't. At the sight of a whole loaf his eyes lit up and for a moment or two he looked almost normal. What was normal for Mikey was still a mystery, and if he wanted to keep it that way Jimmy wasn't going to ask. But there was something else on his mind.

"See here, young Mikey, this won't do."

The youngster, mouth full of bread, stopped chewing. Suddenly he looked hunted, much as he had when Benjy first discovered him.

"Don't be feared, I'm still tryin' t' help," Jimmy went on. "I keeps Benjy in a shed at Mrs Spray's. It smells of the dog, but you seem t' get on. It'd be warmer than here, and soon enough the farmer's going to catch you."

"She'll send for a rozzer." Mikey had dropped his first crumb of information.

"Why are you frightened of the rozzers?"

Too far, too fast. Silence.

"She's a good woman, she's helped me." It seemed the wrong moment to mention she was married to a policeman.

"No!" For the first time since they'd met, there was a firmness in Mikey's voice.

Jimmy's plan would have to wait.

EIGHT

Saturday 5th May 1877

Mill End had seemed long and steep at the end of Friday. By the time Sam had arranged for the body to be taken to Buxton Mortuary and had another look round the quarry, the day was over.

"The thing is, Lizzie, his wasn't the only death."

They were sitting together after tea and telling each other of their day's doings. Little Mary, having gurgled and smiled at Sam earlier, was sleeping, and he had suppressed, for another day, the nagging suspicion that he wasn't deserving of such contentment.

"There was a dead dog there too. The boy from the tramway swore it was his family's and had been lost a few days before."

That Nipper had been more upset by the sight of the intact body of a dog than the mutilated corpse of a man had encouraged Sam to believe him. "My dad allus had summat in his coat fer t'dog." That too fitted with the dead man's torn pocket; the dog must have been hungry. Something else would have gnawed at the corpse earlier when it was fresh.

"At least we know who he is and where he's from."

They were sitting in the kitchen, and spread across the table were such of the dead man's possessions as he carried with him. Business cards filled a section of his pocketbook, and Sam handed one to Lizzie.

Hubert Golightly

Golightly & Schmidt

Cotton Merchants

Manchester – Charleston – Calcutta

"There's a business address on the back and I've a home address in Didsbury on a visiting card here. He looks well-to-do."

In amongst the sovereigns and small change lay a notebook, leather-bound and prim. Whether the random jottings inside would shed any light on the man's death would have to wait for a closer inspection the next day.

"Mary was very good today. She really is getting heavier, I'm sure of it."

Sam tucked a scrap of newsprint back into the pocketbook. That too would have to wait.

"How long, do you think, before Miss Peachment writes back?"

Sam had no idea, but felt it tactful to offer a guess. "Oh, only a day or two, my dear."

In the event a reply arrived the next morning, but by then Sam was on his way to Stockport. Superintendent Wayland had issued no orders about Saturday duties, and until now the two policemen had worked week and week about.

Nothing had been said to alter the arrangement, but both officers arrived as if it had never existed.

"Right, William; you first." Sam wanted to get all the details of Chapel Spike out of the way before the two of them made a start on what looked like a new investigation.

"To start with, that porter. He agreed a woman called Betsy Piggin had been there, had a baby that died, and then left. Let slip that a school inspector comes regular, although the school-age children have moved to a new place in Buxton. Got very defensive when I started asking questions and obviously regretted saying anything on the subject, but Betsy had left an older child, and he'd been sent there with the rest."

"That it, then?" Sam was keen to make a start on what had befallen Mr Hubert Golightly.

"Not quite." William explained about the page of small advertisements as he pulled out his notebook. "Don't know if it means anything, but it was ringed with a red pencil." He started reading from his own notes.

Nursery Services

It is desired to enlist the services of clean and

respectable women to provide for the natural care of infants.

A fee is available to any person making a suitable introduction.

"Then there was a box number." William stared at his own writing. "What does it mean by 'natural care', Sam?'

Sam harrumphed and started into the matter of the dead man. He'd got as far as the empty eye sockets before he faltered. Afterwards he thought it must have been Nipper's description of a cast ewe with hungry lambs looking for milk that brought suckling another woman's baby to mind, but at the time the subject just floated to the surface. "I think it means wet-nursing, William, and we're interested in that subject, aren't we?"

Two nights ago when he and Lizzie had wondered how to find a wet nurse the possibility of a small ad in the *Manchester Evening News* hadn't occurred to them. The women who'd seek such an occupation would, in Sam's estimation, have been unlikely to peruse a newspaper, if indeed they could read at all. But an intermediary, that was different. Someone advertising such services needed women; necessarily women who'd lost their babies, or were prepared to abandon them, for the sake of money to be earned. Such women might be found in a workhouse, and who better than the porter to know who the likely candidates were?

"Another visit to the spike for you, William."

"But, Sam..." His senior officer glared and William wilted. "No matter..."

"Now, let's get back to the cotton merchant..."

The story of Sam's day in Barmoor Clough further unfolded as the contents of the late Hubert Golightly's pockets were spread across the desk. This time much attention was devoted to the notebook. At first glance the contents were unremarkable, mostly referring to incoming consignments of raw cotton from faraway places and deliveries fulfilled nearer home. 'M' figured here and there, and introduced a more domestic note. *Settle M's a/c at Lewis's* was the last entry, but earlier 'M' had issued instructions to *Fulfil Olsberg & Co. order by Thurs week.* There were similar entries scattered through the pages, some with dates attached.

"What's that?" The scrap of newsprint, replaced so casually when it had fallen out the previous evening, reappeared. This time William retrieved it from the floor.

Free Spirits in the Peak

For active gentlemen keen to exert themselves in novel and diverting ways.

Explore

Any crevasse or hillock as the fancy takes. Ropes and other paraphernalia provided as desired. Willing and compliant companions ease your way to a punishing, or energetic, or relaxing, but always

Blissful Experience

"What do you think this is about?" He read it again. "Perhaps it's to do with mountain climbing?"

"It's hardly the Alps out there. There's something I can't put my finger on…" Whilst William pondered the mystery, Sam went back to the notebook. "Every so often he put a little mark and a date. Nothing to show what it means."

There was watery sunshine outside, but set back under the platform canopy the constabulary office benefited not at all. The grate was empty of the fire that had kept it warm and boiled a kettle throughout the colder months.

"No more until October, Sam; I'll go to the refreshment room."

"There you are, my duck; stopped y'r coal, 'ave they?" The gleaming urn gurgled and hissed as boiling water ran into William's teapot. "'Ave these on the company." Two rock buns were slipped across the counter with a surreptitious wink.

With both hands occupied, the journey back was a perilous affair. The two crumbly buns would have ended on the floor had not Sam seen the problem and shot out of his chair to catch them as William navigated the office door. It was at this moment that the light dawned.

"See here; let me look at that cutting again." Tea was forgotten as William thumbed through his notebook. "Sam, look at this."

It was indeed a coincidence. Both Hubert Golightly and the workhouse porter had found their way to separate small advertisements, both with the same box number.

It had been an unsettling five days. Not that he would admit it. Charles Wayland was not a man to concede such weakness even to himself, but he'd disturbed his housekeeper by exploring corners of his establishment that no bachelor had any reason to investigate. On occasion he looked at her in an appraising manner that might have worried a more imaginative woman. At work he'd surprised his desk officer by pouncing on the post as each delivery arrived, and been heard to enquire peevishly if there was any news from the Manchester office.

True, there had been one letter, but its brevity – *Investigation into circumstances surrounding the discovery of a body on the 7.22 dep from Buxton, instigated* – served only to aggravate matters, and finally, on Saturday morning, it all became too much.

"I can be reached at the Manchester office later."

The desk constable looked up. "Sir." Then, muttering as his superintendent swept out, "God help Spray."

It could have been worse. Only crumbs remained of the buns, and they disappeared promptly beneath a sheet of paper, but a chipped brown teapot and two mugs stood defiant.

"Now, Spray," it wasn't clear if there'd been a nod toward Archer, "what's all this about the body on a Manchester train?"

It was the worst possible moment, not because of the tea things, but on account of the state of the investigation. The Whale liked things clear and simple, and his sergeant endeavoured to keep matters to himself until they could be rendered in such a manner. At present the Betsy Piggin investigation was far from fitting that description.

"Good morning, sir. This is a pleasant surprise." Both the junior men were standing now, and by the time they'd shuffled round, the superintendent was in Sam's chair and only William remained on his feet.

"It's well in hand, sir. A few details still to clear up. I thought I'd leave the report until I had it all straight."

A testy harrumph preceded "This all to do with the case?" The contents of Hubert Golightly's pockets still littered the table and were in receipt of a disapproving stare.

"Err… no, sir. That's something that only came to our attention yesterday. It's to do with a body found by the track in Barmoor Clough."

"Another murder, Sergeant? Good God, man, they're coming in faster than you're solving them! There won't be anyone left up in the Peak District if this continues."

"Very droll, sir, I'm sure." No one quite knew whether to laugh.

"Come on, Sergeant, make your report."

Superintendent Wayland was not a happy man by the time the details had been explained. "So you've no more idea who did for these two people now than you had when you found them."

"No, sir."

"And no idea why?"

"No, sir."

"The company expects better than this. The publicity is bad for business."

"Yes, sir. I suppose the Betsy Piggin affair could be in today's *Derbyshire Times*. I haven't seen it."

Constable Archer was dispatched to acquire a copy.

"I can't imagine a national paper will have it yet. The locals are very protective of a story until they've had a first bite, I understand. Maybe it won't get that far." Sam sounded hopeful.

"And Golightly?

"I suppose there might already have been something in a Manchester paper about his disappearance."

"But nothing to link it to the railway."

"No, sir." Sam fingered Golightly's business card. "He looks as if he travels. Perhaps he hasn't been missed yet."

Among the items still on the desk was the newspaper cutting. Whilst he waited for Archer's return the superintendent lighted on it. "This Golightly's?"

"Yes, sir. We weren't quite sure what to make of it."

"I'm glad to hear it, Sergeant." Charles Wayland had, of necessity, served in the past with officers whose inclinations were less than respectable. Whilst deploring their behaviour, nevertheless he couldn't avoid knowledge of it. "This is appealing to a certain type of man."

"Sir?"

"A man…" The superintendent searched for words. "A man whose tastes are…" His explanation was petering out, but he knew it was an important point. "A man who cannot satisfy himself with what is to be found in respectable society."

"Ah… I understand, sir."

Wayland's relief was palpable, and so, it seemed, was his sergeant's.

"We wondered about mountaineering but I see through it now."

By the time William had returned with that week's *Derbyshire Times* and it had been scoured for news of disobliging events on a train out of Buxton, the morning was spent.

"Might have got into the Manchester dailies, sir, but it'll be stale by now. It was five days ago."

"Yes, of course… What you up to next, Sergeant?"

The question hung in the air, and might have trapped Sam but for a moment of inspiration.

"It would be of great assistance, sir, if you could find out something of the system of inspection applied to schools for the destitute, workhouse children and the like."

"Oh, I see… next week, you mean." Then, "Why on earth do you want to know about that sort of detail, Sergeant?"

His brave face couldn't mask the uncertainty of Sam's reply. "I, er… we have enough…" Then, more revealingly, "I believe there may be a connection between Chapel Union Workhouse, an education inspector, and both the dead bodies."

"Good heavens, Sergeant, how do you come to that?"

"Just the odd detail, sir, nothing for sure yet."

The superintendent felt thwarted. Unable to explain to himself quite why, on the spur of the moment, he'd felt the need to journey northward to Stockport, and now he was equally at a loss to explain why a task set for next week had been such a disappointment. It showed, and his expression must have prompted his sergeant's next suggestion.

Sharing a cab with non-commissioned men would have been unheard of in his army days, and on retirement Colonel Wayland had found difficulty in letting go of the distinction in his current role with the Railway Constabulary. He recalled that this was the third time (the fourth if he included travelling by rail, first class, with Sergeant Spray) he had been obliged to do such a thing.

Constable Archer was such an unsoldierly man, too, and yet Spray thought well of him, and he'd been involved in—

"This is the place, sir."

Wayland's reverie was interrupted by the cabbie drawing his hansom to a halt outside a pair of wrought-iron gates. Archer was first onto the pavement and would have extended an arm to steady his superior, but thought better of it and stood by ready to help should he stumble.

"Wait there, cabbie, we won't be long."

Now what did Spray say – *If you were to knock at the front door and talk to the gentry, Archer could see what's what round the back*? Damned underhand, thought Wayland, but nonetheless he waited until the constable had disappeared before pulling a polished brass knob and waiting for someone to answer the bell.

"I wish to speak to your mistress on a matter of some importance."

If the girl wasn't impressed enough by the shiny buttons, the matter of some importance had her scurrying off to "… tell Mrs Golightly. Who shall I say, sir?"

"Superintendent Wayland."

The door closed in his face.

There had been some discussion, back in Stockport, as to how the matter was to be presented. The assumption was that the household in Didsbury would consist of the dead man's wife and possibly a gaggle of children.

"Superintendent Vayland?"

The handsome, bejewelled woman of uncertain years with a foreign accent hardly fitted his expectations, and Wayland had to readjust his opening gambit.

"Mrs Golightly?"

"*Ja*, vot do you vant?"

German, he thought, as he was being patronised through a lorgnette. "Is this Mr Hubert Golightly's residence?"

"He lives here, *ja*, but he is away. Business belongs at the office." The lorgnette resumed its position and Mrs Golightly glared at Wayland through the lenses.

"My business belongs here, madam. It would be best discussed indoors."

The matter of his admission was considered for some time before he was allowed across the threshold and conducted to a morning room. Its east window looked out across the route traversed by Constable Archer only minutes earlier.

"May I enquire, madam, as to the precise relationship between yourself and Mr Golightly?"

Her hesitation perplexed him before she finally answered. "This is an impertinence and has to cease. My family is no concern of yours. I should not have admitted a common policeman. You vill leave."

If Wayland had set out with any idea of how to discharge his task, it was to conduct himself as he imagined Sergeant Spray might do. The word 'common' changed things.

"Madam." He would have liked to speak down to her, but the woman was as tall as he. "Madam, I have come here to inform you of the death of Mr Hubert Golightly. His body was found yesterday beside a railway line. He had been dead for some time."

"Vot, and you did not find him until now? Vy not?" Then, struck by a different thought, "How you know it's him?"

Back in the office this very point had been discussed. It had been decided to present the pocketbook and notecase but edit the contents so that the newspaper cutting was removed. Indeed it had been edited before Constable Archer returned with his newspaper. He would have to know about its importance, but to Wayland's relief someone else would tell him.

"The money doesn't matter, sir," Spray had said, "but we must have the notecase and pocketbook back."

As he presented the items for inspection Mrs Golightly made an unladylike lunge. The superintendent, mindful of Spray's words, behaved in an equally ungentlemanly manner and quickly withdrew them from her reach.

A small victory, but the business card, sacrificed in the tussle, proved decisive.

"*Ja*, this is my son's."

"Good day to you, miss; would you mind if we have a word?"

Between the two of them there would be no 'minding'. William Archer, fresh-faced and smart in his uniform, was so agreeable, as was the pretty girl with striking blue eyes and curly dark hair escaping from beneath her maid's cap, that their conversation soon became animated.

"Two years, Constable, oi bin here two years, give or take."

They had met at the back door and by now were outside in the yard.

"'Tis easier here. Cook's asleep in the kitchen but there's no knowing when the sherry'll wear off."

"How many people live in the house?"

"Well, sorr," the Irish brogue was unmistakable now, "there's Mr Golightly, and then Mrs Golightly, she's a foreigner; cook, nursemaid, parlourmaid – oh, and the scullery maid, but she don't live in, and she ain't no maid; scratchy old besom, she is…"

William expected, in view of the nursemaid, for children to be listed. He waited in vain. Numbers weren't the girl's strong point and she was counting on her fingers.

"That's it – there's Mr Golightly."

"We've had him already, miss."

"No, no, I have the right of it, Constable: there are two Mr Golightlys. The old one lives up in his room. We never see him. 'Tis why we've a nursemaid; she looks after him."

"And the younger Mr Golightly?"

"Mr Hubert; he's away a lot. Not here now, that's why I nearly missed him."

"Mrs Golightly, she's married to…?"

"The old Mr Golightly, and Mr Hubert's their son… well, stepson. It's his second marriage."

"*Saoirse?*" A call came from the scullery and the girl made to go.

"Tell Cook I've just arrived and ask her to come to the door. I'd like to speak to her."

"And you tell her why you're asking all these questions? You've not told me much." The maid was gone.

"And what do you want?" There was to be no friendly chat with Cook. A stout figure in an apron, once white but now stained and encrusted with the detritus of her trade, she was short, but not intimidated as she looked up at William.

"I've come to make enquiries concerning a murder."

The cook was unmoved, but from behind her came a squawk suggesting the maid was within earshot.

"Mr Hubert Golightly was found dead by a rail line in Derbyshire. Can you tell me when you last saw him?"

"He don't come in t' kitchen, so I en't seen 'im fer months, but I know when 'e's here 'cause I've t' cook extra."

"Can you remember how long ago that was?"

"'Bout six weeks. Now then, young man, ah can't go harpin' on." The dumpy body turned for the kitchen. Over her shoulder, more friendly now, "Can't say ah'm surprised."

She disappeared, but such a revelation couldn't be left hanging.

"Very satisfactory, Constable. I think Sergeant Spray will be pleased." Superintendent Wayland had been waiting in the cab for some minutes by the time his constable joined him. Any longer and his patience might have evaporated, but as it was he still had an air of self-satisfaction about him when Archer climbed aboard. "I've established that Hubert Golightly lives at the address and informed his wife of his demise. Formidable woman, German if I'm any judge. Assured her that we will find out the truth and left it at that."

"Very good, sir. I'm sure the sergeant will be impressed with your achievement."

"Don't suppose you found anything useful from the servants?"

"The same as you, sir. The dead man lived there. A few loose ends. That's all."

What could he do, thought William; directly contradict the Whale? Better let Sam do that, and give him first look at the 'loose ends' too. They were all in his notebook: the rumours of "unsavoury men coming to the house", and "Mr Hubert keeping a gun in his room", not that anyone he'd spoken to had actually seen anything, but he'd been assured that another maid had definitely "seen one of those iron bracelet things". Even so, there was doubt about where she'd seen the handcuffs.

More certainty was to be found on another matter. "Oh no, sir, the mistress keeps a very close eye. Us girls never have any trouble." Cook had sounded shocked, and the maid, who'd reappeared, giggled as she answered William's enquiry, but they all knew what he meant. "Very strict, she is; with everybody. I've heard her speak to Mr Hubert like she speaks to us."

Rather than endure travelling further in Superintendent Wayland's company William alighted at Stockport Edgeley, saying he'd call at the office before going home.

"Give Sergeant Spray my intelligence, will you? He'll be glad to know we're on track."

"Very good, sir." William was on the platform by now, and it was with a sense of relief that he closed the carriage door. Even deceit by omission made him uncomfortable.

At least the Whale hadn't given up the pocketbook and notecase. "Had to let the business card go," he'd told William. It probably didn't matter; there'd been more than one and the remainder still lay on the desk as he entered the office. Whilst he walked from the station William had been drafting a report in his head from the mixture of fact, fantasy and supposition that he'd gleaned in Didsbury. He expected to write it out for consideration later, but to his surprise Sam was still there.

"Left the superintendent on the train for Crewe."

"Thank goodness for that. How'd you get on?"

"Bit awkward, really." William explained what he'd found and then gave the Whale's report. "I didn't like to contradict him; he was so pleased with himself. He did say that Mrs Golightly was foreign, probably German."

"That might explain the Schmidt on those cards; perhaps the two families are connected by more than business."

"Nearly missed the last bit: I had to follow the cook into her kitchen and even then she wasn't too keen. Insisted on sending the maid out first, not that it did any good, I could hear the girl outside in the lobby." As if in deference to his subject, William lowered his voice. "She said that Hubert G. frequented prostitutes and that she had heard him and his stepmother rowing about it."

If William thought the subject of prostitution merited hushed tones he was in for a rude awakening. Sam explained what lay behind the advertisement in Golightly's pocketbook.

"So you see, William, there are prostitutes and then… It was the Whale who saw through the advert."

William was speechless. After a while the detective in him reasserted himself. "I suppose that converts the hearsay about handcuffs into a more likely story, and perhaps the rest of the gossip too."

"There's no knowing what the gentry get up to, William. Remember that."

He looks worse than yesterday, thought Jimmy. The huddled figure, wrapped in sacking, barely acknowledged him and, more telling, he'd taken no notice of Benjy, who had raced ahead in the expectation of a bit of fuss.

"I've brought you this." Grease had escaped and soaked into his pocket. The rasher of streaky had looked more appetising on Jimmy's breakfast plate, but it was the best he could do. There'd be hell to pay when his mother discovered the mess it had made of his jacket. "Sorry about the cake."

It too had absorbed a share of the fat. Mrs Spray had given it to him after he'd run her an errand. She'd seen him stuff it in his pocket, and when he'd said, "I'll keep it fer later" she'd insisted on another slice and stood by watching as he ate it. He almost blurted out the truth there and then; that he was helping a runaway and, probably, as Mikey weakened, keeping him alive. What had stopped him was his promise of secrecy. Now, watching the boy's listless attempts to chew the bacon, he knew he had to act.

"Let's have a look at you, Mikey." Illness was given short shrift in the Allcroft household, and most ailments took the hint and were 'better by morning'. Fevers were different; particularly fevers with a rash, and Jimmy knew they were serious. "Well, you ain't 'ot an' you ain't got no spots, but you're not right, that's fer sure."

This was the moment. If the lad could run then he wasn't so bad and good luck to him. But if, as Jimmy thought, things were serious then he would be too weak for that and too weak for things to continue any further.

"You was middling when I first found yer, Mikey, lad, and worse every time I sees yer. If we don't do summat different, you'll be dead soon enough."

The boy's apathy in the face of Jimmy's pronouncement clinched it.

"I got a friend as lets me keep the dog in 'er shed. She's a good 'un an' I'm going to ask her if I can put yer in t' shed wi' Benjy."

By now Mikey was nibbling the cake and Jimmy took his silence as acquiescence.

"Tell me again, Jimmy."

Lizzie had been rereading that morning's post. It consisted of one letter only, Miss Peachment's invitation, which had been eagerly anticipated. But now it was here, apprehension was setting in. What if the ladies assembled on Tuesday morning, at a rather grand address in Chapel, peered down their genteel noses when she made her entrance?

"He's called Mikey, missus, an' he ain't too well."

"And you've been scrounging food for him, including some of Wednesday's leftover stew." Lizzie's amusement at Jimmy's confession was barely concealed.

"He was hungry, see. I got a stale loaf from the baker an' she gev me some sacks but it ain't no good; even wi' me breakfast bacon he's worse than 'e was. So I thought…"

"You thought you'd put him in the shed with Benjy."

"Him an' Benjy get on good and I could give 'em food together."

"Whatever else Mikey is, he's not an animal, Jimmy."

"I found 'im like I found the dog, an' they'd both be goners if I hadn't done summat."

Lizzie couldn't fault the logic, nor could she ignore a distressed child. "You're sure he'd not be bringing contagion here?"

"He ain't got no spots, an' he ain't hot. I looked."

It was no contest. What Sam would say when he came back that evening was for later; just now it was a matter of practicalities.

"Don't worry about the sacks, Jimmy, I'll find some old blankets. Just get him here in one piece."

"Mrs Oldroyd… Mrs Spray," this was important so Jimmy was being careful how he spoke, "Mrs Spray, he's very frightened of being found out. Dunno what for; 'e won't say. I never said Mr Spray was a rozzer and—"

"So we'll be harbouring some sort of disorderly vagrant?" She let the words hang. "You know, Jimmy, I think we'll manage. I'll speak to Mr Spray."

Later Lizzie was indeed speaking to Mr Spray. He'd come home rather pleased with himself.

"The Whale turned up at the office poking his nose in today."

"I suppose it's his office in a way, Sam."

"He cheered up no end when I found something he could do; sent him off with Archer on a little errand."

"Is that entirely fair on William?"

"They worked well together; the Whale made a frontal assault whilst William rootled about at the rear."

"Does William know," Lizzie was amused, "that you think of him as a pig snuffling around after titbits?"

"It was very successful." Sam smiled in spite of himself. "They came back with useful information between them."

Man and wife were at their tea. Lizzie had commented on Sam's early homecoming.

"Well, it is Saturday," he'd said defensively.

She'd laughed at that too. "When you've something important on you stay out till all hours." And then, not wanting to seem a scold, "But it's what I married; I'm not complaining."

"And what about your day, my dear?"

Making the arrangements to house young Mikey had disturbed her daily routine and driven away Lizzie's anxieties about Miss Peachment's invitation. They would return before Tuesday morning, but even then she would be less disconcerted than she was now at the prospect of telling Sam that she had installed a vagrant in her shed. A child about whom she knew nothing but who, in all probability, was running from authority, possibly even the same Union Workhouse where she herself was shortly to assume a semi-official role.

"He's so pale and weak, Sam. Jimmy's done his best, but the boy is starving."

"Out on the moor, you say; the other side of the canal? I wonder how he got there?" His detective's mind probed the situation.

"I don't know, but he was all in by the time Jimmy found him hiding in a hovel."

"What was he running from?"

The question hung for a moment. "Does it matter for now? He's very frightened, and all he's admitted so far is his name, Mikey."

Their meal was over and Lizzie was pouring boiling water onto tea leaves. She saw Sam watching, but from his expression he wasn't seeing. Only when a steaming teacup appeared on the table did he emerge from his reverie.

"I'd best go out there and discover what he's up to when I've finished this."

Lizzie took a sip from her own tea. "Are you sure that's wise, Sam?"

"What do you mean?"

He was sharper than Lizzie had ever heard him. This was something she'd not seen in their newly minted marriage. She pressed on.

"He's a frightened child, not a hardened criminal. He came here because he trusted Jimmy—"

"That boy, he's always getting mixed up in other people's business. Police business mostly… my business."

Lizzie ignored the outburst. "…and Jimmy persuaded him to trust me. Do you know, he flinched when I bent to cover him with a blanket, but in the end he thanked me. He's been mistreated."

"By a woman, if what you say is true." Sam was retreating into detective mode.

"Don't be stupid, Sam." She'd never accused him of that before. "He's been mistreated by authority, man or woman doesn't signify, and you barging in with your policeman's questions and your official boots will ruin everything."

"What if he's running from Chapel Spike; and you visiting there any day?"

She told him, "Tuesday". The letter hadn't been discussed. "It came after you'd gone off earlier."

"I only want to…"

There was a long silence, broken by little Mary whimpering as she slept. Sam, quite unnecessarily, picked up the sleeping baby and by the time Lizzie returned from tidying away the tea tray, was nursing the child.

"I only want to protect our family."

If they'd had their first quarrel, it was over, and Lizzie, bending as she passed behind Sam's chair, lightly kissed the top of his head, noting for the first time that his crisp brown hair was not only shot with grey, but thinning at the crown.

NINE

Monday 7th May 1877

SUNDAY HAD PASSED ALMOST WITHOUT INCIDENT.

In Sam's experience that was the problem with the Sabbath: nothing happened. He'd left behind a childhood of Quaker meetings, where he'd learnt to sleep sitting up straight, without faith, but imbued with the Friends' belief in honesty, truth and personal responsibility.

Whilst the army had ordered him to attend church parade, civilian life had left him with the choice. The hypocrisy of attendance without belief conflicted with the ethic by which he lived, and so he had become used to fretting with inaction one day in seven.

Until… until his day became filled with domesticity. It wasn't that he *did* anything around the house since his marriage – that was Lizzie's domain, as was any significant baby care – but just *being there* seemed meaningful now. Lizzie, for her part, tolerated the extra body under her feet for a while, but in exasperation suggested that he might like to fetch a jug of ale to have with his dinner and have a chat down the White Hart whilst he was about it.

One more customer was hardly noticed in the saloon bar. Busy enough to make finding a seat a matter of luck, Sam found himself slipping into one immediately its previous owner departed. Along with his empty beer mug, the man had abandoned a copy of Saturday's *Manchester Evening News.* Taking that – so satisfying – first pull on his ale, the cutting he'd retrieved from Golightly's pocketbook floated into Sam's mind. It lay, where he'd left it, on his desk back in Stockport. He could picture it well enough, along with its biggest deficiency: the day and date of publication. Just possibly, it might be a weekly posting…

The change of plan necessitated an early start. When they had separated on Saturday, 'excursions' had been their first priority. Whether they were organised from Buxton, where to, how often and by whom? It was all guesswork as Sam well knew.

"We've got to start somewhere, William, and all we know is that a coach with enough plumbing for a prolonged stay has been shunted into a quiet spot for at least an overnight stop, and some weeks ago it left a corpse behind."

Finding another advertisement like the one in Golightly's pocketbook had changed everything. Yesterday, sitting over his beer looking at the Saturday edition, Sam had that stroke of luck that changes everything.

"You see, William; he's been putting in repeat advertisements."

The two of them had met on the platform as William, having arrived from home on a train from Crewe, was setting off for the Buxton connection. It was about-turn and an irate guard as they impeded its timely departure for Manchester by scrambling aboard at the last moment.

"We need to find out how often they appear and when he collects the replies."

"I know where to find the *Evening News* offices."

"Yes, so you do."

They were an oddly assorted couple: William the taller, in his uniform, alongside Sam, stockier, wearing nondescript tweed and a bowler hat, heading zigzag fashion toward Brown Street.

"Best you loiter on the street outside, William; we don't want them recognising you from last time."

William, bridling at the term 'loiter', suggested Sam might be just the character to respond to an advert offering 'Free Spirits' a 'Blissful Experience'. The banter occupied them for a while but gave way to more considered conversation.

"Can't see there'll be any interesting goings-on out here, but you never know."

The disorganised squalor that produced several editions of the *Evening News* each day exceeded anything in Sam's experience, notwithstanding army life and a spell as a clerk in a shipping office.

"What y' after?"

The man had been summoned by a bell on the counter. Having given it a shake, Sam waited. The policeman in him itched to shake it again, but a sheepish demeanour seemed more fitting under the circumstances.

"This box number." Sam retrieved an envelope from his pocket. "I want to leave a reply."

"Give it here." He gave it a glance. "You sure?"

Sam was conscious of the man's curiosity. "Yes; could you tell me when the box will be cleared?"

"Eager, aren't you?" He gave a knowing look. "It'll cost."

"To find out about clearing the box?"

"We're a newspaper, not extortionists." He assumed mock indignation. "The *Free Spirits* offer, it costs."

"How do you know about that?"

The knowing look came back. "That advertisement appears once a month, regular. 'E don't come to put it in every time 'cause it's paid three months up front, but 'e clears it every time on the Wednesday after."

"So he'll be back in two days' time?"

The other nodded.

"What's he like, this man?"

"Smart, middle-aged gent. Well spoken… respectable. That's the queerest thing – respectable. I mean, that sort of business…"

Sam knew he'd give himself away, but carried on anyway. "How do you know what sort of business?"

"Lookee, sir, I'm in and out of the courts fer the paper; I can smell stinking fish a mile off. Take you, sir. You're no sporting man."

Sam was rumbled, but the other went on anyway.

"Them as come in here fer real are shifty wi' money that belongs to another; acting for the high and mighty, they are. Now you, sir, you're acting for another too, but in a very different line. A policeman, if I'm not mistaken."

"Will you take it?" Sam pointed to the envelope in the man's hand.

"It's what we're here for."

"One last thing. This man, does he ever come out of regular… last Tuesday for instance?"

"Mr Policeman, this business – that is to say, the business between the two of us – has all been one way. We keeps afloat on news here, my job depends on it, and I can smell it as well as I can smell stinking fish…"

In the silence that followed each considered what the other had to offer, and how much it might be worth.

"So that was all, but it was enough."

The two policemen were back in the office.

"Him trying to trade, that's what did it. If he'd something to sell it had to be about the man renting the box coming back on other days, possibly last Tuesday."

"Is that important?"

Sam temporised. "Could be."

The discussion moved on.

"You'd better go and see what happens on Wednesday, and don't look too smart. That muckraker has an eye for things out of the ordinary. If he sees you loitering outside he'll think you're a *news story* and stick to you like something nasty on your boot."

"But, Sam… you don't think it's him… do you?" The significance of last Tuesday had dawned on William. "Fewster? We haven't any evidence…"

"Never ignore a coincidence, William; they mean something, until they don't."

"So I'm spending a day *loitering* in a dirty Manchester backstreet on the off chance of a coincidence?!"

"He'd recognise me. Anyway, it'll be better than the post-mortem; I want you to go there tomorrow. Make sure the butcher tells you if Golightly was clubbed, or hit his head when he fell." Then, as an afterthought, "And find yourself a chair; we don't want another scene – it's bad for our reputation."

"And what are you going to be doing whilst I'm sitting down and watching a body being cut into pieces?"

"I'll be finding how to arrange an excursion."

TEN

Tuesday 8th May 1877

A*T LEAST IT'S NOT RAINING*, THOUGHT LIZZIE, HURRYING for her train through the moor grime, *but this is worse.*

A clammy mist had come down from the higher ground, picking up a myriad of smuts and suchlike in the industrial valley, threatening to turn her grey silk dowdy and her lavender bonnet grey. True, her best dress was under a shawl but she was still troubled for the bonnet. She'd hoped to find cover in the ladies' waiting room, but the mist had seeped in there too.

It had been a busy morning, in the way that any deviation from the usual routine seems busy even when enough time has been allowed. Sam at least had left in time for his train, on account of the Buxton service being a little later than his usual one. It would have been a convenience if he'd used the extra twenty minutes to help with feeding little Mary, but he hadn't offered and, knowing his reservations about the workhouse visits, it had seemed politic not to ask. Then there were the baby things to collect up for Elsie. No reservations there; Elsie had been happy to help, although she had warned, "You be careful, Lizzie. They gentlefolk'll not be satisfied till they've turned you into one of them sort, an' if they can't they'll spit you out like a bit of gristle."

Well, that wasn't going to happen. On the short journey, trust in herself and pride in her family came flooding back, and as she stepped out onto the platform at Chapel Station, Lizzie squared her shoulders, as much as propriety allowed a lady's shoulders to be squared, and resolved that she would not be intimidated.

Fortunately the resolve was sufficiently robust to survive her walk up the drive to Pinkstone Hall. They nodded politely, but the other two women stepping out on the same short journey continued their conversation without involving her: *On account of our not being introduced, perhaps?* she thought.

At the door stood a careworn, mouse-like woman of indeterminate years, whose left hand was devoid of rings: a spinster, certainly, but not a servant. She greeted the other two ladies, who had arrived first, by name, whilst inside the entrance hall a servant did her bidding in the matter of visitors' outdoor coats and such. Lizzie, standing back so as not to create an unseemly queue, stepped forward; or was she summoned? It was not quite clear which, but the mouse seemed more formidable at that moment.

"Oh yes, I see, you must be our newest recruit. Mrs… Spray, is it?"

There was the briefest touching of hands and Lizzie was inside, to be relieved of her gloves and shawl. A rather damp shawl by now, and she noticed the maid grimace as she handled the wet garment. Across the room stood a small gathering of perhaps six or seven, if not to attention, then certainly expectantly.

"I'm Miss Peachment. Let me introduce you to the other ladies."

Lizzie was concentrating on not catching her shoe in the edge of an oriental-looking rug as she heard, "And this is Mrs Sp—"

An imperious voice drowned out the rest of the introduction. Their hostess had arrived. "Mrs Oldroyd, such a pleasure to have you join us." Its owner, forceful and bejewelled, gave the impression of looking down, even on those taller. Black-and-white ears flopped over her sleeve and beady black eyes peered out on the world from their vantage point on her arm. "Now let me introduce you; this is Pippin." A pink tongue appeared and Lizzie, had she come close enough, would have been licked by the little dog. "And these ladies will be your companions in our little endeavour."

A roll call of the regulars, completed in peremptory manner, left Lizzie none the wiser as to who was who; nor were the assembled ladies any clearer as to who she was. Miss Peachment had failed to correct the initial mistake about Lizzie's remarriage and she was introduced to those assembled as Mrs Oldroyd.

"Now, ladies, I leave you in the care of Miss Peachment. She has my full confidence." With that, Pippin and Lady Pinkstone retired.

The maid returned with a tea tray and, whilst Miss Peachment poured, offered round a plate of tiny cakes.

"These petits fours are delicious." Lizzie had been drawn into the group. "Don't you think so, Mrs Oldroyd?"

"Indeed they are." Lizzie, who had never heard of such things, stored 'petit four' for future use. She also learned the woman's name.

"How generous of Lady Pinkstone, don't you think, Mrs Entwistle," Miss Peachment was speaking, "to offer us a light collation before we go to our toil?" She turned to Lizzie. "Perhaps you don't know; Sir Wilfred is a baronet and a magistrate, and Lady Pinkstone is employed greatly in ministering to the poor wretches who inhabit several workhouses."

"She hardly ever sets foot in them."

"That's Sir Wilfred's sister," whispered Miss Peachment, but not quietly enough.

"Sister-in-law, Miss Peachment, you must get these things right – if they matter at all."

The speaker turned to Lizzie and presented, on closer inspection, the confusing sight of a woman carelessly dressed in expensive clothes. The gathering as a whole had exerted itself greatly in the matter of presentation, as befitted persons of a lower station when visiting their betters. Here was the reverse: a lady, but with some other sense of what was important.

"Mrs Oldroyd, you look like a woman more used to doing things than talking about them." Clearly this was not meant as a slight as she went on, "We need more action around here and less drinking of tea."

"I must apologise, I didn't catch your name earlier when Lady Pinkst—"

"She thinks she's a latter-day Louisa Twining." Seeing Lizzie's puzzled look, she continued, "Miss Twining started it all – this visiting business. Moved on to higher things now; my sister-in-law fancies taking her place."

He only had one coat, but in any case it was his boots that would suffer most. In this respect Sam was better provided for, and he'd put on his old pair, even now the more comfortable, but shabby and nearing their end. He was going to explore the passenger sidings at Buxton and he'd learnt by experience that rail yards were rough, dirty places and hard on boots. Most of the men working there wore clogs.

"'Ere, what you up to? Y' ain't allowed."

Sam showed his warrant card.

The man grunted. "A bluebottle."

"Your bluebottle." Sam sounded reasonable. "I'm from the Railway Constabulary."

"Does that mek it better?"

"It means I understand what a fine body of men work on the railway."

"Go on; you're 'avin' a laugh…" The man trailed off. "'Ere, what's yer name?"

Clearly he couldn't read. Sam's name was plain enough on his warrant card.

"Spray, Sergeant Spray."

"Him as sorted out all them murders?"

Sam allowed the accolade to stand. "I'm just having a look round and wondering about stock used for excursion trains."

"Not a lot o' they out of Buxton. T' other way, mostly. They come fer t' spa watter. Dunno why; it's just wet."

"What about Wakes Week?"

"They just cobble together any old stock from them sidings." The man waved a hand at a line of elderly coaches, ready for the scrapyard.

"And that one?"

"'Tis th' engineer's coach. 'E rides round lookin', but 'e nivver comes out 'ere."

"So why is it there?"

The man looked vague. "How should I know? I'm paid to stack coal an' clear up clinker and such."

"Is it always just there?" The engineer's coach stood at the outer end of the siding, making shunting it easy.

"'Tis when it is, but it ain't there sometimes. Lookee here, Mr Policeman, I get paid fer what I do, not gabbing on." With that, the yard labourer went about his business.

A shout saved Sam as he traversed the tracks. The line of trucks, rolling silently downhill, would have bowled him over. The shunter in charge was too occupied with controlling their descent to give Sam the bawling-out he deserved, and made do with a black look in passing.

Must be more careful. Sam continued his precarious journey toward the engineer's coach, and was nearly there when there came another shout. This time the man had more time on his hands, standing four-square between Sam and his objective.

"And what the devil d'ye think you're doing? You were bloody near dead back there, and you'll be bloody near dead when I've finished with you."

"I think not." Sam produced his warrant card, exposing the uniform beneath his coat.

"Huh! A Jack, nosing around my patch." Bushy eyebrows were raised. "Well?"

"You must be the yard foreman."

A brief nod.

"The engineer's saloon – get much use, does it?"

"Why do you want to know about that? It just stands there."

"Until it doesn't. It's when it's not there I'm interested in, and I want a look inside."

"It's locked."

"Then open it."

"I can't do that…"

"See here, Mr Yard Foreman, you're obliged to cooperate with the Railway Constabulary. It says so in company regulations. Read them, have you?"

Sam hadn't either, but the threat served its purpose. A standard key with its square-ended shaft appeared. The coach was provided with running boards and gaining access from ground level was easy.

Inside was a revelation. In the saloon a chaise longue dominated, its plum upholstery inviting languorous reclining and arch behaviour. Sam's imagination wasn't up to all its possibilities, but he saw enough to know the Whale had not been mistaken. Further along were two sleeping compartments. Ingeniously, the bench seat in the one he investigated converted into a generous bunk. As he adjusted the mechanism, a cache of coloured ropes, leather bonds and a riding crop opened up.

The yard foreman peered over his shoulder. "What's them about, d'ye reckon?"

For once Sam wished the Whale was there. His own imagination was quite inadequate to enlighten the man. He hardly knew himself.

"What's through here?" The foreman, to Sam's relief, hadn't waited for an answer and moved along the corridor. His curiosity suggested to Sam that he'd never explored the coach, and the two of them crowded into the galley beyond the toilet and second sleeper.

"We have ter refill the gas when it comes back."

"You said it just stands in the siding, but it doesn't, does it? It goes out at times. What I want to know is when and how often?"

"Have ter look at the register…" Reluctant, but more cooperative now.

They were passing a short platform on a spur of track. "There's a gassing point there. It's left during the day before it goes out."

"And there's a gate in the yard wall just by. Got a key?"

"Nah, 't ain't nivver used."

Sam went over to look. Maybe the yard staff didn't use it, probably couldn't; it was a huge double opening and kept secure with an ancient, rusted padlock, but the little wicket had oiled hinges, and no spiders had set their webs across it. Someone had access that way if they had the key.

"Let's have a look at this register." Alongside the yardman, Sam felt safer and they recrossed the tracks without more ado.

By a process of accumulation and elimination Lizzie had finally got to the right of it, she thought. If she assumed that the lady of middling years, with the fourth finger of her left hand unadorned, was a spinster, and Lady Pinkstone was her sister-in-law, it followed that the woman under whose wing she had now been taken must be Miss Delilah Pinkstone, didn't it? She'd heard someone from the house call her Miss Delilah before they'd left together.

"Come along, Mrs Oldroyd, I'll show you the ropes."

Miss Peachment and the others were left trailing as they strode out.

"Yes, I thought you'd do." This after several minutes of brisk walking with Lizzie matching her companion step for step. "Too fond of sitting around a teapot and a plate of petits fours, the others." She nodded contemptuously over her shoulder.

"Miss Pinkstone—"

"Hah! Worked it out, have you? Good, but not quite good enough." This was said without rancour or condescension, but nonetheless Lizzie was much discomposed by the remark. "Either I'm the Dowager Lady Pinkstone, widow, or Miss Arthurs, unmarried lady of indeterminate years. I prefer the latter. Pinkstone was an awful man, even worse than his younger brother; good job he died before Wilfred. I try not to think about him. Miss Delilah Arthurs will do."

Lizzie's feathers had been ruffled, and it must have shown.

"Look here, Mrs Spray, you're here because I told the Peachment woman to write to you."

"But she wrote to me as Oldroyd."

"I hadn't counted on you being so strait-laced. Thought you'd just leave it be."

"But why?" Lizzie felt used, and what had previously been ruffled started to stand up with irritation.

"I'll be straight with you. We need you but you don't need us. You've more charitable achievements to your name than all that gaggle of time-servers and sycophants put together."

By now they were at the gates to the workhouse and the remainder of the party was approaching. Later, Lizzie had a sneaking feeling she was as big a fraud as the rest. Hadn't the Reading Room bequest been a means of reengaging with

Sam? And what she'd tried and failed to do for Mary was out of friendship, and little Mary was just a matter of falling for the child… At the time she allowed herself to be mollified, momentarily at least.

"You were approached because your husband is a policeman."

"Well, really!" Lizzie bristled again.

"And we hoped you and he might help with a problem."

What that problem might be and who 'we' were was left in abeyance. They were inside now, where the lobby smelt of neglect and sweat. A porter had emerged from his cubbyhole and was officiously noting down names. Miss Arthurs had contrived things such that the two of them were the last to enter.

"Ah, Lady Pinkstone…" *Still the widow here*, noted Lizzie, "you have a new recruit."

Mrs Elizabeth Oldroyd's name was added to the list. It was noticeable that her companion was afforded a deference not shown to the others.

"And where will you be going first?"

He got no answer as the visitors made their way deeper into the apathetic mass of humanity that made up the population of Chapel Union Workhouse. Blue stripes were everywhere, some with aprons over, and whilst Lizzie's first impression was that of dull uniformity, it dawned on her that the inmates were better fed and clothed than most of the destitute to be seen on the streets outside.

"Can we go to the lying-in ward?"

"My! You are a glutton for punishment." Miss Arthurs stood looking at Lizzie with an appraising eye. "They're the roughest sort, you know: fallen women and such."

"Nevertheless, that is where I would like to start." If

Delilah Arthurs thought she could use her, Lizzie would return the 'compliment'.

By the time they had traversed an open yard and were outside the door of a smaller building it had dawned on Lizzie that she'd seen no men.

"It's rules; they're kept separate. If they weren't, this ward would be full to overflowing," she was told as they entered.

To the other's surprise, Lizzie had stepped forward and knocked, but Miss Arthurs would have none of it, and pushed the door open. The familiar smell of baby sick predominated and there was a greater sense of purpose amongst the women, all younger than elsewhere. Some were suckling, others just nursing their babies, and of the two without, one still carried, but not for much longer, thought Lizzie.

"Oo-er, it's the quality. Come to gawp, 'ave ye?" The speaker was a coarse, buxom woman whose brazen manner suggested a life on the streets. Others, more demure, stared at the floor or busied themselves with their charges.

"This is Mrs Oldroyd. She is come to engage in improving conversation." Then, to her companion, "I'll be back directly. Don't let them get anything over on you."

And with that, Lizzie was on her own. For a moment she could think only of Mary and how, had she lived, she might well have ended up in such a place. But it wouldn't do; she must gather her wits.

"So it's conversation, is it?" The same woman spoke. "Come to tell us how we deserve our lot, have ye?"

"Do shut up, Maggie, let her speak." One of the others.

"She lost her brat," said the one whose child was yet to be born.

"And good riddance." Maggie again.

Lizzie did her best to hide her shock.

"They're only an encumbrance outside, an' they never thrive."

"They don't let yer go wi'out 'em. Won't let yer 'ave yer things, an' it's up before the magistrate fer stealin' if yer go out in this." The one still to give birth indicated the dress that covered her swollen belly.

"Betsy Piggin did, didn't she?" Lizzie ventured a question.

"Here, how do you know about Betsy?" It was the woman who'd used the word 'encumbrance'. A woman of some education, thought Lizzie. "Anyway, her brat died."

"But she left an older child."

"Ah, well…" The silence hung around until it could be borne no longer. "The man came."

Lizzie waited.

"He allus knows when there's pickings. Says he can help t' get us out of 'ere, but it's just like a ride at the fair. One go round and you're back."

"It's not so bad." Maggie again. "Out earnin' on the streets in the summer, back here when there's one on the way."

"Yourn allus dies."

"It's the gin, my girl, and plenty of it. Works wonders."

"My man says he's coming for me when he's got a roof on 'im." A demure young woman spoke for the first time. "Afore they tek the little 'n'. We'm wed."

Maggie would have none of it. "I tell y' he's not coming; they never do."

Lizzie wanted to know what the woman meant by 'tek the little 'n'', but said nothing as a diffident girl, who put her in mind of poor dead Mary, asked, "Would he get me another place in service?"

Maggie's guffaw left no doubt. "That's not what 'e's about. Whoring and a bit of wet-nursing if ye don' fancy working on yer back, that's his line."

"Did he take Betsy?" Lizzie asked.

"Aye, and that's how she got to leave the boy. That man can fix things and no mistake."

He was not looking forward to his morning's task. It wasn't just the stench of death and the black humour of those who worked there, but the ignominy he'd brought on himself when he'd fainted during the autopsy on Betsy Piggin. But William knew his duty, and took himself off to the infirmary.

"Hah, come back for another try, have ye?" The mortuary attendant was enjoying himself. A smile hovered where one was rarely seen. "How about a chair? Not so far to fall, d'ye see?"

William did see, and was privately grateful not to have to ask. Perhaps he'd be all right this time. It was plunging a scalpel into the woman's distended breast that had done for him. From what Sam had said, the body of Hubert Golightly was less likely to stimulate any fancies.

"P'raps as well. Might end up on your slab else." It was the best he could do, but it served. The man said no more.

The only chair in the place was occupied and the bundle of clothes would have to be pushed aside.

"His stuff; dump it on the floor." The attendant nodded to William. "We've 'ad a look through, no pocketbook or nothing; we don't know who he is."

For the first time, across his two visits to the place, William felt he had the upper hand. A question came to mind. Play his card now, or later? He waited.

"Bits and pieces over there."

William examined the 'bits and pieces'. The contents of a silver case gave it an exotic aroma, even though there was only one cigarette left. Perhaps it had survived unsmoked on account of the dearth of Congreves in the match tin. He was careful with the broken glass and was puzzled by the metal fitments that had been part of the original.

"What d'ye make of this?" He held up a shard.

"I cut meself, that's what." The other sounded resentful. "Cadavers don't do that to a man as a rule."

William looked at the instruments laid out ready for the butchering. "What about these?"

"Them's his business."

There was activity in an adjoining room. The great man had arrived.

"Ready in there, Corporal?" As he entered, the surgeon glanced at William. "You again?" Then, "Very wise, Constable. If you put that bundle down," by now William was sitting on the chair with Golightly's clothes on his knee, "you'll fall more comfortable than last time."

He didn't take the advice about falling onto something soft. Sitting there, willing himself not to succumb, William found he was rummaging through the dead man's pockets. It was an involuntary move. Sam had been the first, in difficult circumstances, and had retrieved the all-important pocketbook. The second bite had been taken in the mortuary with more time and the clothes stripped from their owner. The only point of a third examination was to give distraction from the hacking and sawing on the table.

It was all happening at eye level now that he was seated, making it easier not to see flesh parting under the knife, but then, on the other hand, down with the body, William found himself identifying with Hubert Golightly. Not for long; the pain in his searching finger banished such fancies.

"Damnation." This under his breath. William was not given to swearing.

"What's that, Constable?" The sharp hearing of a disciplinarian.

He didn't really know. After a struggle, and not before pricking his finger a second time, William extricated something akin to a sewing needle, except it wasn't. For a start the shaft ran into a thickened section at one end. At the other it had been sheared off at an angle, with the suggestion of a hole extending along its length. He held it up.

"I've found this, sir."

The surgeon glanced at it. "A hypodermic needle, be careful with it. There'll be a glass syringe somewhere." He beckoned William to look closer at the body. "This man was diseased. He was going to die whether or not he'd cracked his cranium open."

Whatever had caused the damage to the cadaver's skull, it had driven an expanse of bone into the interior.

"See here, Constable." Fragments were being picked out of the wound. "That's his brain, and it's not healthy."

Diseased or otherwise, William's curiosity was stronger than his distaste. He peered, fascinated, at the grey mass with its pinkish sheen.

"There; that's a diseased bit." The surgeon pointed to a whitish area, not so very different from the rest. "Penny to a pound he's been dosing himself with mercury. He'll have had GPI or I'm a Dutchman."

"Don't suppose he'll understand," the attendant muttered as he went about his duties. Whether he was trying to be helpful or the reverse, William was grateful.

"No, I suppose not. Now, Constable Whatever-Your-Name-Is…?"

"Archer, sir."

"See here, Archer, it's like this. That body there suffered what is commonly known as lady's disease. He'll have caught it taking his pleasure with some disreputable harlot and then later it gets him in the brain. Poor chap had syphilis."

William wondered how the diseased woman might have come by her affliction in the first place, but felt unable to ask.

"Only thing is mercury, but he was wasting his money, it don't do for the brain."

Fascinated and horrified in equal measure, William recalled his mission. "How did he come by his injury, sir? He was found alongside a rail track. At one stage a carriage might have stood for some time."

"Hard to say. In his state he could have stepped from it into thin air, fallen, and hit his head on the end of a sleeper. Then again, someone could have whacked him."

Better informed about the ways of the world he may be, but William couldn't see that the case had moved forward at all by the surgeon's findings. He still had hold of the dead man's things and as he went to replace them on the chair something fell to the floor.

"Weren't sure if that went wi' his clothes or 'is bits and pieces." The attendant picked up a short length of crimson cord. "Too fancy for anything 'cept tying knots in a bedchamber. It was round his ankle."

It took a moment or two, but William's offer to return the dead man's effects to his family got a satisfying response from the mortuary attendant.

"You know who he is?" The man was taken aback. "You didn't say…"

"I'm telling you now; he's a cotton merchant from Didsbury called Hubert Golightly."

"So we got the register out." They were back in the office and Sam had the floor. "Keeping it up to date was a clerk's job but he'd disappeared. The yardman did his best. Dockets come in from Traffic. One copy to the yard and the other to the engine shed. The yardman has to have the stock available and the shed sends the locomotive, then off they go."

"What about the register?"

"Ah well; that's made up after it's all happened."

"For one train to leave Buxton there have to be two pieces of paper and an entry in a register?"

"That's not the half of it. Another clerk in Motive Power does the same sort of thing using the duplicate. Then in both places there's a board with the day's work chalked up for the men."

William looked thoughtful. "I suppose it's all got to match up."

"It didn't. Well, it did mostly, but there were several movements in both registers that hadn't been authorised with dockets. There's a procedure for that in case of unforeseen emergencies, but it hadn't been followed."

"What about the clerk in MPD; had he disappeared too, or didn't he get enough warning?"

"He was quite open about it. The other chap was senior, and just walked over and gave instructions by word of mouth."

"Against regulations?"

"If the Whale has it wrong we'd go against orders."

"No *we* wouldn't. You might, but you'd order me to keep out of it."

"And you wouldn't obey… This is nonsense." Sam returned to his report. "In my opinion the clerk I spoke to was weak but I doubt he's a criminal. It's the other one who's a link in the chain. He gets his instructions from someone with a key to that 'disused' gate."

"We need to get hold of him. Do you think he'll be back?"

"I know where he lives and I've got a name for him." Sam relinquished the floor to William. "And how did you get on?"

"Not much help, really."

"You didn't faint again, did you?"

William explained about the chair, and the unhelpful opinion on the fatal wound. "Wouldn't commit himself. It must have been a heavy blow to stave his skull in though." Sam was treated to a description of picking bone out of the hole and the colour of the brain underneath. "He pointed to one bit and said it was diseased, but it all looked the same."

"Diseased?"

William did his best, but Sam had seen army service. "You mean Golightly had the pox?"

"If you say so, Sam. Anyway, to show in the brain like that the surgeon said it had been in his body for some time and might have led him to step out of the carriage and into thin air."

"Egyptian?" They'd moved on to Golightly's 'bits and pieces'. "Came across Egyptian cigarettes a few days past." Sam closed the cigarette case and picked up the cord. "And I saw something exactly like this only a few hours ago."

Whilst William was begging boiling water from the refreshment room Sam pondered the broken glass. He'd recognised the debris as a syringe from the plunger and metal fittings before being told. Mercury treatment? Possibly, but what about morphine used to excess? It might explain the dead dog if the glass had shattered in the fall and its contents seeped out.

"See here, William..."

The tea was brewing and William was gnawing at an elderly scone, too old to sell even to the long-suffering customers of the LNWR.

"It was for free, but it's got me beat." He gave up the struggle. "What's that, Sam?"

Ignoring the interruption, Sam continued. "This is beginning to look like a dead end. All we've uncovered is a writhing mess of iniquity with disease, drugs and perversion at its heart."

"I don't suppose we can prove Golightly was murdered – he probably wasn't, the autopsy findings suggest it was his own doing. If anyone did push him they're not going to admit it anyway."

"So we're left with bribery leading to an infringement of railway operating procedure." Sam was gloomy. "I suppose money was involved; hard to see why he'd do it otherwise."

William's hand was on the doorknob. "That's the Crewe train."

"Tomorrow, then, I'll search out the vanishing clerk, and you go and see if anybody you recognise turns up."

The weather had improved so that Lizzie was able to collect little Mary on her way home in the dry.

"No trouble at all. Took her pap, got her wind up like a good 'un and went to sleep." Elsie was generosity itself. "Any time."

"Would Friday be all right? I'm not sure yet, I'll have to..." Lizzie couldn't quite say what she'd have to do first, but no further explanation was needed.

"Any time means any time, so long as y' heed what I said 'bout them rich folks swallowing you up."

Was she being swallowed up? It had all been very odd. Miss Peachment and her collection of tradesmen's wives had been intimidating at first, but now, in front of her own mirror, Lizzie looked perfectly presentable, despite the earlier damp, and she knew she had held her own.

Lady Pinkstone might have cowed her but she was only there for a few minutes, and anyway the rest of the group shrank in her presence too. It was the other Lady Pinkstone, or Miss Delilah Arthurs, Lizzie was still uncertain how to address her, that was so confusing. She had even wondered, on one occasion, if she was being invited to use the woman's given name, but the moment had passed without mishap.

She had presented Lizzie with a problem. In Miss Arthurs' eyes no doubt it was a simple request. "Could you persuade your husband to look into a little difficulty with the workhouse finances?" An emolument would be arranged, but above all else, discretion was expected.

Problem or not, the present had to be dealt with first. Little Mary would need feeding soon, and supper had to be prepared. In the middle of it all Jimmy put his head round the door.

"Will I tek some o' that through to Mikey when I get back?"

Her eventful day had pushed the waif from her mind but Jimmy, as always, brought her back to earth.

"How's he getting on?"

"Better wi' some proper victuals inside him. Talks a bit more; was saying 'bout his mam."

"What about his mam, Jimmy?"

"Just that he was out lookin' fer 'er." He was back out in the yard now, with Benjy eager for his walk. Further enquiry would have to wait.

Little Mary had gone down without complaint and tea was well under way by the time Sam arrived home. Lizzie had learnt to assess his mood from the tramp of his boot and the time he took to take off his coat. She wished she could do something about that coat. It had been serviceable, if dull, in its day but that time was long gone. The best that could be said of it was that it was clean. Lizzie had taken it upon herself to see it was so, but no amount of sponging would attend to its fraying cuffs and worn collar.

"Is that you, Sam? I'm in the kitchen."

They kissed, and as she embraced him Lizzie fancied she felt the stress of his working day ebbing away; or was it wishful thinking?

"How was your day?"

Given Sam's gloomy assessment of the case earlier it was not a propitious opening. "Looks like an accidental death mixed up with the flouting of railway regulations. All pretty unsavoury, though." Then, brighter, "And what about your philanthropic ladies?"

Lizzie told him about the damp and how well her dress had survived, and the sycophantic tradesmen's wives and the mercifully brief appearance of Lady Pinkstone... At this point she began to run out of words.

Sam waited.

"And then there was a puzzle; the widowed Dowager Lady Pinkstone. One-time sister-in-law to Sir Wilfred, she's in two minds about the family name. I called her *Miss* Pinkstone but she had to set me right. Says she prefers her maiden name anyway, Miss Delilah Arthurs. Very nice about it, but..."

"But what?" He was intrigued.

"She knows who I am whilst continuing with the 'Oldroyd' mistake, and she knows who you are too... and she wants something."

"What's that?"

"They want to pay you to investigate some financial irregularities at the workhouse. That is, she didn't say who she's speaking for but her brother-in-law, Sir Wilfred, is chairman of the Board of Guardians. I'm sorry, Sam, if this is going to turn into a big mistake."

There was a long silence, but it didn't bristle with anger. Perhaps a pause for thought would be more accurate. Lizzie, on tenterhooks at the start, found her worries ebbing. Perhaps she hadn't embarked on an embarrassing escapade after all.

"How did you find the workhouse? Pretty depressing, I'd hazard."

Lizzie explained about the women in the lying-in ward. "They knew Betsy Piggin all right. Said she'd lost the child she was carrying and left an older one there when she went. A man came and took her away."

Sam was no longer pensive. "Did they say anything about him?"

"They said he could fix things, mostly employment of an unsavoury nature, or a bit of wet-nursing if they didn't fancy…"

"What did you think of Miss Delilah Arthurs?"

The question had plagued Lizzie since they had first met. "She's unlike anyone I've ever come across… Whatever else, she's honest and knows her own mind. I'm impressed by her but it's too early to say whether I like her…"

"What did you say to her about me and her investigation?"

"No, it's not…" Lizzie, engrossed in her own thoughts, hadn't heard him. "I *do* like her. She's a breath of fresh air, bracing, but welcome."

Sam had to ask again.

"Oh, I said I'd speak to you but I thought you'd refuse the money and it would be against company regulations anyway."

"I'm not so sure about that."

Sam almost whispered, and Lizzie didn't quite catch his words. She looked at him, enquiring.

"When do you next see her?"

ELEVEN

Wednesday 9th May 1877

He could luxuriate in a leisurely morning if there was some point to it. Not that looking up an old acquaintance, with the expectation of a good lunch, would qualify on its own. That would be a matter of private pleasure and something to be wary of. No; this was in the line of duty.

Best keep his wits about him. Spray would expect no less. What had the sergeant said? "Find out if there's a regime for inspecting workhouses and schools for the destitute, and how it works. Best of all, who's assigned to the area covering Buxton and Chapel-en-le-Frith?"

Having decided on a frontal assault, Superintendent Wayland's plan, if rather sketchy, was complete by the time his train was passing Tring. He hunted around, desperate for something to fill the void, and lighted on a familiar subject. How was it that as senior officer he'd come to be doing the bidding of a mere sergeant? He'd considered this conundrum on previous occasions, although, unimaginative man that he was, he was quite unable to see the thread that connected them all. Or why, when he had done, a warm glow that he'd first felt at the man's wedding should reappear.

With a squealing of brakes the train finally juddered to a halt at its appointed platform. It was a relief to have arrived at Euston without having to confront the subject that was really troubling him: Beatrice Appleton.

Rubin Able had lived up to his name. He would approach a desk swamped in loose papers with relish and turn them into an archive of documents in a trice. Whilst he was at it he'd fire off a terse note in one direction whilst coping with complaints about missing casks of beer from another. Plenty of that had been consumed during the construction of the Grand Crimean Central Railway. The navvies were gone by the time Colonel Wayland took up his command, but Able had remained to assist with operational matters. The position of a civilian in the rigid hierarchy prevailing during the Crimean War had been somewhat below that of a mule, but the man had survived and prospered.

Prospered to the extent that he was now employed by the Home Office. His position was sufficiently elevated to support the membership of a respectable gentlemen's club, and it was there he'd suggested they meet for lunch. Wayland was uncertain. Luncheon at someone else's expense, with an opportunity to talk over old times, had its attractions, but he rather wished business had come first.

"Colonel, a pleasure to see you, sir."

"And you too, Mr Able. I trust you are well?"

They were shaking hands in the entrance hall. Non-members were corralled there until they could be vouched for by a man who'd paid his subscription.

Safely inside, they talked old times over their brandies.

"Beatty didn't last long."

"I didn't know him: before my time."

"Good man; he built the thing, don't y'know?"

"Whatever happened to Campbell? He stayed on a bit..."

The conversation roamed back and forth over their lives together in the Crimea. Wayland was wiping the remains of a spotted dick from his mouth, determined to move things on with the coffee, but was forestalled.

"Now, Colonel, what's all the mystery?"

"I'll explain."

By the time port had circulated and the coffee cups had been cleared, Charles Wayland had learnt more than he wished to about the responsibilities of the Poor Law Board, and Rubin Able had learnt to address his guest as 'Superintendent'.

He'd had a wakeful night. Only recently was little Mary sleeping through, and, lying beside his wife, Sam was loath to disturb her. She'd never weakened but he'd caught her on occasion snatching a brief nap over her tea. Now she could enjoy a good night's rest he was not going to wake her.

So he lay there wondering what was for the best. It was that young scally, Jimmy, that had set him thinking.

"Yes, Mr Spray, said he was looking fer 'is mam. Promised to come fer 'im and nivver did, so 'e ran."

Come for him from where? If only he could tackle Mikey himself. But so far Lizzie had been proved right. By keeping away, details were creeping out into the daylight.

Something Lizzie had said was in the mix, too. The eccentric Miss Arthurs had suggested she went with her to visit the school where older children were sent.

"She wants me to go with her to somewhere in Buxton. Connected with the Chapel Workhouse, she said. Friday would be the day but I didn't say yes in case..."

Sam knew he'd been tetchy about the workhouse visiting, and wished he had not been so, but then Lizzie had been running risks on his behalf. Now that Miss Arthurs had approached her directly things had become less clear-cut... but even more dangerous?

A vision of Betsy Piggin's corpse appeared. He must have drifted off with her in mind because by now light was showing round the curtains and Lizzie was getting dressed. Half awake, he mused on the irony of having a clearer image of the dead woman's body than he had of his wife's. As his head cleared Sam had been surprised to find that overnight he'd gathered up some loose ends and made a serviceable knot with them.

The consequence was that he had more than one destination in Buxton.

Constable Archer had come prepared. He had with him bread and cheese provided by his mother.

"It'll be a long day, William; you'll need some victuals." She was a woman whose life had been devoted to food. As the wife of a master baker and the mother of a family it was hardly surprising. And it showed in her four boys. All healthy and well grown, the quarters above the shop that constituted the family home was a crowded place.

He'd also acquired a discarded newspaper with the notion that it might offer some disguise as to his real purpose, although why a young man should loiter outside the premises of a Manchester newspaper office whilst sporting a copy of the *Shrewsbury Chronicle* was hard to explain, as he discovered.

"Here, 'ave this." The man emerged from a ginnel alongside the offices of the *Manchester Evening News* and was proffering William a first edition. "It's today's; that 'n's nearly a week old, and it ain't much of a place, Shrewsbury."

Confident on the verge of insolence, untidy but not quite disreputable, and above all in control of the situation, the man looked knowingly at William. "He came yesterday."

"I... what? Don't know..."

"Come off it, you an' yer mate are on ter summat t' do wi' that box number 'e shewed me. An' yew was poking about earlier wi' some tale 'bout a dropped wallet, an fer a moment yer had one up on me."

William felt his self-esteem returning.

"Got the bugger's name out of me, ye did. Mostly it works t' other way in my business."

"Just pursuing a line of enquiry."

"We both know the man's name is Fewster, an' what's more, I know 'is first name. Oswald, it is, and you can have that fer free."

William took out his pocketbook and made a note. He couldn't help feeling ridiculous as he did so, the recently bolstered self-esteem evaporating as he scribbled.

"That's a sign of my good faith; that name. I've got more so why don't we make a trade? We could go inside and have a sit-down whilst we're about it."

William, even at this low ebb, hadn't quite lost his wits. "I'll stay out here, thank you." Just because he felt trapped, he didn't have to put his head in the snare.

"'Ave it yer own way..."

A foul-smelling cigarette had been part of the conversation, bobbing about as the newsman talked. William watched hopefully as the glowing end crept closer to his lower lip. At the last moment a packet appeared and a replacement was lit from the stub. He contrived to move upwind.

"Yer see, when Mr Oswald Fewster arrived yesterday, I knew you'd miss him. I'd seen to that by telling t' other fella the wrong day, so as I could foller Fewster myself an' see where 'e went. Ver' interestin', 'twas."

The horns of a dilemma can be very sharp, as William was discovering, and he played the only card he had. "I'm a police constable, and it's not my place to tell you anything. I could lose my job. Now, my sergeant—"

"Oh aye, a've met 'im, didn't know 'e was a sergeant though."

How does he do it? Anything I say turns into his gain and my loss. "If you come to the constabulary office on Edgeley Station—"

"That's it! Got yer. Railway rozzers, that's what y' are."

It had happened again, thought William. But he was wrong. First there was a silence and then, "So you're Archer an' 'e's Spray..." More silence, thoughtful, even respectful now. "Heard 'bout you two... that Fenian business... not much in the papers 'bout yer, but I heard anyways."

To William's amazement, the man took his hand.

"Pleased ter meet yer. I'll come to Stockport termorrer if your boss'll be there."

First things first.

"No, he ain't showed up, an' I reckon it's you and your questions what's done it. Heard you was nosing about

Parcels last week and now they're a man short in that office too."

"You mean the parcels clerk has gone missing as well?"

"That's what I heard." The yard foreman was turning away.

"I don't suppose you have an address for him?"

"No I bloody 'aven't, now bugger off and let me get on wi' me job."

Sam had to make do with what he'd got. It turned out to be a ramshackle building on a road leading out of town. Perhaps once its stone walls had commanded respect, but the door on which Sam knocked needed paint and opening it was a struggle.

"If yer want a room go round the back. This is reserved fer gentlemen, an' we don't get none o' they."

Round the back was even less inviting; a yard and what had once been stabling, disused now, with a sagging ridge. A victim of progress, Sam thought. It would have been a coaching inn before the railways took the trade.

"Now then?"

What had been no more than a voice from behind a part-opened door, turned into a lean, wiry woman. She was small, and Sam wondered how she could be so loud.

"I'm looking for..." Sam mentioned a name.

"Why, what's 'e done?"

"He's not at work."

"He ain't here neither. Him and that pal of 'is, they're a disgrace. The railway should be ashamed o' their sen, employing riff-raff like that."

There's one way above all others to anger a landlady.

"They've gone off owing, have they?" Sam did his best to sound solicitous. "When was that?"

"Di'n't see 'em after Monday night, but I 'eard 'em Tuesday mornin'. Out early, they were; they get no breakfast 'ere." Then, "Tuesday's rent day."

"You'll have it up front, I'll be bound."

In the silence that followed the fiery little woman wilted beneath her apron and mob cap.

"They was good as gold for a start. Polite – well, polite as them sort can be – an' they brought me little things…"

"What sort of little things?" The two of them were indoors now. Mingling with the smell of unwashed bedding and old sweat was something sweeter. "Cigarettes; Egyptian cigarettes perhaps?"

Realising she'd said too much, the woman adopted a sullen silence.

"So you let the rent slip into arrears on account of gifts of goods stolen off the railway. You must have known they weren't honest; I mean to say, *them sort* don't have smokes like that on their own account, or drinks like this." Sam picked up a bottle. He didn't know anything about brandy, but nor did the woman who'd drunk it. "Cost a pretty penny, this; comes from France, y'know." He put on a calculating air. "What with the price of a bottle of…" he stared knowingly at the label, "Napoleon Cognac exceeding two weeks' rent in a fleapit like this, I reckon you've drunk next week's rent already."

She was apprehensive now. "I didn't mean no 'arm, I mean ter say…"

"How about this?" Sam sounded more benign. "You tell me all you know about those two scallies and I might just come to the conclusion that it's their smokes and their bottles that I've just found, and not yours."

It didn't take much thought, but although the offer was snapped up instantly, it was still a tortuous business. "Can't rightly say" kept cropping up, but Sam persisted.

"When they first arrived were the two of them together?"

"Can't rightly say… there were two on 'em, right enough, but not the same two."

"Of course you've had others here, but it's the two off the railway I'm interested in."

"They came 'bout the same time but separate. Two tergether each time, and one were the same one."

As on a damp summer's morning when the rising sun suddenly clears the early mist, so it was for Sam. "You mean, they arrived about the same time but were brought separately by the same man?"

"That's what I'm trying to tell 'ee, but yer a bit slow."

"Do you know this man who brought them?"

The landlady, more confident now she had an escape route, declined to answer.

"Has he got a name?"

She muttered something without intending to inform.

"Do you see him about Buxton?"

In the face of her obduracy, Sam picked up the empty brandy bottle.

"He's been away."

"How do you know?"

"Yer can tell a lag a mile off. Anyways, he had a terrier crop back then."

"Back when?"

She was beaten now. Any sign of hesitation and Sam looked meaningfully at the Courvoisier label on the bottle in his hand.

"'Bout two year ago. Bit more, p'raps; it were snowing. Mind you, it'll snow up 'ere in June if it's a mind."

"I didn't catch his name."

This time the mumble was just audible. "Breaker, Breaker Bill, on account of 'is breaking people's bones."

"Is that all he does?" Sam was thinking of a bit of expert knife work.

"Dunno 'bout that; but he'll be after breaking some of mine if 'e finds out I've been a-talking to a Jack."

Sam had just about squeezed her dry. She'd agreed that Breaker was to be seen about the town times in the last couple of years, and was quite certain that he wasn't local.

"He don't speak proper, not like us."

Buxton was the centre of her world.

There was plenty to discuss back in Stockport.

As his day's work had been curtailed and the return journey from Manchester no more than a short hop, William arrived first.

"You're back early." Sam bustled into the office. "Thought you'd be wandering all over after your man."

It had been a failure and he knew it, but William did his best. "He seemed quite friendly in the end."

"Oh yes, and why d'ye think that was?"

"He wanted to help?"

Sam sniffed. "Like a hole in a bucket. It helps to empty it but *you've* nothing much at the end."

"He's called Snape, and he said he'd come here with some more information tomorrow. He'd heard of our part in the Fenian business."

"He'll want more in return than he gives. His sort always do."

"He did confirm that our man's called Fewster. That might have been a slip, he'd assumed we were sure, but then he gave me his first name." William recalled the newsman's knowing look and the exaggerated display of generosity that had accompanied this insignificant morsel. Perhaps Sam was right.

It was Sam's turn. "The stationmaster wasn't too pleased about it. He carried on as if it was *my* fault."

William would have to wait for a later train home.

Sam continued, "It seems that he was short of a parcels clerk and out of the blue these two lads turned up. They came with recommendations from London. Well, he only wanted one, but he asked in the yard and they took t' other."

"Wasn't he a bit surprised at them coming out here? Better prospects down south, I'd have thought."

"More worried about replacements... I'd like to see the letter of recommendation, wherever that's got to."

The report moved on to the second part of Sam's day.

"Why did you go there, Sam?"

It was a private matter, and Sam didn't know what to make of it himself. Half asleep, he'd been comparing what little he knew of his wife's body to that of a murdered prostitute, and that was definitely not for William's ears, but it was in that moment he'd made up his mind.

"It was to do with what Lizzie said about education for the children."

William had been sent out for hot water and was busying himself with tea. "What was that?

"She's been asked to go visiting at a place in Buxton where the workhouse sends 'em. It's a new arrangement. They've set up a school for the district but they can't find enough young bodies so they're topping up with reform brats sent by the magistrates, and the parish don't have to pay for them."

"Poor little mites."

Sam agreed. On his previous visit to the school, the letter box and a frightened voice from inside had been the only result. This time he'd approached his task with more determination and been rewarded. He went over what had happened in his mind.

An aura of indignation had hung about the man. It was in the sound of the bolts being drawn and the snap of the lock as he turned the door key, and the tightly trimmed beard that bobbed up and down as he'd demanded, "And what the devil do you want?"

It was in his bluster too when Sam had enquired after Betsy Piggin and the child she'd left behind.

"Common prostitute; what d'ye expect? No morals, no self-respect, breed like the vermin they are, spawning evil brats to become a burden on the parish."

It would have continued indefinitely, but for the mention of Mr Fewster. The self-righteous bully is an ugly sight when caught out.

Sam had pressed home his advantage. "Know him, do you? He has business here, I believe."

"But you're from the railway…" Sam had shown his warrant card. "How d'ye know anything of Fewster?"

"His activities are a matter of interest to the constabulary." With precious little evidence yet, but Sam had hopes.

"He's an important personage… influence… Home

Office…" He couldn't distance himself from the man fast enough. "I had little to do with… the porter dealt with it all. You should ask him."

"What position do you hold, Mr…?"

"Figgis, Archibald Figgis, and I'm the master here."

At this point it had finally dawned. The more he said, the deeper he'd be dragged into the mire.

"So you're responsible for everything that goes on. I mean to say, you wouldn't be called master if it wasn't so, would you?"

It was difficult for Figgis to disagree, but then he ought to know what Fewster was up to in his domain. As Sam had watched him wrestle with his conundrum a draught of chill air swept through the entrance lobby where they stood. The door snapped shut behind him and a look of relief spread across the hapless man's face.

"Ah, there you are. Deal with this intruder, will you?"

The new arrival had brought with him an air of menace. It required no effort, just heavy, hunched shoulders, loosely swinging arms and a surprising lightness on his feet. Figgis scuttled out like a frightened rabbit, leaving the two facing each other.

"And who are you?" The question might just as well have been asked by either man, but Sam got in first.

"Never you mind who I am. Who are you?"

Sam had showed his warrant card. "I'm a policeman."

"I can see that, Sergeant Spray – and off your patch too. You ain't got no authority out 'ere, an' you won't 'ave on the railway when I've done with 'ee."

With that the door had opened and Sam found himself out on the street.

He gave William the bare bones of the meeting.

"Not a very fruitful visit, Sam. No better than mine." William had rinsed out the chipped mugs and emptied the spent leaves from the pot. He was heading for the door and the next Crewe service.

"Oh, I don't know. Tomorrow we might find a way of getting at what Chadwick Snape knows. I certainly learned a thing or two before the school porter threw me out."

"I can't see what." William sounded doubtful.

"We now know for certain that Fewster has a connection with the place. We know that the master is not very clever and a nasty little bully. He knows enough of what goes on to be frightened, but the real inside man is the porter. He looks like a bruiser but there's more to him than just violence. He and Fewster are up to something."

There was no doubt about it, the lad was perking up. Mrs Spray's provisions were certainly making a difference, and Jimmy did what he could with the odd little extra. If his ma wondered on occasion at how the cold pie had shrunk, she let it pass.

Mikey was getting more inquisitive and asked where he was.

"Ain't never 'eard of it," was his response to 'Whaley Bridge.' "Must have a railway; I hears whistles, times."

He'd not ventured out, and for the moment seemed content.

"How far's…?" He thought better of it. "I were real frit in the dark."

"Out on the moor?" It was, after all, where Jimmy had found him.

"In t' tunnel. It were real loud."

"You mean you walked through a railway tunnel and trains came past?"

"I were lookin' fer my mam."

TWELVE

Thursday 10th May 1877

He was rather pleased with himself. Not that yesterday's leisurely morning was to be repeated. It might turn into a habit, and that would never do. A hot drink as he arrived at his desk was, however, a necessity, and as he sipped tea from the only china cup in the office, Charles Wayland would rather it had been coffee.

But drinkable coffee was well beyond the capabilities of his desk constable. The only man in his command who could make it had by virtue of his rank excluded himself from such tasks. He was now in charge of the Manchester office. The thought of Sergeant Spray led on to yesterday's expedition and the information that he wanted. A written report would be quite sufficient, Wayland had decided. It was dry stuff and the thing had pretty much written itself by the time he'd arrived back the previous night.

Why then was he putting his greatcoat back on and donning his top hat, somewhat hurriedly heading for the next Manchester train?

"Now then, gents, it's a pleasure to meet you both… again." Chadwick Snape, true to his word, had journeyed to Stockport and was making himself at home in the constabulary office. Both chairs were occupied so his backside was propped against a desk.

"I hope your journey won't be wasted." Sam was treating the visitor with some circumspection.

"I can see you're an honest couple of coves with a name to live up to."

The two policemen put on an air of indifference.

"I got friends in Minshull Street. That inspector from down south they had there last year said you was good. Catching them Fenians was down to you, he said."

"Mr Snape, why are you here?"

"Well now, the way I see it, you're on to something to do with Fewster."

Silence.

"I follered Oswald after he left the office on Tuesday." At this point Snape adopted an exaggerated air of contrition. "Sorry about that…"

Silence.

"I arrived at a flash house in Didsbury."

It took an effort, but Sam remained impassive whilst experiencing a moment of inspiration. "Oh, there." He let slip the address on Golightly's visiting card. "We know all about that."

Chadwick Snape seemed to shrivel, all his swagger gone. Sam, still impassive, concealed his relief. The gamble had paid off.

"Stop long, did he?"

Snape, off balance now, was in the middle of an explanation of how long he'd watched and how he'd had to return to the office before Fewster reappeared when, without warning, the door banged open. One person only would assume the right to such an intrusion, and he stood in the doorway.

"Good morning, sir. We didn't expect you today."

Constable Archer hurriedly stood up and Superintendent Wayland came to rest in the vacated chair. By now the modest little room was becoming crowded. Snape, still propped on the desk, was above those seated, but it didn't stop the new arrival glaring at him.

Sam stood up. "This is Mr Snape, sir. He thought he might have had some information pertaining to our enquiries, and was kind enough to come to us with it. He's just leaving."

They shuffled round until both he and Snape were outside on the platform.

"Kind of you to come, sir." This in a firm voice that carried. As they shook hands Sam's voice dropped. "Perhaps we might meet again if you come across anything else. At some stage we may have something for the press. You might as well be the first."

He watched the retreating figure as Snape set off for a Manchester train. The man looked as cocksure as he had when he arrived. Sam on the other hand was troubled by doubt. Snippets *read* in a newspaper were all very well; snippets *given* to a newspaper were quite another matter. But there was no doubt that Snape, unknowingly, had been useful.

"Unsavoury character, Spray. Don't suppose he was any help."

"He didn't think he was, sir." No need to tell the Whale more than he had to. "This is an unexpected visit."

"Went to up to London, met with an old Crimea hand at the Home Office." Luncheon at the club and the brandy beforehand weren't mentioned, nor the port that came after, but by the end of the report, Sam had a clear idea of how things stood.

"All to do with Andover." The Whale didn't know what had happened, but he was sure that a scandal there had something to do with the current state of things. "The parishes have to get together and set up these Union places." Then he went on to education. "Two sorts of school, one to educate the workhouse brats, and another to control the delinquents. The Home Office pays for the miscreants. They're supposed to be kept separate and they send out inspectors, but Mr Able didn't think much to them."

"Mention any names, did he, sir?"

"Come to think of it, he went very quiet when I asked him about Derbyshire. Don't suppose it means anything..."

Sam, silent now, wasn't so sure.

"You'll think of something," Sam had said. And he had done the *thinking*, but the *something* wasn't very palatable. It consisted of hanging around a respectable neighbourhood without attracting attention, and keeping an eye on a pair of wrought-iron gates which may or may not serve to let the servants in and out of the house behind.

There was one consolation: Saoirse. Not that she'd told William her name, not that he'd ever heard the name before last Saturday, and he certainly couldn't spell it, but he'd heard the cook call her '*Sear-sha*', and he wanted to see her again. For entirely professional reasons, he told himself; and it was going to require the involvement of an intermediary, and *she* was a ‘scratchy old besom’. That was Saoirse’s description, and since, by now, everything the maid had said had become the word of an angel, in William’s eyes at least, he believed it.

What mattered about the ‘scratchy old besom’ was that she was a casual. She lived away from her place of employment; so William waited.

Not at all what he expected; the scullery maid, when she finally appeared, was a trim little woman wearing a black bonnet and bombazine. True, close up the coat was well worn and had been mended times, but it was clean and its wearer carried herself with purpose.

“And what d’ye want, young man? I seed y’ earlier, hangin’ ’bout. You makes a respectable widder woman nervous.”

“I need to speak to one of the maids and I—”

“Oh, it’s that Saoirse, is it? Heard she’d been thick with a bobby days ago. Come back for another try, have ’ee?

William, his secret longing laid bare, did his best. “It’s constabulary business. I need to ask her a few more questions, and I’d rather not be seen at the house.”

“If you say so, Constable… I’m off fer me tea.”

“Do you think…?” William jangled coins in his pocket. “Do you think you might set your tea back by a minute or so and slip inside with a…?”

“Will that be constabulary money you’m throwin’ about?”

“Never you mind about that, missus.” William, struggling to keep control of the conversation, pulled out a coin. “This is yours if you’ll slip back inside with a message for the maid.”

After that it was a matter of waiting; and getting wet. To begin with, a plane tree just in leaf offered some protection, but later its leaves bowed under the weight of water and what was a fine mizzle out in the open turned into heavy droplets. When a slight figure in a shawl slipped through the gates the rain no longer mattered, to William at least.

"'Tis mighty wet out here, Constable, you'd best be quick."

"Miss Saoirse—"

"How d'ye know my name? I nivver telt ye."

At least she's noticed me, thought William. "I'm a detective, I find things out."

"Huh, and you're finding things out from me, are ye?"

"Miss Saoirse, when we met a few days ago..." *I fell in love at first sight* was what he wanted to say, but duty called, "I should have asked you about visitors to the house. Are there any that you know about?"

"Really, Constable..." She sounded shocked. "Mr Hubert wouldn't..."

"No, no, not ladies; men, friends of Mr Hubert's. A Mr Fewster, perhaps? He might have visited last Tuesday?"

"Oh, him. No, you've got the wrong of it. I don't know his name but he visits upstairs. I think 'e's a friend of the old Mr Golightly; the mistress always opens the door and takes him up. I've never really seen the man, but we always know it's him; he leaves his gloves and a silk topper in the hall."

"Have you ever met the old Mr Golightly?"

Saoirse looked thoughtful. "I... I don't believe I have. The nursemaid looks after him, an' she don't speak... well, not 'bout him, anyways."

"So does he really exist? I mean to say, you've never seen him, the one person who knows doesn't talk... what about his wife, has Mrs Golightly ever mentioned him?"

"Constable, I'll be missed if I don't go back, an' I'm getting soaked. Anyways, you don't understand nuthin' 'bout service. The mistress don't talk to the likes of me. She gives orders, and I don't answer back." The maid turned toward the gate. "He eats; Cook gets something for him mealtimes. Mostly slops, but it all disappears." She started walking.

"Saoirse." William kept pace for a few steps. "Saoirse, do you have a time off when we might meet again?"

"Huh, more constabulary business is it, Constable?" The gate was getting close now and the gap between them widening. Over her shoulder, "I get an afternoon every other week."

Then as she closed it, fainter now, he thought he heard "Next Wednesday" from the other side.

"It's getting to be quite a habit, and one I'm not inclined to encourage."

Lizzie's mind was on other things. "She smiled back at me today, Sam. She did it twice."

The conversation ran on separate tracks for a while. Sam, tetchy at the Whale's meddling, had to give way in the end to more important matters.

"Look, she's done it again… Oh, Sam…"

Unable to see both Lizzie's and little Mary's faces at the same time, Sam was unsure whether the earth-shattering event had run to a third showing, but he agreed, the baby was indeed progressing well.

"Go on; see if she'll do one for you."

The child started crying and, judging from the smell, she'd done something quite different for Sam.

Later, little Mary asleep and the tea things tidied away, Sam was able to return to his day. "Came all the way from Crewe just to tell me about why they're called Union Workhouses and how they do the children."

"I'm visiting a school for destitute children tomorrow. What do I say to Miss Arthurs if she asks about you?"

"You can tell her I am in the middle of an investigation, and I'll bear her suggestion in mind. Did she say who had put her up to it?"

"I don't believe she did." Lizzie seemed doubtful now. "I'd assumed it was her brother-in-law…"

"Is that how to call the connection now her husband is dead?" Sam wasn't really after an answer; he was wondering how a middle-aged widow came to be interested in the financial affairs of a workhouse.

"I'm sure of it now; she never mentioned a name… though she did talk about 'we'."

There was a knock on the parlour door. Jimmy seemed to feel no compunction about venturing so far into the house before announcing himself.

"Left something in the meat safe, missus. Young Mikey's doing all right." Then he was gone.

Sam hadn't been listening, perhaps on purpose. What now resided in the pantry was no doubt a rabbit, poached by Jimmy's lurcher.

"Is that school you're visiting connected to the Chapel Workhouse?"

"I don't know, Sam; I can ask."

"I wonder if Betsy Piggin's child ended up there?"

THIRTEEN

Friday 11th May 1877

IT SHOULD HAVE BEEN EASIER SECOND TIME ROUND. THEY were to visit the school alone without the polite conversation and petits fours that had preceded Tuesday's episode. Lizzie, having decided she liked Delilah Arthurs, could have looked forward to the expedition but for her parting shot.

"We'll go and take tea afterwards. There's someone I want you to meet."

Beyond a snatched cup of tea and a bun in a railway refreshment room, Lizzie was not versed in the etiquette of eating out. Tuesday's 'light collation', as she had heard one of the ladies call it, was quite enough for one week. True, it had taught her about petits fours, but of dealing with waiters and giving an order and whatever else was involved, she was totally ignorant.

The grey silk and lavender bonnet would have to serve again. It would have to serve again and again as it was her only dress refined enough for the company she was now keeping. On this score at least she felt more at ease. Delilah

Arthurs may have spent a small fortune on her gown, but she was so careless of her appearance that Lizzie was untroubled. And there she was on Buxton Station, waving like a mother trying to attract the attention of her child. By arrangement they had both travelled on the same train, but boarding at different stations had made meeting before arrival difficult.

For a brief moment Lizzie wondered if she was to be embraced.

"Mrs Spray, such a pleasure." Said as if it was meant. "Come, we'll get the visiting over with first."

"Perhaps we could continue with 'Oldroyd'?"

"As you wish." Delilah Arthurs looked quizzical, and then, "Oh, I see; the good sergeant has agreed to my request."

Lizzie found herself bristling at this description of Sam. She wasn't quite sure why; but she wasn't having him patronised. "My husband is pursuing enquiries on behalf of his employer." It was true as far as it went, but try as she might, Lizzie couldn't remember him saying anything definitive on the subject of working for anyone else. Indeed, he had been uncharacteristically opaque on the matter. "He feels it would be improper to accept any fee." Of this she was surer. "I can say that his present investigation has taken him into the world of the workhouse."

Should she have said that? Lizzie was uncertain, but she felt that Miss Arthurs was owed something. They were walking now, brisk and purposeful as before, and were appreciating the company of each other.

"I visited the Reading Room, Mrs Spray. Your library is remarkably well stocked."

"How kind, although it's hardly mine. It belongs to the community now."

"It must have made a splendid place for a wedding breakfast."

How on earth did she know about that? wondered Lizzie.

"Sam thought so, and that's what mattered." And then, "I suppose I did assume a little privilege on that occasion."

"No more than you deserve, Mrs Spray. At least let me call you that in a conversation about your wedding."

Lizzie let it pass. "And where do you live, Miss Arthurs? Up at the Hall with your brother and sister-in-law?" Was this polite conversation, or was there a hint of the detective about it?

"Oh no. I stay there times, when I have to; I live up in London. Tell me, have you met a man called Downes? He's something at Scotland Yard."

No longer a hint; a full investigation. "I've heard my husband speak of him; I believe he's a detective chief inspector now."

"He speaks very well of your husband, Mrs Spray."

They were expected, and the school door opened before the conversation was quite over. The man on the other side stood four-square in the doorway.

"We're here by arrangement." Miss Arthurs took a step forward, and to Lizzie's amazement, he moved away and they were inside. "Thank you, my good man. Perhaps you would show us to the schoolrooms."

The porter led and the two women followed. Even from behind he radiated menace. With hunched shoulders and swinging arms, his lightness of foot belied his bulk. The children had been divided into two.

"Mrs Oldroyd will take the younger ones." Miss Arthurs turned. "Does that suit you, Mrs Oldroyd?"

At least she's remembered 'Oldroyd', but what about the conversation at the door?

Did he know what he'd done? Of course he did. Sam couldn't hide from truth, try as he might. He'd been ejected from premises which were at the heart of an investigation and he'd prompted his wife to risk her own safety by asking questions to which he'd failed to find answers himself. Her only protection was her anonymity and Delilah Arthurs' connections.

He'd manipulated her; hadn't he?

Momentarily he found comfort in Lizzie's earlier assertion that she was 'volunteering', but he was still agonising when a grimy youth barred his way into the office.

"You Mr Spray?"

"I'm Sergeant Spray, yes. Who are you?"

The young engine cleaner gave a name that Sam didn't quite catch and went on, "He's in a trough, face down. I found him; foreman telt me ter fetch you."

"You mean he's dead. How do you know?"

"'Cause he ain't moving, an' there's blood, an' he just looks… dead."

"And where is the trough?"

The boy looked at Sam pityingly. "In t' yard, of course."

Patiently, Sam drew out from the laconic lad that he'd gone for a jimmy riddle before going home from his night shift in the Buxton engine shed.

"Yer know, where they used ter shift parcels afore they started keeping 'em in t' new place."

"The trough was there for the delivery horses?"

"S'pose." The lad wasn't interested in anything so old-fashioned. "'S all in them weeds now."

"How did you see what was in the trough?"

"'T were all knocked down just by."

"So you could get close to the trough. Do you have a jimmy riddle there regularly?"

The answer was yes; and no, he hadn't seen a body the previous night; and yes, he would have noticed it. That, thought Sam, would be helpful in determining the time of death given the uncertain behaviour of rigor mortis in a body immersed in water.

They were aboard a Buxton-bound train now. "You don't seem very upset at finding a dead body."

"Well… he ain't one of us, so who cares?"

"What do you mean?"

"You'll see…"

And Sam did see. The business of the yard was progressing normally when they arrived.

"Told the lads ter get on with things." The yard foreman, unapologetic. "Yer'll know where it is. You was nosing round there earlier." He pointed in the direction of the engineer's coach. "Watch yer sen. You was near killed last time."

Even in early May the undergrowth was thick and matted, sheltered as it was beneath the yard wall. The nearest rail track was several yards away, leaving plenty of room for the horses when the trough was still in use. They walked past the old gate. He'd investigated it earlier, and three days later there still wasn't a spider's web to be seen across the wicket.

"See what a' mean, mister?" The engine cleaner kicked something out of the grass by the trough.

Sam was looking at the back of a body, lying face down in the shallow water. Its once-smart coat was not only wet and soiled; it had been pierced on the left side about halfway down the chest. A smear of blood had trickled from the wound.

"Here, leave that and lend a hand."

The lad stopped playing football with the silk topper, and helped Sam lift the corpse of Oswald Fewster onto dry ground.

"See what a' mean… 'e's a toff. Not one of us."

She hadn't thought about the noise. It was a long time since Lizzie had been in a classroom, and back then her young ears must have become accustomed to the scraping of chalk on slate. Not now: she found it excruciating.

"Good day, Mrs Oldroyd, they said you were visiting." A bright young woman turned from the board where she had just written out the letters of the alphabet. "You can stop writing now, children," the squeaking stopped, "and greet Mrs Oldroyd."

In unison, "Good morning, Mrs Oldroyd." Eager young faces looked up expectantly.

A startled Lizzie, who had given no thought to how she might reply, could only answer, "Good morning, children."

The squeaking resumed. Working her way through lines of bowed heads, the teacher would, on occasion, stop and gently correct a mistake, as she came toward Lizzie.

"Come outside, Mrs Oldroyd, the children will be settled for a minute or two."

Lizzie was impressed, not only by the sense of purpose about the place, but the atmosphere of care, and the intelligent manner of the teacher.

"Now, Mrs Oldroyd, what do you want to know about us?"

For the second time in a few minutes Lizzie was taken aback. At the workhouse in Chapel, mingling with the inmates had been an end in itself. Here, where idleness had been banished, it seemed an intrusion.

Her reply was forestalled. Children's voices from within the classroom, amplified as they echoed round its high vaulted ceiling, had the teacher's full, dark skirt swirling as she whipped round to quell the insurrection. It took some time and a miscreant was dispatched to stand outside as punishment.

"'S not fair." The child seemed unaware of Lizzie and was talking to herself. "He started it." Her sleeve was about to wipe away tears, now in danger of dripping to the floor. Lizzie offered a handkerchief. It was taken without a word. There were no sobs; the tears were shed for rage.

"What did he do?"

"He pulled my hair."

Lizzie could see the temptation that her pigtails might offer.

"That Herbert, he's always doin' it." Indignation waned. "I hit 'im on the nose." She giggled. "That'll show 'im."

They discussed the naughtiness of boys, and Lizzie asked if she knew one called Piggin. Surnames didn't rate much attention, and anyway, boys were hateful. So far as the girl was concerned her world would be well rid of them.

"No, I don't know no Piggin, but he'll be just as bad as the rest."

The conversation proceeded and the passageway, poorly lit at best, darkened as the porter approached. Lizzie would have been more than content to let things rest, but the little girl went on.

"Funny name, Piggin; sounds like the piggy-wigs Miss drew on the board."

The man passed, and Lizzie had the uncomfortable feeling that he didn't miss much.

Minutes went by and peace was restored. After the child was recalled the teacher again turned her attention to Lizzie.

"Now, Mrs Oldroyd, you were going to tell me why you are here."

In the few minutes that had elapsed since the question was first aired, Lizzie had thought of something. "We think that those confined to institutions might benefit from a little contact with people of good will from the world outside."

"So you feel that the presence, for an hour or two, of a respectable lady of means will direct these children towards a better life?"

It was as painful as it was sudden. Lizzie was forced to view herself in a new light. In her guise as companion to Delilah Arthurs, those with whom she felt she belonged attributed superiority where she had seen none in herself. Elsie's warning had been prescient.

"I only," not 'we' any more; it was her own integrity at stake. "I only hoped that I could let them see that they were cared for by others. I see now that my concerns were misapplied. You look to take very good care of them."

"If I do, I'm the only one here who does." The two women had found a community of interest. "It isn't any good just saying it; you must show it. Why don't I stop the class for a few minutes and you can tell the children who you are, and perhaps they can ask you questions?"

Lizzie felt she was on trial; the more so when: "They'll see your colours if you don't mean it." She swallowed hard and turned to face the children.

The class learned that Mr Bennett had been a railwayman.

"Did he drive an engine?" One of the older boys.

"No, he was a guard, but they're very important because they look after the train. Mr Oldroyd was a clerk."

"What does he do?" The girl had missed the past tense.

"I'm afraid he died some time ago..."

"Oh, missus..." A murmur of sympathy ran round the class. Here was something they understood. "But he looked after the records when he was alive?"

The questions went on until the teacher intervened. Sergeant Spray and Lizzie's present marriage had escaped mention.

Afterwards the two women were alone in the classroom.

"Tell me, do you recall a child called Piggin?"

"Why do you ask about him?" Then, the imparting of gossip being more pleasurable than the receipt of it: "There was a terrible to-do over it."

Lizzie waited quietly.

"His mother went off from Chapel, leaving him there. She's not supposed to do it but... Anyway, young Piggin arrived here for the school but he never settled. Kept saying his mother would come back for him."

Lizzie ventured a comment. "He must have felt betrayed when she didn't return."

"But that's the thing. She did return, quite recently, and they wouldn't let the boy go."

"Do you know why?"

"Nobody will say, but it was the boy disappearing that really upset them. And I just don't understand it. They don't care about these children, the people who run this place."

It was getting expensive. Sam wasn't sure what it cost, but he knew that every time he requested a post-mortem the Railway Constabulary had to pay. The Whale had said as much after the second one, and he didn't seem to be joking. Nonetheless, it was important. The stab wound hadn't bled much. Perhaps it had killed him, but what if his lungs were full of water? It made a difference.

Much of the morning had been taken up arranging for the body of Oswald Fewster, together with his once-smart top hat, but minus the contents of his pockets, to be transported to a mortuary. Sam was back now, asking questions.

"Notice anything unusual yesterday?"

The yard foreman was not pleased to see him. "You! You're allus makin' aggravation. These bodies are your doin': they foller y' round."

Sam bit his lip. It wasn't any use telling the man. He repeated his question. The foreman looked round. "No… not yesterday."

"What do you mean?"

"That coach you was so interested in…"

Sam looked across the yard. The engineer's coach stood much as it had three days ago.

"It were booked out last night fer two nights. We 'ad to gas it up yesterday. It were due ter stand in t' platform last night an' go out after last reg'lar service."

"How is it still here?"

"I don't bloody know, an' I don't s'pose anyone else do neither." Truculence was turning to desperation. "I ain't got no clerk. They took mine to replace the one as ran from MPD."

"So you're trying to keep up with the papers yourself."

"And failing."

"Mind if I have a look?"

Not waiting for an answer, Sam set off, the other man hurrying alongside him with an occasional "Watch it, mate" and a restraining hand. He was warned more forcibly on another subject. "Shut the bloody door. It'll be like a snowstorm in here else."

At first Sam wondered if a draught would make much difference. The place was littered with paper. Later he realised there was a semblance of order: similar items formed individual stacks, some impaled on spikes and others kept in place by heavy ledgers into which detail had yet to be entered. But there were enough random sheets with no apparent home to give the impression of chaos.

"Only taken three days to create this mess; they'd better be sending a new man soon."

"How do you get the instruction to prepare a train?"

The work of the yard continued apace and required attention. The foreman, halfway out of the door, turned and pointed – "It'll be in that one" – and was gone.

Looking through the ledger Sam identified a series of late-night departures designated 'E' – possibly 'engineer's'? Here was a schedule of the *Free Spirits in the Peak* excursions. Maybe 'E' stood for 'excursion train'. Nothing was entered after the 2nd May in the permanent record, but trapped underneath were a number of sheets referring to the last three days. Each had a large tick scrawled across, presumably by the foreman in the hope that someone would enter them up later.

All but one, that is. In the neat hand of a clerk was written the word *Cancelled.* It referred to an 'E' train for Thursday 10th May, a late departure, as the others had been. The handwriting seemed familiar and, looking back in the ledger, Sam realised why.

Setting off for the motive power department office, Sam had to navigate on his own. The locomotives made some noise as they moved, or at least, he thought they did; though even here he would have met his end but for the warning shout of an alert driver.

"Yes, sir; promotion and a bit more money." The newly transferred clerk was pleased with his new position.

"Smoke, do you?" An innocuous question but it made the young man uncomfortable.

"N… no, sir."

"No one else does in this office either." Sam gave an exaggerated sniff. "But you don't have to light those Egyptian smokes. They smell whilst they're still in the box."

The clerk was sitting, and Sam stood over him. "He came back, didn't he? The chap who was here before."

Silence… uneasy and fearful.

"You remember him, he's only been gone a day or two. He used to come over and tell you to make up dockets for those *Free Spirits* excursions, and you did what he wanted because he was senior to you."

Silence.

"That's what you told me. I remember it clearly."

Silence.

"Did he come alone?"

"He... he..." Defeated now, the young man put his head down to the desk. Sam might have seen a tear. The voice was muffled, his arms trapping the sound as he cradled it. "He frightened me."

Seeing the lad's shame at his own fear, Sam pulled up a chair and took a more conciliatory line.

"Lookee here, I can see you've been bullied into things you didn't want to do. Perhaps when you first arrived it seemed usual for a senior man to nip over with alterations to the schedules." Sam made a sweeping movement with his arm. "I mean, this lot'd defeat me." The ledgers and piles of spiked dockets were a malevolent presence. "Then, once you got master of the job, you realised that it wasn't quite jannock. But it was too late and you were in deep. He came back yesterday and after work he had you nip over to the yard and write *Cancelled* on that night's excursion docket... and that was after you'd cancelled the MPD docket here."

"Yes, sir." The clerk lifted his head sufficient to be heard clearly. "That's just how it was."

"And when you'd tried to get out there was this man... Tell me, what does he look like?"

"I hardly ever saw him. Just once or twice, p'raps, I'd see the previous chap with someone different. Once the clerk from Parcels was there too. They all disappeared sharpish but I could see he wasn't a man to mess with."

"How d'ye mean?"

"Big shoulders, light on 'is feet, walked swinging his arms, low bowler, and that's from behind. Never saw 'im head on, an' I didn't want to."

"Does he have a name?"

"I half-heard it once…"

"Go on."

"Breaker, or it might have been Butcher… scared the life out o' me, it did."

"Right, my lad." The time for a sympathetic approach was over. "It's like this. Looked at one way, I have enough evidence to have you dismissed."

Silence.

"In your defence, you might claim to have been acting under duress."

Silence.

"The rule book has nothing to say about duress. Its only concern is with the proper conduct of the railway."

This time a sob broke the silence.

"I am in a position to interpret the rule book. Were I to remedy its omission concerning duress, things might look rather different."

For the first time a light flickered in the clerk's dark place. "Oh, sir…"

"There is a condition."

The flickering light dimmed.

"You know where those scallies go drinking; you've been with them a time or two, I'll be bound."

"Yes, sir."

"You take me there after work tonight and point them out to me. If you see the back view of Breaker you can point that out as well."

"Ugh! That Figgis man is appalling."

The two ladies had been walking briskly, but were now seated on a park bench. Lizzie had never ventured into the

Pavilion Gardens before, indeed she hardly knew of them. Buxton had always seemed rather grand for the likes of her.

"Who is he, Miss Arthurs?"

"The master. He struts about like a cockerel. Do you know, he asked me what good I thought I was doing? I gave him a piece of my mind. Told him to keep to his own business."

"The teacher in my class asked me the same." Lizzie went on to repeat what she had said and tell of her talk to the children, only to be discomfited by the long silence that followed.

"I wish I had been able to say that, Mrs Spray." Delilah Arthurs resumed in a tone of contrition. "Some of us think we're doing good in this world by reordering things in our own image."

Lizzie wondered who 'we' were. The gentry, perhaps?

"You, on the other hand, Mrs Spray, see it in generosity and kindness, and you have the right of it. We are the sinners here."

Lizzie tried to hide her confusion. If this was a compliment, and she wasn't sure of that, even, what should she do with it?

"Come along, it's time to meet another sort of sinner."

They were walking again. Lizzie's apprehension at the prospect of afternoon tea in the Old Hall Hotel would have resurfaced but for her curiosity at meeting 'another sort of sinner'.

"He's my cousin, known him since we were both in skirts. Even at that age he was a dirty little boy."

Lizzie wondered what sort of dirt? Perhaps below the age of five it was just to do with nappies. But no, there was more.

"He used to love helping the gillie with gralloching. He was always better with a knife than a gun."

Lizzie made no enquiry as to what 'gralloching' might amount to.

"Our sort of family looks down on work, Mrs Spray… I suppose you're shocked by that." Then, more pensively, "And rightly so."

They'd left the gardens now and were nearing the hotel.

"There's money, you see, and it's corroded the soul of the family. My cousin's squandered his share, and he's obliged to work."

The intimate revelations, the greeting by a uniformed flunkey: "Good afternoon, Lady Pinkstone"; followed by a dismissive nod – "Madam" – in Lizzie's direction, the glittering chandeliers above and the thick pile underfoot, together with the bone china and… it was all too much for Lizzie.

They had arrived to find Cousin Ossie was late. Both had looked around before entering the hotel but no gentleman was seen to approach, although later Lizzie found herself puzzling over the familiarity of a briefly glimpsed retreating figure.

"Most unlike him, he's usually here first if it's at my expense."

Lizzie couldn't suppress her surprise. "Oh!"

"He's run up an account, but he never settles…"

A contraption of three plates on a central support had arrived at the hand of a waiter, less flamboyantly dressed, but no less intimidating, than the man at the entrance. It was adorned with little cakes, and Lizzie gained fleeting comfort from remembering the name 'petits fours'.

"We'd better start. I can't think what's happened to him."

"Before we do, I must say something." Lizzie could bear it no longer. "Miss Arthurs, you and I met for the first time three days ago. You have favoured me with details of your family sufficiently intimate to be quite inappropriate, considering the duration of our acquaintance. Furthermore, I am about to meet a sinning cousin in circumstances I find… intimidating." She drew breath. "I would like an explanation."

"Ah, but Mrs Spray, you are not *intimidated*… that is one reason why you are here."

"I don't understand."

"We are being used, all of us – you, me, Ossie and your husband."

By the time Delilah Arthurs had finished, the cake stand was almost empty and a fresh pot of tea had been consumed. Lizzie had learnt that an institution of which she was only dimly aware was beset by fraud and that a senior officer from Scotland Yard was investigating.

"You see Oswald was ideally placed, being a school inspector, and he could hardly refuse given the delicacy of his position."

Quite what gave rise to that delicacy was never explained, but it seemed to have given Detective Chief Inspector Downes power over him.

"The chief inspector wanted more action. I could have told him Ossie was unreliable, he always has been. He gets distracted by—"

"Good afternoon, Lady Pinkstone, Mr Fewster not with you today?" A rather more imposing functionary was at the table this time. "Will there be anything else?"

Lizzie waited until the conversation, too quiet to overhear now, ended when what seemed to her an indecent amount of money changed hands. Later she wondered if she had seen the profligate cousin's account being settled.

"Downes knew of your husband and persuaded me to involve him through you."

They were walking back to the station now.

"Miss Arthurs, have you any idea how patronising it feels to be used in this way?" Whether the denizens of Delilah Arthurs' world would have found this remark acceptable, Lizzie didn't know, but in hers it was entirely appropriate. "I find your conduct unbecoming."

There was no apprehension now. Lizzie walked on with her head erect.

"Mrs Spray, please…" The other woman was having difficulty keeping up. "Let me apologise and try to explain. Judge me then if you must."

It was close-run but he'd managed it. Fortunately the train was standing just across the platform outside the constabulary office. It would have been a perverse official who waved it off whilst a stout gentleman with a limp hurried toward a first-class carriage.

A damned strange thing. Charles Wayland, seated now, out of breath and a little flustered, looked again at the telegram.

ATTEND HQ SOONEST STOP EXPECTED FRIDAY STOP CRC

On occasion he allowed himself a little latitude of a morning, and it had been a lucky chance that today he had arrived promptly.

The boy must have been close on his heels. Wayland barely had time to shut the outer door – "Morning, Superintendent, can I get your cup?" – when it had burst open and a squeaky voice announced, "Telegram for Wayland."

Why are they so irritating? He hadn't the imagination to connect the squeaky voice of a fourteen-year-old telegram boy with the problems that their messages usually brought him. All he knew was that earlier he'd been irritated and now he was worried.

He'd known the chief of the Railway Constabulary not well, but over many years, and had to admit that he owed his position to the man. Montague Archbold had rescued him from the constraints of a modest pension and restored a sense of purpose to his life. It left a sense of obligation that irked.

In the three months since they'd last met the man had become more genial than he remembered. Back then, in the company chairman's sumptuous office, the two policemen had been a little in awe of their surroundings despite the congratulations being showered on them, and the tumblers of Scotch. Neither would have admitted to being intimidated at the time, and certainly not now when the more senior of the two was on his home turf. As Superintendent Wayland eyed him warily the chief of the Railway Constabulary was doing his best to set his junior at ease.

"Good journey, Charles?"

It was a half after midday and the morning train had arrived on time.

"Fine, thank you, sir." The inconvenience of arriving at his office on Crewe Station moments before a telegraph boy, whose missive instructed near-instant embarkation for London, was not mentioned.

"No need for formality today, old chap; Montague, please."

It had been different back in India, thought Wayland. They had been junior officers together, where he'd been known as the Whale and the other man as Monty, but Montague had stayed where he was in the regiment, rising to full colonel, whilst the Whale, unable to pay his way in a fashionable cavalry unit, had transferred to the Engineers. There, advancement was without purchase, and he'd risen to a lesser rank; a more modest achievement in every way.

"I hear your men have been busy out there."

Wayland knew that 'out there' was anywhere north of Euston; alien territory to the police chief, and was grateful for it.

"Don't get north too often."

Whisky was being offered. Inferior to the chairman's, and in smaller glasses too. Wayland endeavoured to make his sip look like a good mouthful. "We've a couple of investigations that are taking up the men's time."

"And yours too, I hear."

My visit to the Home Office? thought Wayland. How the devil had he heard about that?

"Best if you leave the London stuff to those who know their way round the metropolis, Charles. Just tell us what you're after and we'll see to it… What were you after, by the way?"

"Just a few details about official provision for the poor and needy." He'd done his best to avoid the trap, but without a doubt he'd been warned off.

"Good thing if you keep your chaps on routine matters, Charles. Excellent fellow, that sergeant of yours, no doubt about it: bit like a ferret, don't you know. Gets his teeth into things… most commendable, but best if you prise his jaws open and let this one go."

They chatted further, and more whisky was poured despite Wayland's protestations. The conversation ranged across their past life, together and since their ways had parted. One name came up: "You remember him, Charles; not up to your standard on the polo field."

The only thing Wayland could remember was a harangue on the advantages of Freemasonry for an aspiring cavalry officer.

"Made grand master, y'know."

Somehow Freemasonry hadn't seemed so influential when he'd transferred to the Engineers and his connection had lapsed. He'd wondered at the time if a residual obligation remained, but had never found it demanded of him and he'd not thought of it for years.

Their meeting over, they were taking their leave when he felt the (by now unfamiliar) pressure of a Masonic handshake.

FOURTEEN

Saturday 12th May 1877

IT MUST HAVE BEEN THE CLICK OF THE FRONT DOOR catch, but by the time Lizzie was fully awake she could hear him doing his best not to disturb the household. This was the latest he'd returned home since they'd been married, and a succession of emotions had chased each other across the previous evening. *Poor Sam, he'll be ready for his tea* was followed by *I suppose I'd better keep his warm* and then *He really should have told me.*

Only the next morning was Lizzie able to tell Sam of her day.

"It really was too bad but I don't suppose Delilah Arthurs could help it; she was being used along with her cousin Ossie…"

"Did you catch the man's surname?"

"Downes, that policeman?"

"No, not him – the cousin. Ossie does for Oswald, I imagine."

"Oh yes, she said Oswald once. But he didn't arrive anyway. I do wonder what sort of scrape he was in. His cousin used the word 'delicate', but I suppose she was saying as little as she could on the matter."

It was a few moments before Lizzie noticed the change. "You've gone very quiet, Sam."

"I suppose… his family name is the same as hers."

"Oh no, not Arthurs. I think I heard the waiter say it…"

"Go on, you must remember."

He startled her with his abrupt tone. Sam ignored the reproachful look she gave him and waited impatiently.

"Fewster, yes, that was it, Fewster. Odd name, never come across—"

Later, looking back, she was able to clarify what happened next, but at the time…

"Damnation, I've had the wrong of this all along."

He wasn't quite shouting, and he certainly wasn't talking to her, Lizzie was quite sure of that.

"What a fool…" Then after a long, tense silence, "Downes, she said?"

"Yes, Sam, Chief Inspector."

"It has to be the same. At least he's a sound man."

Then, as quickly as it possessed him, Sam's mood evaporated and he was calmer if not quite his usual self. "Lizzie, my love," the endearment worried her even more than she had been by his previous mood, "this is going to shock you."

Sam entered into a preamble about engine cleaners, locked wickets, troughs…

"For goodness' sake, Sam, none of this is shocking. Say what you have to."

"I know why Miss Arthurs' cousin failed to appear yesterday."

It was Lizzie's turn to be exasperated. *Why doesn't he get to the point?*

"He was found dead in a water trough in Buxton's LNWR railyard yesterday morning. Murdered."

Now that he had come to the point, Sam must have been surprised at his wife's reaction. It was less of distress than curiosity.

"That would explain it. His position is hardly delicate any more."

"At the moment no one else except the murderer knows who he is. I've arranged for an autopsy and it will have to come out there..."

Only then, with the word 'murderer' running loose in the conversation, did Lizzie lose her equanimity. "Oh, Sam, how awful! What will Miss Arthurs make of it? Someone should tell her... I'll write..."

In the quiet that descended on them both something more worrying, if less tangible, occurred to Lizzie.

"Sam, I've not told you." Now that she'd started she realised how nebulous it was. "I saw this figure... no, it was a man of that I am sure." It was the only thing of which she was certain. The rest... "I only caught a glimpse as he turned... he disappeared. It frightened me."

His professional facade dissolved and it was as a husband that Sam put an arm round her shoulders. "Lizzie, we've only been married a few months, but one thing I'm sure of is your courage. If you were frightened there was something to be frightened of."

"I thought... I thought he'd been following me. I suppose I mean us, since Miss Arthurs and I had been together since we'd left the school. But I can't say why."

It hadn't been in his plan for the day, but with the way things had developed, the investigation needed the involvement of higher authority. Whether he liked it or not, that meant the Whale and a trip to Crewe.

As his train trundled southward through the Cheshire plain Sam wondered what he was to do about Lizzie. She'd been adamant, she was part of the investigation, and neither he nor the Whale, if it came to it, was going to dissuade her. He blamed himself; he'd put her up to it in the first place, hadn't he? What's more, she was on her way to Chapel-en-le-Frith to see the Arthurs woman and it was a pound to a penny she'd think she was a detective too.

What did they want, these women? He'd given no thought to how a marriage might develop and now, faced with intransigence, he was floundering. Undeniably, she'd turned his enquiry upside down with her information, and it was all the better for that, however inadequate it made him feel. And he had to admit that the Arthurs woman was already there at Downes' instigation.

Downes... he was the real reason for today's journey. The body of Oswald Fewster on its own would have merited a written report, but if he was to get involved with Downes, the Whale would have to know. He wouldn't like it, particularly on a Saturday morning.

"Mornin', Sergeant, we don't see you round these parts much." In the outer office the man's surprise was hardly concealed.

"Superintendent Wayland in?" Sam hoped so. It was raining.

"Just arrived; in a funny mood, he is. Had to go up to Euston all of a rush yesterday and didn't come back here after. Must have unsettled him."

Sam knocked and received a very unmilitary invitation to enter. Inside the Whale sat staring at the ceiling, apparently daydreaming. It was a disturbing sight: the Whale was not equipped for abstract thought, nor was he given to startled looks of shock, but he was unable to suppress one when he realised who was standing in front of him.

Seeing how things stood Sam offered to find tea, and was thanked for his trouble despite there being a chipped mug standing half full and cold on the desk. By the time he'd returned things had reverted to normal.

Grudging acknowledgement was followed by a peremptory "What are you here for, Sergeant?"

"There's been developments, sir."

The Whale looked as if developments were the last thing he wanted. He gave a reluctant nod.

"A man's body was found in a trough in Buxton LNWR railyard."

"When was that, Sergeant?"

"Friday morning, sir, and my enquiries so far suggest he wasn't there late Thursday evening."

"How did he die?"

"That's still to be ascertained." Sam had to own up to the expense of another post-mortem. "It all depends on whether he has water in his lungs. If he does we can assume he was drowned in the trough where he was found. If not the stab wound must have done it and he could have been killed elsewhere."

"And earlier." The Whale was shuffling papers around, and retrieved an unprepossessing yellowish slip which, even from its back, was clearly a telegram. "When's the autopsy?"

Why was the telegram so important? Sam watched as his superior officer balanced a pair of pince-nez on his substantial nose and peered at it intently.

"It's promised for Monday, sir."

The Whale appeared not to hear. "Must have been sent on Thursday." At this he looked up, a happier man. "Very good, Sergeant. Monday, you say; bring me the report in person. No reason to put yourself out until then; you can be on your way. Why don't you spend the rest of today and tomorrow with that charming wife of yours?"

"Sir, there's more." Sam watched the mood collapse as he filled out the story. "So you see, sir, I think we have to contact Detective Chief Inspector Downes. Fewster was his man and..."

Sam put Wayland's bluster down to frustration at having his orders questioned.

"Of no consequence the Piggin woman, a prostitute most likely. Golightly was... dissolute: ropes, whips and the pox. He probably fell to his death, and good riddance. Even if he was given a helping hand by one of those women you'll have to find 'em first and there'd still be no proof. Fewster was different altogether... a school inspector, wasn't he?"

Sam had one last try. "Fewster was on visiting terms with Hubert Golightly's stepmother. By your own account, sir, a handsome woman. A woman in the prime of life with an infirm husband who never leaves his room."

"Oh, very well, you can tell Downes and let him have sight of the post—"

They were interrupted by a knock on the door.

"Message for Superintendent Wayland."

A look of relief spread over the Whale's face as he lumbered to his feet. The desk constable, surprised by this, was slow to get out of the way and in the confusion a number of papers, already disturbed by the draught, found their way to the floor. Had anyone been watching they might have thought that Sam's attempt to prevent this happening only made matters worse. At any rate, he assumed responsibility for the accident and, in setting things to rights, found he was holding a telegram.

Of course she had to go, no matter what Sam thought about it. Not that he'd said much, one way or the other.

Somehow things had changed between herself and Delilah Arthurs. After Lizzie had been sharp with her, an exchange which she had to admit might have ended the connection, and the obligation the poor woman had felt toward her cousin explained, a comfortable familiarity had sprung up between them. Later, on her way home the previous afternoon, she'd recalled Elsie's stricture about 'not being turned into one of them sort', but it seemed to Lizzie that the association had been forged on her own terms, not 'them sort's', and she was content.

Now, sitting in the train to Chapel-en-le-Frith, she wondered if Miss Arthurs would be at Pinkstone Hall. She had said she was only visiting, but when they parted yesterday she'd certainly alighted at Chapel. It would be a disappointment if she had departed for London, and a waste of much energy on Lizzie's part since she had been obliged to bring little Mary with her, not wanting to put on Elsie any further.

It was a breezy walk from the station and by the time she arrived at the front door of the Hall she had begun to think herself a little windblown. It was opened by a liveried servant who took one look at a woman with a baby in her arms and glared.

"Round the back fer your sort."

"I think not, my man." Afterwards she marvelled at her performance. "I have an urgent matter to discuss with Lady Delilah Pinkstone."

The door was shut in her face after a grudging "I'll see if she is at home. Who shall I say?" With that and a disapproving look at little Mary he'd gone.

Things were different again when the door reopened.

"Mrs Spray, what a surprise. A pleasant one, I may add; we weren't to reconvene until Tuesday."

The two visitors were ushered in and an indulgent smile bestowed on the sleeping Mary. It seemed an unconscionably long time before they were settled with tea, brought in on a tray by a maid but, to Lizzie's relief, left for Delilah Arthurs to pour.

"Can I have anything brought for the baby?"

In the rush of the morning Lizzie hadn't considered how little Mary might be received. No mention had been made of her existence thus far, and it wouldn't require much knowledge of babies to deduce that the child was some months old at the time of Lizzie's wedding to Sam.

"Thank you, no. She had her pap before we came out. She'll sleep for a while yet."

"Now, Mrs Spray…"

Lizzie would clarify the matter before she departed, but for the present appreciated her host's delicacy.

"What is it I can do for you?"

"I'm distressed to say, it is something I must do for you."

Whilst knowing it had to be done, this moment had hung over Lizzie's morning, but in the event it was easy enough. After she'd told of Oswald Fewster's death, of his murder indeed, for that was how Sam had described it, and offered simple condolences, there was a long silence, punctuated only by the discreet sipping of tea.

"He courted disaster all his life. It's a disgraceful admission but I suppose I've been so attached to him because of it. If only he'd had some purpose..."

There were no tears, but a deep sadness prevailed until little Mary, awake now, called attention to herself. Lizzie put a finger into the child's mouth, and with something to suck she was pacified.

"Such a pretty baby." Miss Arthurs gazed down at the child with fondness. "I was never favoured during my marriage to Pinkstone... but then he didn't... wasn't interested."

It would be indelicate, Lizzie felt, to enquire as to quite what it was that failed to interest the late husband, but she used the remark to explain her own situation in the matter of parenthood.

"So you see, Mr Spray and I felt we should – no... that's not it – we wanted to give the little orphan a home."

At this point Delilah Arthurs briskly pushed her grief aside. "If you'll excuse me I really have to go up to London. Downes must be told and it had better be me that does it. Perhaps then I shall be rid of the man."

Lizzie, glad to have matters concluded, made her excuses.

"Until next Tuesday, Mrs Spray. I will be back by then."

Whatever Superintendent Wayland imagined a Saturday afternoon of family life might be like, it was not for Sergeant

Spray. The entrance to the constabulary office faced onto the main up-platform of Crewe Station, and this provided something of a hazard for Sam as he waited for the next London-bound train.

Now in the safety of a compartment full of rustling newspapers and tobacco smoke, he had time to contemplate the Whale's exact words. The matter of spending time at home was an invitation, not an instruction, and he hadn't been ordered to wait for the autopsy report before contacting Downes. If it came to an issue of discipline Sam might just escape with his skin, but…

ATTEND HQ SOONEST STOP EXPECTED FRIDAY STOP CRC

Sam had memorised the telegram before tucking it discreetly into the middle of the papers he'd replaced on the Whale's desk. He hadn't needed pince-nez to establish the date of origin and delivery either, but the Whale had gained satisfaction from them, and Sam wondered why.

The passenger opposite was hidden behind a copy of the *Times*. The outside, as always, was covered in advertisements, their print sufficiently small to turn the page into a blur, but standing out in a narrow banner across the top was a date, Friday 11th May. The man's copy was out of date and it set Sam thinking of the speed at which news could be spread. To appear in the man's paper, someone of Chadwick Snape's ilk could have uncovered a matter of interest as late as Thursday afternoon, turn it into a printable report by early evening, and as if by magic it would appear in print at a gentleman's breakfast table on Friday morning.

If Oswald Fewster's body wasn't in the trough when the engine cleaner had gone to work on Thursday evening, there would be no news of his death until after that. It was difficult to see how CRC could have known of it before summoning the Whale with a telegram originating at 5.30pm.

As proof of anything, it leaked like a colander. What if Fewster didn't die with water in his lungs? He could have been stabbed to death earlier, elsewhere. *The post-mortem will sort that out.* What if the cleaner had arrived at work early? Another trip to Buxton would deal with that.

What if… what if, but there was no denying the Whale had been intent on closing the investigations into the deaths of Golightly and Piggin after a summons from Archbold, but was reluctantly allowing him to contact Downes about Fewster. *Even if he doesn't see a connection, I do.* Things were taking an awkward turn.

As a consequence, when he arrived at Euston, Sam decided on walking. A cab would be an expense he could ill afford, and putting in a claim for it might, under the circumstances, seem… provocative.

He'd never been to London and set off in all innocence. The ticket collector he'd asked had made it sound reassuringly simple, perhaps because he was busy.

"Out through the Arch, cross the road, turn right and go along for a bit and then turn left. Keep going downhill to Trafalgar Square."

He took the turns as he understood them and in the end found himself walking steadily downhill. The variety of people surprised him. A smattering of coloured faces mixing in with the white, grimy or otherwise; the jangle of languages he couldn't understand in some parts giving way to the more genteel voices.

On occasion he'd joined the crowds in Manchester, but whilst it had its share of gentlefolk it was an altogether more workaday place. Not that London was all of a piece. Handsome squares with railed-off gardens gave way to mean streets and sinister alleyways. He was offered anything from a loose woman to a meat pie by way of a bunch of flowers from street vendors, or expensive jewellery from behind one shop window, or umbrellas from behind another, and books from a third. There was poverty and filth just round the corner from respectability, and further on, untold wealth… and confusion.

The confusion overtook him and by the time he found himself staring across a litter-strewn foreshore to the wide expanse of water beyond, he knew he was lost. Of course it had to be the Thames, that much had been retained from his schooling, but whether he needed to be on the other bank to find Scotland Yard, he didn't know.

He wasn't as lost as all that.

"Don't get many going there voluntary." The uniformed policeman found the enquiry amusing until he was shown Sam's warrant card.

"Whassat then? Ain't 'eard of no Rail Police." He was still holding the card.

"I'm based in Stockport."

"I ain't 'eard o' that neither. What yer doin' in these parts?"

"That's between me and Detective Chief Inspector Downes. Do you know of him?"

"Huh, Downes… Knows everything and does nuffink."

"That wouldn't be the chief inspector I know, Constable…"

Sam's tone caught the man's attention. He looked more closely at the card.

"No, Sergeant, of course not. I'm headed that way so I'll show you."

The Metropolitan Police Headquarters at Scotland Yard was the most eminent of the country's police stations and also one of the busiest. Newly arrived, Sergeant Spray sat on the same hard bench, in the same atmosphere of unwashed bodies, surrounded by the same dingy buff walls and the same unwelcoming air to be found in lesser establishments of the burgeoning constabularies around the country.

"You say you want to see the chief inspector, and you're from where?"

"From Stockport."

"Stockport." The desk sergeant had finally deigned to take Sam's particulars. "And you're a sergeant in what?"

Sam showed his warrant card.

"Ain't never 'eard of it."

"I think you will find the chief inspector has."

"We'll see about that. Constable…" A man was summoned from behind the desk sergeant's position. "Take this and knock very quietly on Mr Downes' door." Then to Sam, "He won't want disturbing, he's got the quality with him." Turning back to the constable, "If 'e calls y' in, mind yer Ps and Qs and tell him this man says 'e's known to 'im and claims it's urgent." Then, under his breath, "Which I very much doubt."

It took a few minutes, but the desk man had to watch as a very senior officer came in person to greet an upstart from nowhere, and, after shaking his hand, as the two were disappearing, catch, "Sergeant Spray, I can't tell you how glad I am to see you. I've someone here…"

As the voices faded from the front desk they could be heard, with increasing volume, through the partly open door of Detective Chief Inspector Downes' office. Its walls were the same depressing colour as the rest of Scotland Yard, but several frames, hanging from a rail above, broke the monotony. True, they largely concerned professional matters: a carefully posed group fronted by Downes having his hand shaken by a man in full regalia, and a citation celebrating some distinguished service to the state were prominent amongst them.

Of the two women to be found in the room, one was standing with her back angled to the door, obscuring the other, whose image, surrounded by ormolu, contrasted with the rest, less elaborately framed.

"Is this of your wife? She's very beautiful." Hearing steps, the lady inspecting the photograph spoke as she turned.

"She was." The tone invited no further enquiry.

By now Chief Inspector Downes and Sergeant Spray were inside the room, facing a self-assured woman dressed as for a train journey, first class if the quality of her clothes was anything to go by.

"Lady…"

The lady in question glared.

"…Miss Arthurs, may I introduce you? This is Sergeant Spray."

The enthusiasm of her response took both men aback.

"Sergeant Spray, such a pleasure. Your wife and I are acquainted, perhaps I could say friends. I certainly hope that to be the case, and I have so wanted to meet you, quite apart from this shabby business."

They were shaking hands.

"Ma'am. My wife certainly speaks of you."

Sam's guarded response was allowed to pass as the shabby business was addressed. Both visitors had come with the same news; Delilah Arthurs clearly the winner, but Sam brought the all-important detail. Initially reticent at disclosing it in front of a civilian, Downes insisted.

"Miss Arthurs is already embroiled in this affair and I fancy it won't be resolved without her. I'm happy for her to remain if she wishes."

Sam was in no position to argue, as Downes ignored his unease. He explained the need for post-mortem findings and their relevance to the time and place of death, and was able to explain his identification of the body by producing the contents of Fewster's pocketbook.

"There have been two more violent deaths in the area. Although their discovery was only days apart, one predated the other by weeks. The earlier one may indeed have been an accidental fall. More recently, however, a young woman was clearly murdered, by an expert with a knife."

At this Miss Arthurs gasped and put an elegantly gloved hand to her mouth. Both men ignored the lapse; perhaps the stark description of a young woman's death was too much for her, but it was out of character, and notable for that.

"So when's the autopsy?" Having allowed Miss Arthurs to remain, Downes was in no mood to spare her. The forensic examination of her cousin's corpse was as much part of the investigation as anything else, and she accepted it with equanimity.

"Monday morning in Buxton."

"That's going to be difficult; I'd like to be there."

"I'm returning to Whaley Bridge tonight, sir. I could enquire about accommodation and send a telegram, although I'm not sure..."

Downes saw the problem. "Most kind, Sergeant. It would be down to the Metropolitan budget of course."

Miss Arthurs, finding little to interest her in such mundane matters, made to leave. "Do you think one of your men could hail me a cab?"

The others stood and a call through the now-open door brought a constable.

"Yes, sir, of course, sir. If it's for the lady wouldn't she prefer a growler?"

"No, she wouldn't." This from Delilah Arthurs. "It's a ridiculous convention."

The officer, suitably chastened, ventured to ask where he should tell the driver it was for. Miss Arthurs gave an address which Sam committed to memory but, ignorant of London, had no way of knowing the prestige of being resident in such a place.

"Sergeant, if it would be convenient my cab is available to take you back to Euston."

Neither Delilah Arthurs nor Chief Inspector Downes had any idea of the dilemma in which Sam now found himself.

"It's on my way."

Only a raw provincial could fail to note that it was no such thing, but an experienced detective would surely have recognised the telling of a lie had he not been distracted. In the end he supposed his failure to go into Oswald Fewster's many lurid activities didn't signify as nothing further was contemplated until the autopsy. By then he would have had an opportunity to remedy the omission unencumbered by the presence of the man's cousin.

"There'll be no increase in the expense."

That settled another matter. Sam tried, but could find no hint of condescension, only an eagerness to help. Perhaps Lizzie had the right of it; Miss Arthurs was a worthy companion.

It was unusual; no doubt about it. True, most times he'd arrive earlier but there were always errands of a Saturday morning and they had to be done first. Even so, the missus was always about early. Jimmy conveniently forgot the two days recently when she'd left the house by the time he'd returned from Benjy's walk, but at least there'd been something for Mikey's breakfast.

The runaway had changed in the last couple of days. Since the admission that his journey had taken him through a railway tunnel he'd been more open, and it seemed that wherever he'd started from had a station, and he'd arrived there by train in the first place.

"Tryin' ter g' back to me mam," he'd said.

Jimmy thought it was all down to victuals, and all the lad had needed was food. He was very concerned that with the missus absent Mikey would miss out today. He needn't have worried.

"She brought me a bite o' bread an' cheese."

Not only had he eaten, but the slop bucket was empty.

"Went ter t' privy. Don't need a bucket no more."

He'd been venturing out for other purposes too. Benjy had been chasing down sticks and learned to sit at Mikey's feet in the expectation of his trophy being thrown the short length of the yard again.

Jimmy didn't have the words to explain why, but felt something swell inside at the lad's progress.

"Where's this place?"

It was the first time Mikey'd shown any curiosity about where he'd ended up, but the answer didn't appear to register. The three of them were walking toward the centre of Whaley Bridge. It had seemed the most natural thing in the world – "I'm tekin' Benjy out; you cummin'?" – and the lad was coming. He was even kicking a stone down Mill End.

"Mikey, when you went looking fer y' mam, did yer know where you were heading?"

"Chapel Spike."

The stone was being contrary and required a lot of concentration. Conversation lapsed. Further on the town's Saturday-morning bustle made kicking it impossible and the three of them stuck together as they made their way down to the canal. High up the valley side a train whistled as it started away from the station. By some freak of acoustics the sound magnified, and Mikey flinched at the noisy clanking of the locomotive's driving rods.

"Must ha' walked up there." The lad pointed.

Jimmy didn't contradict him as they made their way, single file, along the towpath. Further on they would come close to a different rail line that ran near to where Benjy had found the runaway. Where it ran to and from Jimmy wasn't sure, but it was a good place to practise his playing without upsetting anyone, and it was the best place he knew for rabbits too… as long as the lengthman wasn't about. A rabbit and a cornet were about the same size, and he was carrying his cornet case today…

"What's that?"

Jimmy explained. "I was practising when Benjy found you."

"Are y' mekin' a noise wi' it today?"

Jimmy let the case fall open a crack.

"Why yer got it empty?"

"You'll see."

By late morning the fruit of Benjy's prowess was snug in the instrument case, the lengthman had been avoided and the little trio were heading for Number 37. If anything, Whaley Bridge was busier now and the game with a stone could only resume when they regained Mill End. It was a different matter going uphill and Mikey's progress was slower than the other's. Benjy ran back and forth between them and was at Mikey's side when Jimmy, who was opposite the house, caught sight of the figure peering into a downstairs window. Whether he'd knocked on the front door wasn't clear, but after glancing back over his substantial shoulder he disappeared down the ginnel to the backyard.

"Mikey."

Benjy and the stone were occupying all the lad's attention. Jimmy didn't quite know why he thought the matter was urgent, but he ran back.

"Mikey, come on." He grabbed the boy's wrist and called to Benjy.

At Jimmy's urging all three ran uphill past Number 37. Jimmy was in charge now and ordered the other two to stand on the uphill side of a pillar box.

"Stay there wi' Benjy. Grab 'im if yer 'ave ter."

They waited, Jimmy out in the open keeping watch. From time to time Mikey's curiosity got the better of him and he peeped from his hiding place.

"I'll be goin' that way," Jimmy said quietly, pointing back the way they'd come. "When yer can't see me any more tek Benjy round the yard and keep hid till I'm back."

In the interminable minutes he wondered why he was concealing Mikey. Perhaps it was all a great mistake, the man was just an innocent visitor; nothing to worry about… then he reappeared. In a flash of panic Jimmy saw the risk. What if he turned uphill, away from the town and toward the hiding place?

In the few seconds it took the intruder to come round the house and turn into Mill End, all doubts evaporated. It was the look around that gave it away, the furtive action of guilt. Jimmy recognised it this second time. He was a wrong 'un, right enough, and the boy wanted to know where he was going.

Lizzie's day had been difficult. Not only had she had to tell Delilah Arthurs of her cousin's death, but she'd arrived home to be met by Jimmy. An intruder nosing round the house was one thing, but…

"Follered 'im down Mill End an' up t' station."

"Did he get on a train?"

"Train came in an' I didn't see 'im no more."

"Did you see him get aboard?" Sam had taught her such details mattered.

"Weren't near enough. Should 'ave got closer."

"What was he like?"

"Only saw 'im from the back. Big shoulders, swingin' arms, bowler 'at, walked funny."

Lizzie had waited and listened.

"Sort of up in the air. Feet di'n't seem t' hit the ground."

That was enough; a chill swept over her as vague memories and half-sightings came together into one picture. The man must have followed her to know where she lived, and then, with no one at home, come nosing around. But for what?

"Where's Mikey and Benjy?"

"In t' yard. I kep' 'em safe."

"I'm sure you did, Jimmy." Later she would marvel at the boy's resourcefulness but just now other matters occupied her. "We'd better get Mikey indoors, and Benjy too. I'm going to lock everything up. You'd best have a key."

Even in her citadel Lizzie didn't feel entirely safe, but initially there were things to do. It was an inconvenient arrangement on account of its size, but Benjy was bedded down in the scullery. Mikey was taken up to the attic. Nothing was said about the fate of its previous occupant; indeed, nothing much was said at all.

Lizzie's silence was out of concern for the runaway. She felt she might betray her fears; Mikey hadn't spoken since she'd returned. Jimmy, back later to feed his dog, confirmed that Mikey had been silent ever since the intruder had emerged onto Mill End and presented his back view to the two lads. Only after feeding little Mary and making the tea, now spoiling as she waited for Sam, did Lizzie have time to consider her actions, which she did at length.

Where was Sam? She needed him now as never before, and as the evening wore on her worry fuelled a desperation she tried to allay by picking up the sleeping baby and holding her close.

Sam's day had been difficult too. That his problematic interpretation of the Whale's instruction had been followed by a failure to fully inform Downes about the scale of Fewster's activities was bad enough. Worst of all was the cousin's reaction when the manner of Betsy Piggin's death was mentioned. *She knows something.*

In the hansom conversation had been slow at first. He'd offered a hand to assist boarding but it had been politely declined. She'd given directions for Euston to the driver.

"Most kind, ma'am."

"Miss Arthurs, please, Sergeant," was all they could manage for the first minutes. But by the time Sam stepped down at Euston, the Crimea had been mentioned, as had the deplorable conditions under which the poor and destitute lived, and the iniquity of the oft-used description 'undeserving'. He'd found no difficulty in the discourse up to that point, but the movement for women's suffrage was a mystery.

"It's a national society now, Sergeant, you know."

He managed to disguise his ignorance of the word for long enough to learn its meaning, but, never having enjoyed the right to vote himself, kept his own counsel.

"A pleasure to meet you, Sergeant; please give my regards to your admirable wife. I so enjoy her company. Tell her I am looking forward to our meeting on Tuesday."

A firm handshake, and the hooves of the cab horse were clip-clopping over the cobbles toward the Euston Arch.

Sitting in his train, Sam had much to think about. Not too many travellers were for the north of a late Saturday afternoon and there was little press of fellow passengers in his compartment; but time pressed. The timetable assured him that it would arrive at Stockport with a full five minutes to spare before the last Buxton service of the day, but this was only a happy coincidence, not an official connection. There would be no 'holding the train' to allow passengers to transfer in good order at Edgeley if the Manchester express was running late.

He pictured Lizzie feeding little Mary, preparing their tea, perhaps having hers and then maybe reading a little. He even acknowledged that she might be a bit short with him about his lateness, but he'd weathered that little storm once already. One problem he hadn't solved by the time he put his key in the front door at Number 37 was accommodation for Downes; all the hotels on his way home were unable to help. He'd have to try a different tack.

The door was locked as he expected, but by the time he was in the hallway he felt there was something wrong. Perhaps the faint smell of Benjy was the first intimation, but the catch in Lizzie's voice as she called to him confirmed it. Fear, relief, irritation; they were all there, along with a barely suppressed tear.

"Oh, Sam, where have you been? I've been so worried." Benjy and Mikey both got a mention. "And Jimmy was so good; he kept them safe until I arrived home with Mary."

Into the confusion of Lizzie's explanation, muffled on account of her arms being wrapped round Sam's neck and her face being buried in the lapels of his coat, came a cold, wet nose. Unused to managing a dog indoors, Lizzie had left the scullery open. For a while the three of them stood embracing, relief, incomprehension and curiosity each having a representative.

In the end Sam gently detached himself on the pretext of removing his greatcoat, but in reality not knowing what to do with the outpouring of emotion. Not that it was distasteful, just confusing. It was easier to deal with the dog.

"I thought he lived in the yard."

"I brought him in for safety, and Mikey's in the attic."

"Safe from what? Tell me from the beginning."

They were well through the story before the real reason for Lizzie's distress emerged.

"It was the same man, you see. I didn't connect him up until Jimmy tried to describe him. It was the porter from the Buxton school; he must have overheard me asking about the Piggin child and followed me to the hotel, then followed me here yesterday and come back today… for what?"

Sam didn't have an answer. Instead he told Lizzie of his day, perhaps only briefly in connection with the Whale's curious reluctance to continue his investigations, but at length in the matter of Delilah Arthurs. "Made very good time; would have set off soon after you left."

"She was very calm when I told her."

"I had a ride to Euston in her hansom. She speaks very warmly of you." Sam described their conversation. "Do you know anything of the movement for women's suffrage?"

"They're for women's votes. Miss Arthurs told me. She said she'd loan me one of their magazines if I'm interested."

"I've never had a vote, and I haven't missed it. I've never come across anyone wanting public office that deserves it."

"But, Sam, you're a householder now."

"It's your house, not mine… anyway, there's something else." The subject of Downes' accommodation had been left to last. "Lizzie, Mr Downes needs to be in Stockport early

Monday." The subject of the autopsy had so far escaped mention. "I said I'd book him a hotel but there's nowhere will have him."

"Is that because he's devious and takes advantage of vulnerable women without scruple?" Lizzie couldn't keep a straight face. She giggled. Suddenly the day's tension evaporated. "Very well, Sam, on one condition; I am free to say what I think to him."

FIFTEEN

Sunday 13th May 1877

For a moment it frightened her, the sight of Sam's silhouette in the doorway as he set out for the telegraph office, but it wouldn't do, Lizzie told herself. She wasn't going to allow her life to be dominated by fear. *Sam'll be back soon anyway.*

Jimmy had arrived earlier to collect Benjy for his morning walk. On account of the dog spending the night in the scullery he'd had to knock, and that had caused a little shiver of fear until she'd seen who it was.

"I'll see if Mikey's coming. He did yesterday."

But the answer had been no, or rather, there was no answer.

"He ain't speakin' agin."

Little Mary had been attended to and Sam had gone out by the time Lizzie gave any more thought to Mikey. The runaway had been easier to put out of her mind when he was sharing the shed with Benjy. She'd made sure he had bedding and wasn't starving; beyond that he'd felt like Jimmy's responsibility. Now, up in her attic, she couldn't pretend any more.

"Mikey, Jimmy said you wouldn't go out." The room smelt of beef fat from the bread and dripping she'd sent up earlier. It lay uneaten by the low bed. "You haven't had your breakfast."

The lad was no more than a hump beneath the bedding.

"Are you all right?" Lizzie pulled the covers aside, and as she did he flinched. "I'm not going to hurt you." She stroked his forehead. The silence was broken by a loud sob, and after that the weeping started. She gathered him up and cuddled him despite the grime and smell of his unwashed body. By the time he'd stopped and been coaxed into eating, Lizzie could hear someone downstairs. Mikey still hadn't spoken.

"Is that you, Sam?"

"It's me, missus; Jimmy."

She unlocked the door into the yard.

"Ye'd best look at this."

He led her to the shed. "Benjy were all mucky. Ye'd not want 'im in th'ouse till 'e'd dried off so I were goin' t' put 'im in 'ere… Look!"

When she'd had occasion to look in the shed previously Lizzie had been impressed. Indeed, its tidiness had been the mainstay of her allowing things to run on. Not now.

"Oh, Jimmy, it's awful." Another shiver of fear crept over her. "He must have been in here and done all this."

All this was the chaos that ensues when a determined search has been undertaken by someone in a hurry. That was what Sam said when he returned. "Now see here, boy, you'd best come with me."

Gloom descended, and Jimmy followed Sergeant Spray into the parlour. He was about to get a wigging.

"Come on, sit down, Jimmy – it is Jimmy, isn't it?"

"Yes, sir." *Strange*, he thought.

"Constable Archer's always thought well of you."

Jimmy, unsure where this was going, said nothing.

"I, er… Mrs Spray speaks well of you… I'd like your help."

On the outside Jimmy remained calm. He even managed to keep the excitement out of his voice. "Yes, sir." Inside he felt like bursting. *He was going to be a detective!*

They didn't start with the man at the house. Policemen start at the beginning, and Sergeant Spray started with the cornet.

"So you go out regular to practise by the canal?"

"Yes, sir, in the mornings before school of a weekday. Tek me dog."

"And it was the dog who found the boy, Mikey?"

The questions went on long enough for Jimmy to have second thoughts about the detective life. Everything he said was gone over twice.

"So Mikey started walking along the railway from where he'd arrived in the first place. Did you say station or terminus?"

"What's the difference, sir? He just said from the place he'd arrived… I think…" By the end Jimmy was exhausted.

"Stay there, lad." Sergeant Spray left, only to return with a tray. "Tuck into that. Mrs Spray will be along with the teapot… you drink tea, do you?"

He'd have preferred lemonade, but it would have been rude to say so. In any case his mouth was full of the missus' cake.

Sergeant Spray was actually smiling. Jimmy had finished every last crumb and wasn't sure if he should go or not.

"You're a better witness than most, without a doubt." Sam went on to explain the difference between a through station and a terminus. “I’d like to know which sort Mikey ran from. Could you ask him?”

“Yes, sir.” This was better; proper detecting. “’Cept he ain’t talkin’ since…” Jimmy gathered his thoughts. “Since that man were here. We watched ’im, the two of us did, down the hill for a bit till I took off after. I reckon he knew the man that done it.”

Jimmy had been a good witness. So far as Sam could see he hadn’t made things up and if he didn’t know the answer, he’d said so. In the few minutes before the train arrived there was time to check one small gap in the lad’s story. Having followed the intruder at a distance, could it be that the man had given the impression of boarding a train whilst taking cover and then… then what?

“Ah, Spray, good to see you.” Hands were being shaken, ticket given up and a porter waved aside. “I’ve only one bag… travel light… ready for a quick getaway.” Detective Chief Inspector Downes was in a jovial mood. “Now, where have you put me?”

“Well, sir…” They were heading for the Jodrell Arms. “I couldn’t find a hotel to take you but—”

“Policemen from the idle south not welcome in the industrious north?”

“There weren’t any beds, sir, but Mrs Spray has agreed to take you.”

“Most kind. It must be on sufferance, from what Delilah Arthurs had to say.”

By now the men were seated in the saloon bar with two pints of best bitter, at Downes’ expense, in front of them.

“My wife does intend to say her piece, sir.”

Downes laughed. "A roasting for the guest as well as the joint."

By the time the two were climbing Mill End the omissions in the previous day's report had been remedied.

"Not such a wise decision after all. Looked good when I thought it up but I'd underestimated Oswald Fewster."

"He certainly had a wide range of interests, sir."

"I can see him running *Free Spirits in the Peak*, not without some inside help, mind, but an agency for wet nurses, Sergeant?"

"An act of desperation, sir. He'd been visiting a Mrs Sturgis whose husband had been away for the last eighteen months in Africa. She died in or shortly after childbirth and a wet nurse would have come in useful. Then the baby died and the woman had to be discharged."

"So it was Fewster's child and..."

"He was known to 'visit' at least one other household. I've not met Golightly's stepmother, but Chief Superintendent Wayland was impressed when he did."

"You don't mean you let him loose...?"

"Seemed like a good idea at the time, sir. All he was doing was informing the family of the man's death. I sent Archer with him; he came back with the real story."

The Golightly household was explored and Sam explained.

"Upstairs is an elderly Golightly who's never seen, and may not even exist. The servants Archer spoke to said they understood he was the object of Fewster's visits. The problem is that none of 'em had anything to do with that part of the house."

"He must eat..."

"The cook says she sends 'slops' upstairs, sir."

"It must be getting pretty smelly up there if no one eats."

They agreed that Golightly Senior was probably still alive, but that he was not the object of Fewster's visits.

"So Fewster made 'friends' with married women whose husbands were…"

"Unavailable, sir?"

"Very fastidious, Spray; I'd have said he was a bounder… yes, a rake and a lecher."

Taken aback by Downes' vehemence, Sam embarked on a different topic. "This intruder, sir; what do you think he was looking for?"

"You see, Spray, my investigation revolves around fraud. The Home Office pays for delinquent brats to be confined and money for the waifs and strays is raised locally. Mostly they are housed in separate establishments, but in some places that is not so. It's come to the notice of someone high up that money is being lost through double-counting."

"How d'ye mean?"

"Registers are kept, with all those present at a weekly roll call noted down, one register for each class of child. The suggestion is that the same individual can appear in both registers."

"So Fewster was told to get hold of the registers?"

Downes sighed. "He was told to get a look and leave them there. If the same names appeared in both we were going to raid the place."

"But instead he must have taken them, been rumbled, and been killed for his trouble."

"But I think the registers are still missing, Spray, and the murderer's after anyone who might have them; your good lady being one possibility."

They were both out of breath by the time Sam unlocked the front door of Number 37. Lizzie must have heard them entering for she was there in time to welcome their guest.

"This is Detective Chief Inspector Downes."

Hands were being shaken and social niceties observed.

"Mrs Spray, a pleasure to meet you."

Sam, more than a little anxious, was not reassured by the look in Lizzie's eyes. She was not one for devilment but… and there was amusement to be seen as well.

"Come into the parlour, both of you." Downes was shown to Lizzie's favourite chair. "You should be comfortable there, Chief Inspector."

"In the circumstances I think we could dispense with all that; Downes will serve, Ernest Downes, ma'am."

"I think, Chief Inspector, things had better stay where they are until you've heard me out."

Sam, courageous in the face of manly threats, found he had urgent business in the backyard and, ashamed of his cowardice, retired to the privy. He returned to find matters unresolved.

"It would have avoided all this if you had gone straight to my husband. I know he thinks well of you."

"And I of him…"

"Instead, by involving Miss Arthurs, a connection which has come to mean much to me, and which this business may well have destroyed—"

"I think not, ma'am. I was with Miss Arthurs yesterday, and she spoke most warmly of you. She felt I had made an unwarranted interference in her life too." By now Ernest Downes, policeman and austere upholder of the law, was twinkling. "Perhaps I may venture to point out that this association, so valued by you both, might never have been born had I not played the part of midwife."

Lizzie burst out laughing. "Perhaps, Mr Downes, you have the right of it."

Sam, cowering still, was standing in the hallway, unseen, but possibly heard by the sharp-eared policeman.

"Had your husband been less steadfast in the path of righteousness, I might have approached… Ah, there you are, Spray."

Sam stepped into the room.

"The roasting of policemen is finished, and judging from that delicious smell, almost over for the joint too."

SIXTEEN

Monday 14th May 1877

By the time their meal was over and the two men were back in the parlour, relations had warmed. The presence of two children in the household had been explained, and Lizzie's generosity applauded, though with a certain reticence on Downes' part.

"Don't you know anything of the waif's background, Mrs Spray?"

Lizzie described what little she knew.

Later Jimmy had made an appearance. "Just tekin' Benjy out. I'll see if Mikey'll come wi' us."

After the pots had been washed and the kitchen tidied, Lizzie had sat with the men. Mikey, it seemed, was staying put.

"That young man seems very much at home here, Mrs Spray."

"The dog proved important in your last investigation in this part of the world, Mr Downes, so I let the boy keep him here."

In truth, Benjy had already been in residence before his significance emerged, but Lizzie wasn't totally in thrall to her guest. She had treated him to a long tale of Jimmy's father making difficulties on account of upsetting a pig, fattening in the Allcroft backyard.

"The dog's very good for getting rid of leftovers."

"I dare say fattening a pig takes care of that too."

Lizzie admitted to a certain squeamishness in the matter of slaughtering pigs.

"But not deterred from taking on more formidable challenges, I understand."

Unsure of what to say, she'd remained silent.

"You see, Mrs Spray, here's our problem. We think we know who the intruder was, we think we know what he's looking for, we don't believe he's found it, and it is possible that he is still searching."

"Mr Downes." Lizzie, seated on the hall chair, brought in so their visitor could be accommodated in her favourite button-back, was already sitting upright. She'd endeavoured to straighten her back further. "I thought our earlier discussion had made it plain."

Sam, with no escape this time, sat mute, fearful and admiring as his wife returned their guest to the oven for a further roasting.

"You are drawing me back into your investigation whilst feeding me scraps but no explanations. If you want my cooperation you will have to be more open."

This time there'd been no clever riposte and no ensuing laughter. A thoughtful silence had broken with Downes' capitulation.

"Very well, Mrs Spray, I can see I have misjudged matters and must apologise."

He'd spared the victor no detail, giving Sam and indeed Superintendent Wayland their due.

"There is a class of person – perhaps 'class' is the wrong word since their proclivities are spread across society – who are not satisfied by the comfort of the marriage bed. They seek entertainment elsewhere. Fewster was such a man, both in his appetite for other men's wives and in his provision for the depraved desires of others: at a cost. It was Superintendent Wayland's particular insight that revealed the depth of that depravity."

A sombre mood prevailed by the time Downes had finished.

"You must understand, Mrs Spray, our immediate problem is the safety of this household. Tomorrow your husband and I must attend the autopsy in Buxton. Constable Archer was to accompany us but Sergeant Spray suggests we detail him to remain here."

"The constable and I are well acquainted."

"Tuesday is the more likely day for the intruder's return. I understand you have a prior engagement with Miss Arthurs and we believe he knows of your movements. Were you to conduct yourself as normal, your husband, the good constable and myself might provide him with a suitable welcome."

"And what about the poor little boy upstairs?"

"With the presence of three policemen in the house you can assume his safety is assured, Mrs Spray. And of course I offer you my guarantee that any expense incurred in the matter of accommodation will be met from constabulary funds."

It was settled.

Sergeant Spray of the Railway Constabulary had to exert authority that neither he, nor the stationmaster at Whaley

Bridge, were entirely sure he possessed. Their debate over the issue was sufficient, however, to delay the Buxton train's departure long enough to find Constable Archer already aboard, and instruct him, if only briefly, in his duties. The two senior men then embarked and the train resumed its journey.

William Archer had a spring in his step as he set out for Mill End. His day had taken a turn for the better. Not only was he excused watching the professional mutilation of his third corpse in less than two weeks, but he was to spend the day in the company of an agreeable friend. It was odd, though, to find the place so tightly locked and barred.

"Who's there?" It was certainly Lizzie's voice, but he couldn't remember her calling through the door before opening it, on previous visits. "Oh, William, I am glad to see you."

He was inside now and the bolts were being replaced. Mrs Elizabeth Spray, known to Constable William Archer for some time now as Lizzie, went so far as to deliver a peck on his cheek. *She's not done that before*, the detective in him noted.

"Chief Inspector Downes assures me you will explain matters, Lizzie. There was hardly time whilst Sam was arguing with the stationmaster."

As tea was brewed he admired little Mary, and as she gurgled and smiled he went to pick her up.

"She's due for a sleep just now."

William contented himself with smiling back. Then it was down to business.

"It seems the intruder may come back, and that is why you're here."

As Lizzie concluded, he saw his day of comfortable domesticity for what it was: a matter of keeping two vulnerable souls from harm.

"No, William, there are three of us." Mikey had thus far escaped mention. "He's up in the attic room and no one can get a word out of him."

William was curious. With younger brothers of his own he was well versed in the ways of small boys, and in his experience they couldn't keep quiet for long.

"Don't frighten him; he's a poor little thing."

William went upstairs and discovered the same unhappy lump under a blanket Lizzie had found the previous day. Perhaps things weren't quite so bad. Nothing was left of breakfast and he placed a piece of Lizzie's seed cake where the bread and dripping had been.

"Hello, Mikey, I'm William. I've brought you something."

No answer. William settled as best he could on a rickety chair. He didn't run to a regular newspaper but one discarded on the train was different. No matter it was Saturday's *Manchester Evening News*; he started to read.

First the cake disappeared, no doubt leaving crumbs in the bed. Then a pair of dark eyes stared out from under the blanket, and finally, "What yer doin'?"

"Reading."

The staring continued for some time. "What's 'at?"

"Looking at words written down."

"Nah, words is fer speakin'."

"They can be turned into marks on paper, and still be words."

"Don't believe yer."

"Come and look."

Had he gone too far? William sat very still, not daring to look away from his paper. It took a while but it was the smell that told him the child was standing just behind him.

"Them's just dirty marks."

"They're different shapes."

There was nothing wrong with Mikey's eyesight. "Oo-er, they are so." Then, "Some on 'em's the same."

"There are twenty-six different ones." It didn't seem the time to go into capitals and small letters.

"That's too many." He held up a grubby hand. "One, two, three, four, five. My ma taught me that. Said she'd tell me more when she's come back."

"Hasn't she come?"

"Wouldn't let 'er 'ave me. I 'eard 'em shoutin' and 'er screamin' an' then the door slammed."

No more curiosity; this was reality, painful and unresolved. The child dissolved into tears; this time tears of rage. With no one else to vent it on he started to aim blows at William.

"Grand and grim at the same time." More of an inner thought than a comment, but spoken nonetheless.

For Sergeant Spray, born in Derbyshire and familiar with Buxton, the Devonshire Royal Infirmary was, in architectural terms, just there. Its original function, as stables and accommodation for servants, had been eroded so that horses and grooms shared the grandiose building with a lately established hospital.

"Hadn't expected anything quite like this up here in the wilderness."

Downes and Spray had travelled on from Whaley Bridge and, although signs of habitation and industry had intruded, mostly the view from their carriage window had been of the Peak in all its fearsome majesty. As a man from the gentler south, and whose experience of the north was largely confined to the grubby interior of Manchester police stations, it was a revelation.

Less impressive was the autopsy room. Tiled, with a flagged floor and cold, it was also rather crowded with two policemen and a lugubrious mortuary attendant upright, whilst the corpse of Oswald Fewster occupied pride of place, horizontal on the slab. Everyone was familiar with at least two others present, although the attendant's acquaintanceship with the corpse was entirely post-mortem.

"You was 'ere a few months back." This directed at Sam. "Can't remember what about."

"You were taken with pneumonia after we met but before the autopsy."

"Get what ye wanted?"

"I had a helpful report from the doctor."

"Oh, 'im; the sawbones only does what 'e's told. It's us workers what keep things going."

"I heard that, my man," said the doctor as he entered.

It was difficult to know how the arrival of one individual could cause so much commotion.

"Here, take my coat... Where's my apron?" This as its strings were being tied for him. "What's been done with my instruments? Who's this chap?"

Oswald Fewster was the 'chap' in question.

"Scum of the earth work here."

Muffled, as he was now bending to his task, it was the first acknowledgement of his visitors.

"That makes two of us." Spoken by the attendant under his breath.

"I heard that; damn your insolence."

"Yer were meant to." The exchange of pleasantries was over and the attendant had the last word.

With his external examination complete the sawbones straightened up. 'Country gentleman' might have described him, perhaps more country than gentleman; muscular rather than stout, moustachioed and, in Sam's eyes at least, looking rather ridiculous wearing an apron that Lizzie would certainly have had in the wash some days ago.

"Now then, you two, what do you want to know?"

"He was found face down in a water trough, but there was blood too. Was he drowned or knifed?"

"Well, Sergeant…" A pause. "Who are you?"

"Sergeant Spray, sir, Railway Constabulary, and this is—"

"Well, Sergeant Spray, that is a most pertinent question. See here…"

The heads of the two policemen vied for space, peering at a deep wound in Oswald Fewster's left shoulder.

"That's where the blood's from, but it wasn't fatal. Now look at this." Bruising around Fewster's left wrist was displayed. "Don't suppose you know if he was right-handed?"

Sam had to admit ignorance in the matter of handedness.

"Found a weapon?"

A further admission of failure.

"There'll be one somewhere – stout knife, sharp, blade shape like this only heavier…" One of the tools of a surgeon's trade was displayed. "Can't say how long; didn't penetrate too far, started as a slash, then forced into the muscle. Plain what happened."

Not plain at all, even if you were a police sergeant with military experience. The two visitors received pitying looks.

"Two men face up to each other, Friend Oswald here with a knife, thinking he'll have the best of it. Man in the opposite corner quicker and more powerful, grabs Oswald's right wrist and forces it across his chest and injures him with his own knife. Trough just behind… tips him in and holds him under. There'll be water in his lungs, I'd bet my life on it."

"We'll have to empty the trough."

Retrieving Oswald Fewster's body had been unpleasant enough, but at least he'd been floating on the surface and there'd been a grubby engine cleaner to help. Now it was only the two policemen.

There'd been water in his lungs, right enough, but not much. What had done for 'Friend Oswald', as the doctor had insisted on calling the body under the knife, was a lump of decaying vegetable matter.

"See here," he'd waved his trophy aloft, "jammed across his windpipe."

When it had been teased apart on a dissecting tray, it had looked very like the fibrous scum the two men were now contemplating.

In the doctor's judgement, the knife went into the trough with him, unless his assailant took it away.

The two men had debated the importance of the weapon before setting off for the rail yard.

"It was his own blade and it didn't kill him." Downes' contribution was dismissive.

Sam, more ambivalent: "Someone else ended up a corpse as the result of the expert use of a knife."

"You fancy Fewster for it?"

"Hmm."

They set to work with a bucket. As the level went down, water was thrown into the yard, and try as they may, it flowed back toward the trough, creating a foul mess underfoot. Constable Archer was sorely missed. As the junior man he would have had the pleasure of groping in the sludge for the missing weapon. As it was, Sam rolled up his sleeves.

He found nothing, and Downes, standing well back, wondered about bucketing the mud out. There was no offer of help. Sam set about sifting through buckets full of stinking detritus.

It was there all right, with *Finest Sheffield Steel* etched into its eight-inch blade and *OF* engraved on a brass plate attached to the flat end of its horn handle. Sam was lucky not to have pierced his finger with its sharp point or cut himself on its well-honed edge.

"Can't fault the sawbones," was the senior officer's conclusion.

Their trophy gleamed after a wash down in clean water, but although it was in his hand, Sam had something else on his mind.

"Fewster had something the other man wanted. All right, the assailant had to deal with the knife first, but that wodge of stuff the doctor waved about in triumph could have been almost as much of an inconvenience to him as it was to Fewster."

"You mean he was trying to get at where the ledgers are hidden?"

"That's it, sir. Fewster was to be held underwater for as long as it took to convince him he was drowning. When he emerged he'd be frightened enough to do whatever was demanded, and if he wasn't, then it could be done again."

"Except he died first. You're right, Sergeant; manslaughter rather than murder."

"I'm not sure that makes him less dangerous."

The smell came with them up Mill End, as it had followed them across the rail yard and into Buxton Station. Sam had done his best at a pump, and Downes politely avoided mentioning the matter, but Lizzie had no such scruples.

"Where have you been? It's awful."

There had been a moment or two of uncertainty at the outset before she determined which of the two men had brought the malodour into her house. That established, she continued, "Don't you go near little Mary smelling like that, Sam Spray."

Whilst Sam was banished to the yard with a bar of carbolic and a scrubbing brush, Ernest Downes was again being settled in the button-back. A glass of sherry wine was offered.

Much thought had gone into the purchase earlier in the day. It had necessitated the leaving of little Mary in the care of another. So far not even Sam had been given such responsibility; only Elsie Maida had been trusted. Today things had changed.

"William, I have to go to the shops. Mary's asleep and I won't be long."

Once said, her worries dissolved only to be replaced by something more intractable. The grocer stocked two different sorts of sherry. It had seemed a good idea earlier. Having gained total victory over the chief inspector she had no desire to make an enemy, if only for Sam's sake. Anyway, she'd decided to like him. Behind the policeman's facade she detected something softer, tragic even. So the sherry project was born. But which one?

"Gentlemen generally prefer the dry, Mrs Spray." What did he mean by 'dry'? The stuff was liquid, wasn't it? "Ladies prefer it sweet."

That had settled it. "I'll take a bottle of the dry."

It wasn't clear whether the pale yellow liquid was to Ernest Downes' taste, but he took the peace offering in the spirit in which it was given.

"Most kind, Mrs Spray, thank you." He was still sipping it when Sam returned, smelling as strongly of carbolic as he had earlier of putrefaction.

"No thank you, my dear." Sam had never taken sherry and didn't intend to start now. "We can send Constable Archer out for a jug of ale before… where is he?"

Such had been the distractions of soap and sherry that no enquiry had yet been made as to the events of the day at Number 37.

"Not out chasing an intruder, I presume?" This from Downes.

"Nothing untoward at all, I'm glad to say." Feet clattered on the stairs. "That'll be him now. He's been talking to our waif."

For the moment at least, a homeless child proved less interesting than a trophy from the scene of a murder.

"The sawbones put us onto it."

Both William and Lizzie were paying attention.

"Said it wasn't the cause of death, but there'd be a knife around somewhere."

After some moments of contemplation, Lizzie asked why.

"Because the deceased—"

"You mean Oswald Fewster." It was Downes who had spoken, and Lizzie wasn't having any backsliding, no matter how well the sherry had been received.

"Because Fewster had a knife wound in his shoulder." The injury and how the dead man might have received it were described, as was how the shape of the blade conformed to it. "Anyway, it's got *OF* engraved here."

As she looked at the brass plate, engraved with the initials of Delilah Arthurs' cousin, a question occurred to Lizzie. "Mr Downes, what is the meaning of 'gralloching'?"

It was William who answered. "Getting the guts out of a newly shot deer."

"Good heavens, how do you know that?" Sam was impressed.

"We had all sorts in Father's shop. There was this Highlander who'd been a gillie; he'd use the word. I asked him what it meant and he admitted I'd caught him out on account of there not being a lot of deer-stalking in Cheshire."

"You see," Lizzie explained, "Miss Arthurs said her cousin had taken to deer-stalking when he was young and he'd been particularly inclined to the gralloching."

It was as much as she could manage. She took refuge in the kitchen. "I have to attend to the tea." It was indeed true, but once the meaning of the word had been revealed, it was rather too close to slaughtering pigs for comfort. Getting on equal terms did have a downside.

Before William went for the ale, he insisted on being heard. With nothing of note having happened at Number 37, or so they thought, the two senior officers paid attention only reluctantly.

"I spent some time with the lad upstairs."

To Lizzie's relief Downes accepted more sherry, perhaps a better investment than it had seemed at first, but still Sam didn't pour any for himself.

"He's been too frightened until now, but he's started talking."

A small boy's conversation could usually be ignored.

"He says he lived at Chapel Spike with his mam. Then she had a baby and it died. After that she disappeared, saying she'd be back to fetch him."

Perhaps this was of interest after all. Downes put down his glass, and both men sat forward.

"Then he says he was taken very early one morning on a train. He was with other children and they were told to get out with all the other passengers."

"Does he know where?"

"No, sir." In the presence of a senior officer William and Sam were back on more formal terms. "But he did say that all the passengers got out and the train went backwards."

"That has to be Buxton." Sam spoke with authority. "It's the only terminus station in the Peak; two stations side by side, the LNWR and the Midland. He could have arrived at either from Chapel-en-le-Frith."

"And he said he was frightened by the man who came here… but he still won't say why."

SEVENTEEN

Tuesday 15th May 1877

HER GREY SILK WOULD BE SAFE ENOUGH TODAY, AS would the lavender bonnet. Lizzie had been up betimes and, glancing out, had seen the clear sky and the early sun as it made its appearance. There'd been plenty to do before putting them on, though. The stove was out but the pan of porridge, left standing overnight, was still warm and only needed a good stir and heating through. Not for some time had she catered for so many at breakfast, and she didn't have a small baby to care for when she last took in paying guests.

Jimmy popped in, and before going off with Benjy, had taken a bowl upstairs. Lizzie hoped porridge didn't remind Mikey of the gruel so prevalent in the workhouse diet. To help it down she'd added the luxury of a small dab of jam. If the three policemen felt they were missing their bacon and eggs they didn't say so. Indeed, Mr Downes complimented her as she was leaving.

"My, you do look a picture, Mrs Spray."

Rather forward, she thought, but reassuring nonetheless. Jimmy hadn't returned by the time she was making her way down Mill End with little Mary in her arms, but she had much on her mind and it didn't register. It was not matters of etiquette that troubled her; with a light collation at the Hall and afternoon tea at a hotel behind her, not to mention the confrontation with Sir Wilfred Pinkstone's flunkey, she was confident on that account.

No; it was how to tread delicately round the subject of Oswald Fewster. Did Delilah Arthurs know her cousin was a – Lizzie searched for the right word – dissolute, and partial to other men's wives? Of one thing she was sure: there would be no more half-truths and obfuscations. To that end the subject could not be avoided.

Constable William Archer, the most junior of the three-man squad, drew the least enviable posting.

"He'll come through the backyard. You take the shed and block his escape if we don't secure him," were Sam's instructions.

There was scant ease indoors for the others. The curtains would usually be open at this time of day so that was how they were left, and although the net remained, movement in the room behind might be visible to someone bent on illicit entry. With both the parlour and the dining room fronting Mill End, that left the back of the house, but both scullery and kitchen looked onto the yard, without even the benefit of net.

Sergeant and chief inspector sat in discomfort and gloom in the hall.

"He could have found Fewster's hiding place already." Downes was getting bored, and the ambush was only half an hour or so in the waiting.

"I'd have expected him as soon as he'd seen Lizzie onto the Chapel train. There's a good place to keep out of sight near the station entrance." Fifteen more minutes had elapsed before Sam ventured this opinion.

The moment, when it came, was deceptive. A key rattled in the back door.

A whisper from Downes: "Do you think that's Mrs Spray returning early?"

"No." Sam's response was instant and without thought. It took a moment or two to work out why. Lizzie had left by the front door and wouldn't have the back door key with her. But why no crashing entry?

They retreated, one each to the two front rooms. No prying eyes from the road now. Muffled sound from the kitchen, but not for long. There weren't a lot of places to hide a ledger there. Too big to fit in pans, and the stewpot was full of tonight's supper. Drawers slammed, as did the pantry door. Then steps in the hallway had the two waiting policemen on high alert.

The prolonged silence since Lizzie's departure had emboldened young Mikey. He too was bored and, in more confident mood now, resolved to come downstairs to return his porridge bowl to the scullery and, since his slops bucket was perilously full, visit the privy in the yard. He was on the lowest flight when a pair of heavy shoulders, topped by a cap with spikes of hair protruding beneath, quietly filled the hallway below. His foreshortened view was limited, but the sight was familiar enough. Mikey cried out with fear, and as he turned, the man below saw him.

"By God, the buggers have the Piggin brat…"

In that moment the indoor policemen joined the intruder. The two doorways into the hallway were staggered and he was caught as a rasher of bacon in a butty. What ensued was a melee in which, confined by the hallway, friend and foe were at times indistinguishable. Flailing arms on occasion hit the wrong target, and the hallstand joined the fray as it was brought down by the writhing mass of bodies.

Observing the fight was William Archer. A crack in the shed wall had allowed him a glimpse of the intruder, and he waited for the noise of breaking in. Confused by silence, his curiosity got the better of him. As William entered the hallway he heard Mikey's surname clear enough; after which, chaos. Duty would have him join in to support his fellow officers, but common sense suggested otherwise. He retreated to the kitchen and took up the heaviest pan he could find. Returning to the fray, it seemed there was no advantage to be had in numbers. Spiky hair, now without its hat, followed by a pair of enormous shoulders, was emerging unscathed from the conflict and apparently wriggling free.

The sensation of Lizzie's favourite skillet, cast iron and newly acquired, landing fair and square on the man's head was to be treasured long after the event. He went limp, and as the other two staggered to their feet, William dragged his arms behind his back and snapped a pair of handcuffs on unresisting wrists.

The victory was not without its awkwardness. The junior man, cool and unharmed, had undoubtedly saved the day. The others, breathless and bruised, had laboured in vain. As they stood, composure was slowly retrieved in silence, whilst William tactfully attended to the hallstand. He knew he had an important piece of information, but was he the only one to hear that young Mikey was the late Betsy Piggin's son? For the moment discretion suggested he kept it to himself.

"Oh yes, Ossie had a special knife for the gralloching."

The best of friends now, Lizzie and Delilah Arthurs walked together from the workhouse.

"He was very proud of it as a youngster. I didn't realise he still had it."

Earlier they had travelled to Manchester.

"You're new to this, Mrs Spray. I'm going to show you how a workhouse should be run."

Whilst the rest of the well-meaning ladies had gone as before to the establishment in Chapel, they had made their way to Crumpsall.

"I wish Pinkstone would visit, he'd see how it could be done. You know my brother-in-law is chairman of the Chapel Board."

Perhaps it was impossible to eradicate the odour from an institution caring for upward of two thousand souls, it was the same here as in Chapel workhouse and the Buxton school. Despite this, the kindly middle-aged woman with starched collar and cuffs who showed them round looked smart in her pristine apron and, from what Lizzie could see, was well liked. Although they had toured elsewhere, most of the time was spent with the children. Their care was the particular responsibility of Mrs Pincher and both she and her charges had appeared content with the arrangement.

Hands were shaken, thank-yous said, and the visitors had set off for London Road Station. They had arrived by hansom, but this far from the centre of town was not the natural habitat of the cab trade and they had to walk a mile or more southward before one could be found.

Hailing a cab was far beyond Lizzie's experience, but Delilah Arthurs' umbrella, waved with an admirable panache, proved sufficient. The matter of expense had been settled earlier.

"This is my expedition, Mrs Spray. It's the least I can do for one who vanquished Chief Inspector Downes."

Lizzie had been open with her companion about what was known of Oswald Fewster's death. As a fellow recruit of Downes', it was the least she could do. Anyway, if in the interests of openness she'd had to hear the details of drownings and knife slashes, not to mention louche behaviour, it seemed only fair that Delilah Arthurs should too.

"I've no wish to be seen as the victor. Only that I'd managed to rearrange matters so things were more equitable."

"But you had to fight hard to achieve your objective."

"But surely it is well to know when a matter is settled and end the conflict straight after. Otherwise you make an enemy for life, and I should be sorry for that. I rather like Mr Downes, and the connection can only be in my husband's interest."

Delilah Arthurs laughed. "Oh my, Mrs Spray, I wish I had your restraint, but you're right about the chief inspector." She went on to describe a photograph of a beautiful woman in his office. "There was definitely something tragic about it. I thought she might be his wife, but Downes warned me off when I asked."

They were at the station now, and the cabbie was paid off. Lizzie couldn't ask but she would have loved to know the cost of their ride and, most of all, the tip. It all belonged in such an alien world.

"Would you mind if I leave you here? The Midland is so much more convenient."

With the two railways running services to Chapel-en-le-Frith, Lizzie could hardly blame her companion for the choice. The Midland station was central to the town whilst the LNWR, as Lizzie well knew from personal experience, deposited its passengers more than a mile away. In one respect it was a relief. It decided a matter she'd been putting off all day. Should she tell of whatever was going on at home? Details of Delilah Arthurs' cousin and his fate was one thing, but was the ambush different?

"Of course, most sensible. Shall we meet on Friday as before, Miss Arthurs?"

With no further opportunity for conversation the decision was made and the two ladies separated.

Afterwards Lizzie could remember little of her journey until, walking from the station, she met a distraught Emmeline Allcroft.

"Emmy, my dear, whatever is the matter?"

"He's not been home all day, and I asked one of his friends, and he wasn't at school either."

"You mean Jimmy?"

"Have you had sight of him? He spends time with you."

Lizzie admitted seeing him go out first thing with his dog, but, "No, I didn't see him come back before I went out."

The distraught mother rushed away, leaving Lizzie feeling somehow negligent for gadding off to Manchester. By now she had little Mary in her arms.

"Not a scrap of trouble, Lizzie." Elsie Maida was her usual unruffled self. "She'll need a feed when you get home."

On the hallstand was a note: *Successful arrest, back later, William.* The hall didn't seem quite as normal; certainly the wooden upright chair usually to be found there was still in the parlour, or perhaps… There was no time for further thought; the baby was insistent, she was hungry and she wouldn't be ignored.

Part way through Mary's tea Lizzie became aware she was being watched. If she had given Mikey any thought, and there'd been precious little time for it since getting home, she'd have expected him to be upstairs. But there he stood, two solemn, dark eyes fixed on the messy business of spooning pap into the mouth of an infant.

"That yourn bab, missus?"

"Yes, Mikey, she's Mary and she's ours."

Something had happened to loosen the child's tongue. "My ma done that but it died." There was a long silence. "She were comin' ter get me but that man wouldn't let her."

"Which man, Mikey?"

"'S all right now. They got 'im. There were a set-to out there." He indicated the hall. "That thing fell ower an' William 'it 'im wi' that."

Lizzie found herself indignant that her new skillet had been sullied by such violence, but the moment passed.

"Then they put things on 'is… 'is…" Mikey held out a skinny hand and pointed to his wrist. "Made a lot o' noise, 'e did. 'E weren't 'appy."

By now little Mary was in her cot, asleep.

"You got summat t' eat, missus?"

The sound didn't carry beyond the scullery, and it was only by chance Lizzie'd gone in there, but there was no doubt: something was scratching at the back door. Benjy had never done it before but there he was when she opened it, and scratching wasn't his only first. The dog took a mouthful of her hem and gently tugged it.

"Benjy, no! Naughty dog."

"Wants yer t' go wi' 'im." Mikey, cake in hand, was watching the tussle. "Did that ter me when I lost Jimmy."

Benjy let go the dress and rushed off to scratch the yard gate.

"That's what 'e wants, missus, an' no mistake."

Minshull Street Police Station hadn't changed much in the eight months or so since William had last visited the place. The difference was considerable; this time the detainee was Breaker Bill. He was not a policeman arrested on a misunderstanding, as William had been on a previous case.

It was Sam who'd casually called the prisoner by his nickname and elicited, "How d'ye know that?" It had been an inspired guess; and, realising he was giving too much away, the prisoner spoke no more.

Their journey hadn't been without incident. Sam, as Sergeant Spray of the Railway Constabulary, carried just enough authority to evict those already in possession and obtain sole use of a compartment for the journey to Manchester. It was perhaps as well that law-abiding citizens were denied the sight of a senior officer of Scotland Yard bringing his truncheon down with some force into the angle between the prisoner's neck and right shoulder. It required accuracy to obtain the desired effect, but they had no more trouble until the man regained the use of his arm.

A black police wagon, waiting at London Road Station, was Downes' doing too. His standing with the Manchester

Police was sufficient for a wire ahead to arrange it, so they were saved a repeat of their walk through Whaley Bridge.

Now for the interrogation. It was an open question: whose prisoner was Breaker Bill? He'd been apprehended in Sam Spray's house, and the Railway Constabulary were present in larger numbers than Scotland Yard. Indeed, Constable Archer was responsible for the successful denouement. On the other hand, Downes' investigation was the reason for the attempted burglary. Then again, Bill was wanted for questioning in connection with a murder on railway premises. At this stage it was no more than an allegation, though Sam was sure. But the victim had been Downes' man… In the end, possession being nine tenths of the law, and the detective chief inspector being the senior by some margin, Downes had first dibs. What he didn't know until Sam told him was Breaker Bill's occupation. The man in the cells was the porter at the reform school in Buxton.

"See here, Archer," a certain familiarity had grown up over the last day, "you'd best get back to Mrs Spray, and let her know how things stand. That all right with you, Sergeant?"

As a search after information the questioning was initially a failure. True, the prisoner didn't deny being porter at a reform school, but that was in the face of being told it was so by Downes. He was confronted by the name J. Burford, found stitched into his coat lining, and denied it. The policemen had to accept that the jacket was sufficiently ill fitting for its original owner to have been relieved of it by Breaker Bill.

Sam took his turn and started after Archibald Figgis. "You know him, of course, I've seen you together. He's your employer."

No more than a contemptuous shrug.

"Must have been a shock when Fewster pulled that knife on you? I suppose you challenged him about the ledger and he came at you."

Silence.

"That must have scared you…"

"A worm like Fewster? I ain't scared of the likes of 'im."

"So we've established that you knew Oswald Fewster."

"I di'n't say that…" Rattled now, the prisoner, having regained the use of his right arm, struggled against the cuffs. Two burly policemen could barely restrain him.

"How do you know you weren't frightened of him if the man wasn't known to you?"

"I ain't scared of no one."

"What about the noose? You killed Fewster and that's a hanging matter."

"It were self-defence…"

By the time they had finished, Billy Spatcher had admitted to his name, accepted his position of employee as porter at the Buxton Reform School and agreed that his superior was Archibald Figgis. "'E's a worm an' all." By claiming he'd had to defend himself against Fewster, he couldn't deny responsibility for the man's death.

"It's not much, is it?" A rueful Downes was on his way to the station with Sam. "I must be in London by tomorrow morning and I'm empty-handed."

"Could I suggest, sir, that we meet with my superintendent in Crewe on Thursday? I'm sailing close to the wind as it is and I've a plan for tomorrow that might put me in irons."

"Hadn't got you down as a seafaring man, Spray."

"No more I am, sir, but I was posted to the Crimea and had to take ship to get there."

"Learnt a bit on the voyage, I don't doubt."

"Learnt more things after I went ashore, one of which was how to manage…"

"…senior officers. Yes, I see; just as you're managing me."

"Oh no, sir, I—"

"Of course not, Spray; you leave that to your wife…"

Downes burst out laughing, and in the merriment quite forgot to enquire after Sam's plan for the morning.

If only Jimmy were here. But of course, that was the problem, he wasn't, and Lizzie was loath to disturb little Mary, who was now peacefully asleep. The dog had transferred his attention to Mikey but that was no good either. She could hardly send the child off on his own.

All she could do was wait and hope Jimmy would come back to explain what was going on in Benjy's head. She was still waiting when William arrived. He, his head full of the day's successes, was disappointed to find Lizzie had already had an eyewitness account of the arrest, not to mention her acerbic view on the misuse of her new skillet.

"But, William, the dog hasn't been himself since I got back."

They were in the kitchen now, where Benjy's efforts were renewed, this time in the hope of catching William's attention.

"He certainly wants something… where's Jimmy?"

Unbidden, as they talked, a loose end dangled. It demanded his scrutiny even more than the tugging at his ankles.

"Lizzie, since you've been locking the dog up in the kitchen, has Jimmy been able to get to Benjy when you're out?

"Oh yes…" Lizzie didn't see where the question was leading, and went on with preparing the tea.

"So how does he do it?"

"I've given him a key. I'll have it back from him now…"

As she spoke William was making for the door; Benjy, finally vindicated, at his heels.

"William, where are you going?"

"To find Jimmy. Benjy knows where he is."

The door was closing but Lizzie wrenched it open. "Why do you think that?"

"Spatcher got in without breaking anything. We all knew it was strange but in the excitement didn't think about how. He must have had a key: Jimmy's key. And he must have…"

Hanging, unsaid, was the possibility that he'd killed for it.

Outside on the street, Benjy took charge. The tension in his lead reflected urgency; William felt it too but, less nimble than the dog, had difficulty keeping up. He stumbled from time to time as he was dragged down Mill End, along Market Street and onto the canal towpath. Hurrying on, the detective in him started to reconstruct the kidnap.

Must have seen Jimmy on Saturday. William gulped for air as he almost tripped. *Spatcher stayed to watch his movements and guessed he had a key.* "Sorry, sir," he apologised as he bumped into a passer-by, "the dog's got the better of me today." *Knew Lizzie was out on Tuesday* – oops, at least he hadn't fallen into the cut. Benjy could only see it as time-wasting but William needed a moment to get to his feet and scrape away the worst of the mud. *Didn't think about the dog, or Mikey come to that – hey, watch out, there's a rope across the towpath. Stole the key from Jimmy; best not think about that for now… Oh please, it can't be much further, can it? Walked straight into our ambush – thank heavens for that.* The lead had slackened and Benjy barked.

The tumbledown building wouldn't make a prison, of that William was sure. The walls, such as still stood, gave some hint of what it might have been, but was no longer. Roof timbers lay where they'd fallen in the remains of an open-sided hovel; and yet Benjy, off the lead now, was down the embankment and whining whilst nosing about in the rubble.

Unsteady and sliding, William joined the dog and, coming closer, saw some of the timbers had been rearranged recently so that they looked rather as a funeral pyre. Old and dried out in the recent fine spell, they would have burnt too, but the body on top was missing. Benjy continued to whine at the base, whilst attempting to drag a timber aside. William would have assisted, but the pile of wood suddenly let it go and the dog staggered back, revealing a pale and bloodied hand.

Too slow, William bent to feel for signs of life but was beaten by a cold, black nose and the rough, pink and, more importantly, warm tongue of its owner. The fingers twitched, or could it just have been Benjy gently nosing into its palm? No, he was sure; the hand not only twitched but tried to stroke the familiar nose.

Desperate now, William started to dismantle the pile of wood. *Not too fast, don't want it collapsing*, but quicker than quick just the same. He'd no idea what he was going to find, but as he laboured he was talking.

"Jimmy, can you hear me? Jimmy, it's me, William, William Archer…"

No reply.

He feared the worst, but Benjy knew better. Each question produced a squeeze from the hand he was cosseting, and as the work progressed, its arm moved. Finally William saw the movement too and renewed his efforts.

"I blame you – you policemen – for all of it. There was none of this sort of thing in these parts before Lizzie Oldroyd took up with that Sergeant Spray."

Emmeline Allcroft was cradling her son, as best a small woman can with a well-grown thirteen-year-old on the verge of manhood. In other circumstances he wouldn't have permitted her caresses, but the walk back had been exhausting.

William, in dismantling the woodpile, had realised it had been constructed with no regard to the body beneath. It was fortunate that none of the bigger timbers had further damaged the boy. All he'd suffered was a single blow to the back of his head which must have knocked him insensible. Most probably Spatcher thought him dead; why else would he have risked leaving his victim without restraint or gag? It seemed an inopportune moment to bring such details to the attention of Jimmy's mother.

"We kept him at school extra so as he'd better 'imself, an' look what's 'appened."

There was no possible reply, and William stood mute in the face of this outpouring of maternal anxiety.

"You took him all the way to Manchester that time, and there's no knowing what might have befallen him there... and he looks up to you. I don't know what his father's going to say."

All the while Benjy had been circling mother and son in an attempt to join their embrace, but Mrs Allcroft was having none of it. She adjusted her position, perhaps to berate William to greater effect, and an opportunity arose for Benjy's snout to find its way to Jimmy's hand. Lovingly he caressed his dog, and unable to avoid seeing the tableau, she burst into the tears that had been threatening all day.

"I've left Benjy at Mrs Allcroft's house." William was back at Number 37, trying to put Lizzie's mind at rest. "Said I'd take any scraps you've put by for his feed."

"But how is Jimmy? Emmy must have been very relieved when you brought him back safe and sound."

William's description of how matters stood was truthful, but perhaps incomplete. By the time he'd left the Allcroft household Emmy's tears had largely dried and a brew of tea had been proffered. She'd asked how he knew where to find her son, and even resigned herself, on account of the answer, to Benjy spending the night on Jimmy's bed.

The problem for William, as he received her belated thanks, was the sneaking suspicion that she was right. The Railway Constabulary had indeed been responsible for putting her son at risk. He didn't say as much to Lizzie, but as she prepared their tea, he and Sam, back home now, retired to the parlour to examine the entrails of their day.

"So he tried to kill the boy... just for the key?"

"Not sure he tried, but he very nearly succeeded. The poor lad can't remember a thing."

"Perhaps there's nothing to remember. A blow to the head from behind is all it would have needed… then oblivion."

"We still haven't retrieved the key." William, first to recognise the problem, had a proprietorial interest in its solution. "Think, Sam; he might even have had it in his hand as he came into the hallway. It certainly isn't in the door or out in the yard, I've looked."

Tea being ready, Lizzie had come to call them through and, catching a snippet of their conversation, went on to comment adversely on the repositioning of her hallstand. "The wallpaper's less faded behind, and now it shows. I suppose you detectives have looked underneath?"

With the spare back door key restored to its rightful place, they seated themselves around the kitchen table. Food, very good food, in the form of Lizzie's shepherd's pie, would ordinarily have filled the silence, and indeed no one spoke whilst they shared their tea, but for three of the diners another matter preoccupied them. Lizzie was the only one to attempt a resolution, but bringing Mikey to the family table served only to amplify the problem. How to tell a child, of perhaps seven or eight years, who'd risked running off in search of her, that his mother had been murdered?

If anything good had come out of Spatcher's intrusion it was to connect up Mikey and Betsy Piggin. Allowing the boy to her table and letting him sleep in her house was poor recompense for the loss of his mother, and Lizzie knew it. All three of the adults present knew it, but settled for procrastination.

EIGHTEEN

Wednesday 16th May 1877

It was the second time in two days that William had told less than the whole truth. This time he was rumbled.

"So you found out the maid was free on alternate Wednesday afternoons, for purely official purposes?"

William answered with an indecipherable mumble.

"And you discovered her given name, but not her surname, for official purposes too?"

Sam didn't wait for a reply, mumbled or otherwise.

"And you didn't enter the details in your notebook because you couldn't spell it?"

It couldn't go on much longer. Sam might have suggested William attend to the front door whilst he went round to the servants' quarters if he could have contained himself, but as it was he burst out laughing.

"Bonny Irish lass with dark hair and blue eyes…?"

William, blushing now, attempted to retrieve the situation by repeating what Saoirse had told him last time he'd been at the Golightly house. Sam relented.

"We're bringing news of Fewster's death. I'll see to Mrs

Golightly trying to hide how upset she is on the front step whilst you talk to the servants. I don't suppose they'll care one way or the other. What we're really interested in is anything he may have left at the house. It's almost certainly two ledgers, probably wrapped to disguise what they are."

It had been a fair walk out to Didsbury from the station, and the two policemen were getting warm in the spring sunshine. William would have preferred to dawdle. He had no idea what time a maid with half a day off might be released and he'd much rather find out by waiting casually on the street, but Sam was having none of it. Inside the gate they went their separate ways.

At the front door the maid found Sergeant Spray even less important than she had Superintendent Wayland some eleven days before. The door was closed in his face without it being clear it would reopen. In the event she reappeared.

"Your sort should go round the back. In any case, the mistress is unable to see you."

The gap was shrinking, but Sam's boot was too quick.

"Here, you can't do that."

"Now, listen here, missy, you tell Mrs Golightly that I have urgent news of a Mr Fewster who visits here regularly. Whilst you are about it I shall wait in the hall." As he pushed his way inside, Sam hoped her name wasn't Saoirse.

It must have been Fewster's name that did it. Superintendent Wayland's description had hardly done the mistress of the house justice. Mrs Golightly, in her forties, had lost the bloom of youth, but she retained an imperious beauty that boded well for a graceful old age. It was marred only by the air of disdain that had so riled Wayland. For Sam it was less of a problem; he'd dealt with the 'superior' before.

"Spray... vot do you vant?" No greeting, no handshake, just a withering stare.

"I believe Mr Oswald Fewster is known in this household."

"Such insolence... get out."

The maid had departed, and Mrs Golightly moved to usher out her unwanted visitor. Sam held his ground and the protagonists stood toe to toe.

"You may wish to know, madam, that Oswald Fewster is dead."

The contest was no longer between the two of them. Mrs Golightly struggled to prevent her feelings surfacing, and stepped back as she did so.

"He was murdered in Buxton six days ago."

In other circumstances Sam might have felt some compassion, but he needed information, and as the woman shrivelled, he suggested her husband should be informed and he was happy to oblige.

"No, no, no... he doesn't... there is no need, I will... that is, he's resting at the moment."

"You see, Mrs Golightly, we believe that Mr Fewster died because he had something his assailant wanted. Not with him, you understand, but left elsewhere. He must have refused to divulge its whereabouts." Sam was happy to sound like one of his written reports for the Whale. "We think he may have left it here." It was guesswork, but he used his hands to frame a package containing the ledgers. "It would be about this size, and forms an important piece of evidence in an investigation." Then, as an afterthought, "It could help to convict Mr Fewster's murderer."

Whether it was natural resilience, or the mundane matter of a lost packet, Mrs Golightly composed herself as Sam watched. Less haughty now, she answered his questions but had no knowledge of anything that might have been left for collection later. It was too much to expect an opportunity to look for himself, but servants were sent for and the lady of the house repaired upstairs to do he knew not what.

All to no avail; no one had seen anything. Mr Fewster was well enough known, even if by sight only, for any of those who might have opened the door to him to be sure. Nothing had been left for safekeeping.

Only when he was out of the door did it strike Sam that he'd not heard an Irish accent on the lips of any of them.

Given the freedom, William dawdled, if only on the path around the house. It would buy him half a minute, perhaps sixty seconds at most, before he had to knock on the back door and start being all official. Perhaps it was luck, or just possibly that Saoirse, hearing a disturbance in the entrance hall, decided to leave for her afternoon off rather than get caught up in it, but they came face to face.

"Well really, Constable," she said as her blue eyes sparkled, "what's a girl to think with y' lyin' in wait by the bushes?"

Just in time, William recognised he was being teased. "I hoped to meet you."

Both of them were smiling, and without another word made their way out to the road.

"Now, Constable, I hope you're not taking advantage of a poor servant girl and bringing policeman's questions along with you."

Of course it had to come but he'd hoped to leave them till a bit later. He blushed at what followed.

"So you's just here to ask questions, are ye? In that case I'm off."

But she wasn't.

"I've been sent with questions, yes, but I wanted to see you anyway."

"Really, Constable, d'ye think I'm just off the boat?" But still she didn't walk away.

William continued his questioning. "Mr Fewster, the man who leaves his shiny top hat and gloves in the hall when he visits the mistress—"

Saoirse looked shocked. "I never said that."

"But you know who I mean?"

She nodded.

"He was murdered some days ago."

It was not the suggestion of impropriety that shocked her this time, but fear. Fear and something else... guilt perhaps, guilty knowledge? William wasn't sure.

"We've caught the man who did it." He was gratified to see the relief on her face. "But we think he was killed because he had something the murderer wanted, and he refused to say where it was."

They walked on in silence until, "Constable, can we stop talking about such disagreeable things until we've had our walk? Then, in return for telling me your name, I'll give you something when we get back to the house. You'll have to behave yourself, mind, and you can tell that sergeant of yours how difficult it was to get what you wanted."

It was Saoirse's turn to blush when she realised what she'd said.

"I'm William Archer." And then, in an attempt to move away from constabulary matters, "My pa's a baker and I live in Crewe."

"'Tis a long way away, I'm thinkin'?"

"Under forty miles from Manchester."

"Till I came here I'd never been more than an hour's walk from home."

"Oh, it's not far, it doesn't take long on the railway." William tried to reassure her.

"You English folks, ye think y' own th' world… just 'cause ye can catch a train and get there from here before y' set off. We got railways in Ireland, y'know, 'cept the likes of me never get t' ride 'em."

Saoirse was nettled and William knew he'd done the nettling, but he didn't know how.

"I only get to travel on them because of my job."

"Just 'cause y're a policeman for 'em."

He'd only made things worse, so tried to improve matters. "Tell me about your family. What work does your father do?"

"What d'ye think the da of an Irish servant girl does? We're Catholic and he's a farm labourer. Don' y'know nuthin' 'bout Ireland?"

William knew a bit about the Fenians, having helped to catch some at their treasonable work, but it seemed he'd learnt nothing of use in his present predicament.

"I'm sorry, Saoirse, I only want to be friends, but I don't know how. Why don't you tell me about yourself, and I'll just listen?"

He was treated to a tale of grinding poverty, starving infants, punitive rents and an overweening gentry. Suffusing it all was a sense of loss, of family, of home and above all, self. However heart-rending it may have been, William could have listened to the lilting voice with its barely suppressed youthful high spirits forever. However, a half-day off consisted of only three hours of an afternoon and all too soon they were back at the Golightly residence.

"Have I behaved well enough?" he asked her.

"That's always the way of it, William Archer, my mother told me. A feller gives a girl a good time and then wants something."

Said in jest… wasn't it? William hoped so with all his heart.

Saoirse disappeared round the back of the house, giggling. "I'll get ye what ye want."

NINETEEN

Thursday 17th May 1877

"SMART AS YOU CAN AND STAND BY FOR FIREWORKS." THAT was Sam's parting shot last evening.

They had met up at the office, having made their separate ways back to Stockport after the Didsbury expedition. William arrived to find his sergeant already at his desk.

"Spent the afternoon romancing that Irish maid, I'd hazard." As he didn't look up he failed to notice the package William had brought with him. "In company time too."

William held his fire.

"It was a long shot, I suppose, but I'd have liked to have something for tomorrow."

"Tomorrow?"

"I've a meeting with Downes and the Whale in Crewe. You'd best come here. We've both been out of the office lately."

"You don't sound hopeful."

"The Whale tried to close the Piggin investigation down last time I spoke to him, and I don't think Golightly's death was murder. I'd hoped Downes might change his mind."

"What about Fewster?"

"Pound to a penny he'll want to leave that to Downes."

"Will this help?" William showed Sam a grimy package, inexpertly wrapped in brown paper. "I haven't opened it; the Irish maid hid it in the coal cellar on Fewster's instruction."

It was painful to allow Saoirse's dismissal as 'the Irish maid', but worth it. As Sam tore at the wrapping, William watched his expression go from irritation through hope to triumph as the embossed lettering on two leather-bound registers emerged: *Workhouse* on one and *Reformatory* on the other.

"These were Fewster's death warrant, William, and they're going to save our bacon."

William's mother wasn't one to waste anything, and certainly not an opportunity to feed up her eldest son. He'd been away nights recently, but even when at home, catching the Stockport train was always a rush each morning.

Today was different. With time to spare before the first arrival from London he'd sat down to bacon, eggs, black pudding and a chop, washed down with cups of tea and time to spare.

"I do worry, William; all this rushing back and forth to Stockport can't be good for the constitution."

He'd strolled down to the station and, as instructed, awaited the morning arrival from London. It was onward bound for Holyhead, and as he stood on the busy platform looking for Detective Chief Inspector Downes, he realised intercepting him would be touch and go.

"Catch him before he gets to the Whale's office and give him the registers. Make sure he sees these entries." Slips of paper had been inserted to mark certain pages. "There'll be others but that should clinch it for now."

The two of them had pored over the lists until they'd found the name in both registers. Fewster had got the proof. The question now: what had he intended doing with it?

"Blackmail." Downes was clear once the duplicate entries were pointed out.

William fortunately caught him in time and they repaired to the refreshment room to examine their trophies.

"Good work, Constable. You smoked him out."

"Well, sir, it was Sergeant Spray's idea to go to Didsbury…"

"Damn it, Archer; take what praise comes your way. There'll be plenty to go round before this is over."

Tetchy at the delay and wondering what the meeting might throw up, Superintendent Wayland had only one outlet for his frustration.

"I'm not certain that was the London train, sir."

Sergeant Spray was doing his best. It was a fiction and both men knew it. The disturbance on the platform outside could hardly be caused by anything else, but it served for a minute or two.

"Are you sure he's coming? Probably thinks it not worth his while."

"He'll be here all right…"

"You seem very calm, Sergeant; this is your meeting…"

"As you say, sir…"

Rat-a-tat. Tension eased as Sam answered the door. Downes' arrival was acknowledged, but his companion received a frosty look from Wayland.

"What's he doing here?"

"Constable Archer has advanced matters significantly in the last twenty-four hours, Superintendent." Downes defended his presence.

William stood meekly in a corner whilst Sam was happy to let the senior officers bicker. A third chair was brought in and, with the most junior man still standing, Wayland was satisfied that the matter of precedence had been settled.

"Now, Mr Downes, Spray here seems to think we have business to conduct."

Ernest Downes started with the Home Office. Reform schools were paid for by the Education Department and they had become more expensive than had been anticipated. It was difficult to lay the blame at the door of the inmates, though many would like to have done so. They were, after all, delinquents. Fraud must be responsible, and Scotland Yard had been called in.

The setting on of Fewster by Downes was described, as was the man's death on railway premises, the reason for it and the arrest of Spatcher. Two exhibits were produced and credit for their discovery was given where it belonged. The name of Mikey Piggin was shown to appear in both the reform and the workhouse school registers.

"So you see, Superintendent, that's how it's done: the parish pays for their children, and the Home Office pays for the delinquents. A child can only be one or the other but this Piggin appears to be both and—"

"Yes, yes, I can see that. But what's it got to do with the railway?" He knew it was a mistake before he'd finished speaking.

"Apart from Oswald Fewster being murdered on your premises, there's the woman to consider. The mother of the child Piggin was found dead in a train at Stockport. We're pretty sure Fewster murdered her. The question is, why?"

A knock on the door, and William found himself receiving a tray of chipped mugs and a teapot that had seen better days. Refreshment having been distributed, the conversation resumed. Mikey Piggin was of interest to William, and so far the child had hardly had a mention in his own right. He determined to speak.

"What if Betsy Piggin threatened to expose Fewster? It would have been him who persuaded her to go wet-nursing and leave the child behind at the workhouse. Then when they refused to release Mikey…"

The Whale glared. A constable's place was to be quiet, to be ignored, and to do it on the other side of the door.

Downes had been listening to Archer. "I suppose she might have been one of his fancy girls, or at least known some of them."

"Or possibly she threatened to publicise Mikey's incarceration. Workhouses aren't prisons. They're usually glad to see the back of inmates, to lower the charge on the parish." This from Sam.

Downes moved on. "Then there's the matter of railway property being used for immoral purposes. Fewster was at the bottom of that too, but he must have had help from the inside."

Lacking imagination, Wayland was unused to visions, but one appeared at the periphery of his consciousness. It consisted of a handshake from years ago, reprised in an office at Euston Station. It was a reminder of loyalties worn thin by age and uncomfortably roused from the dead. He couldn't escape the realisation that Montague Archbold, one-time colonel of cavalry, Freemason, and currently in control of the London & North-Western Railway Constabulary, had attempted to close down an investigation that would have exposed wrongdoing both at the Home Office and within his own jurisdiction.

From there, even Charles Wayland could make the connection between a hearty lunch in the company of Rubin Able and, two days later, a summons to Archbold's office. Downes had yet to point out that a senior man at the Home Office must be at the centre of the conspiracy, but there had to be one.

It wasn't getting any easier, this exchange of old loyalties for new. A year ago, painfully, he'd had to choose between a Peer of the Realm and the testimony of his sergeant, and now it looked as if he had the choice again: truth and the common man versus deceit and gentlemanly camaraderie.

"I have some information..." Wayland overcame his reluctance to discuss such things before the lower ranks. "I made a visit to the Home Office..."

The whole story came out: his request for information, the invitation to Able's club, the summons to Euston, the exhortation to call off the investigations into Piggin and Golightly's deaths, and the pressurising handshake.

"So there you have it, Downes. It's not exactly proof, but at least you know where to start looking."

In the long silence that followed, Wayland watched the other three. The relief on Spray's face was puzzling, but Archer's look of discomfort was as it should be. The less a constable knows about the misdemeanours of his superiors, the better. Downes' look of quiet satisfaction was only to be expected.

"We need to be careful." Scotland Yard was about to assert its primacy. "We don't want to alarm anybody."

"Won't they be alarmed already?" Sam, thoughtful now. "We've arrested Spatcher; that's enough to set the cat among the pigeons."

"It was only two days ago, and hasn't been made public yet. Figgis must know he's a man down, but probably not why."

"So we go for Figgis?" Sam was eager to get started.

"Chief Inspector Downes, I can't see that this matter is one for the Railway Constabulary any more. Figgis may well be your man in Buxton, but his fraud has nothing to do with the London & North-Western Railway. It's a Scotland Yard matter, I would have thought."

Why was Downes looking so exasperated? Wayland couldn't understand it.

"Superintendent, have you considered how to deal with the involvement of your commanding officer in this affair?" Downes allowed time for his comment to register. "Ticklish problem, I would have thought."

So far Wayland had avoided thinking about it. No longer.

"Could he have come across them by chance?" Sam didn't like loose ends, and this one was troubling him.

"It couldn't have worked it without them?" William, too, wanted it cleared up.

"Spatcher introduced them to that rooming house; just a matter of rogues helping each other out?" Downes had been told about the two delinquent clerks.

"Or they're part of something bigger, and chance had nothing to do with it."

The wider conspiracy would have to wait. They had arrived and were making their way through Buxton to the school.

"He might just make a run for it." Downes was making a plan. "You go round the back, Archer; Spray at the front, and I'll go and confront him."

Getting through the door proved difficult and it took a while before his persistent knocking produced a response.

"What d'ye want?" To Downes' surprise it was a woman's voice that squeezed through the crack.

"I'd like a word with Mr Figgis."

The crack widened sufficiently for him to get the toe of his boot in it.

"Yer can't. We'm short-staffed. He's busy."

"I think he'll find time for an officer from Scotland Yard." Downes gave the door a hefty shove and it crashed open.

"Hey, you can't do that. If Mr Spatcher was here he'd keep you in your place."

The bombazine skirt was topped by a once-white blouse. Both were well filled, in contrast to the angular face above. It was grim, and bore more whiskers than would be considered becoming in respectable society.

"But he isn't, ma'am. Take me to Mr Figgis."

Kicking the door shut with his heel, Downes set off along the lobby. The woman could do little else but follow him.

"Which way?" A passage crossed at the end, offering a choice.

"To the right." She was resigned now, and went past him to open a door. "Figgis, there's a man to see you. Says he's a policeman…"

The manner of her address gave it away. They were man and wife, or perhaps wife and man. He, all pomposity and pretension, would be no match for this stony-faced woman in a family quarrel.

"I'm Downes, Detective Chief Inspector, Scotland Yard." He had his warrant card out, but it barely received a look.

"Now see here, my man, you've no right to push your way in here. Be off with you…" At first Figgis blustered, then looked puzzled. "What are you doing with those registers?" Downes had produced them from his bag. "Mrs Figgis had no right to give them to you."

Both men turned to look… into empty space. Downes' surprise turned to realisation.

"You didn't know they were missing?"

"Of course not. The porter keeps them up to date, Mrs Figgis does the roll call, I look at them—"

"Not often enough. Any idea where she might have gone?"

"I… she…" Downes stood by as the man floundered. "Mrs Figgis and Spatcher usually deal…" Then, in an attempt to retrieve his dignity, "I've more important things to do."

"Did you engage Spatcher?"

"I, er, Mrs Figgis… she's the matron…"

"So you're telling me that as master you don't have control over the hiring of your senior staff?"

Downes didn't wait for a reply; he was hurrying, registers in hand, back to the entrance. Through the door and onto the street, he found what he was looking for. "Has anyone come out of here, Sergeant?"

"No, sir. A woman came from there." He pointed to a ginnel that emerged from the side of the school building. "It must lead to the back. Archer followed her out and I told him to keep his distance and see where she goes."

"Thank God someone's kept a clear head. We've had the wrong of this. Figgis isn't our man, it's his wife. Fierce-looking woman with whiskers."

"I wasn't close enough to see the whiskers, but she looked fierce enough."

"D'ye see where they went?"

Sam confessed he hadn't, but an idea struck. "I can hazard a guess, sir. You stay here in case we've got it wrong again, and I'll send Archer for you if I'm right."

The place hadn't changed in the eight days since his last visit to the dilapidated rooming house. William looked relieved as Sam appeared.

"Wasn't sure whether to come and find you or keep an eye here."

"Downes thinks she's the one we want, not the man Figgis."

"She's still there; are we going in?"

Archer was sent back for the senior man, and then, as befitted his rank, was left outside. The others, in search of the elusive Mrs Figgis, went round the back as Sam had done before.

"You again? Thought I hadn't seen the last of you." It was the same wiry little woman, but the fire had gone out of her. The sweet smell of Egyptian tobacco had been replaced by something coarser, and there were no brandy bottles to be seen.

"You havin' trouble, missus?" Before Sam could speak there was a clatter of boots from deeper in the house and two young ruffians had burst through the door. "We'll soon have these two out of here for—"

"Come back to pay the rent?"

The one-time parcels clerk faltered and fell back. The other, who had never met Sam, would have fought.

"Leave it; he's a rozzer, only railway, mind."

"I'm from Scotland Yard." Downes stepped forward, for the moment uncertain, but prepared to back Spray.

The two would have run but the way out was blocked.

"Don't you be tekin' 'em. They owes me rent."

"No more cigarettes and brandy, then?" Sam was keeping up the pressure. "You were promised money, but by whom? These two haven't any..."

"He said I had to tek 'em back. Promised money later."

"*He* hasn't been back." It was a statement, not a question. "He's had more on his mind lately, wondering about a hangman's noose."

The effect was palpable.

"You got Breaker Bill inside?" A look of relief spread over her face. "Better'n the rent; he'd nivver 'ave paid anyways."

The other two saw things differently.

"We ain't done nuttin' t' get us topped." It was the former parcels clerk who spoke. "Half-inched a few smokes..."

"Who stole the key?"

It would all have come out there and then, but Mrs Figgis made an appearance, complaining loudly at being manhandled, dragged in by Constable Archer.

"Tried to make a run from the door to the road." Archer was holding tight to the struggling woman.

"It's nivver used." The landlady looked surprised. "I likes t' see who's cummin an' goin'."

"So you knew Mrs Figgis was here. Do you know why?" It was Downes' turn.

"She said she was lookin' fer a Mr Spatcher. I didn't know who she were after. I only knows 'im as Breaker Bill."

It would not have surprised Sam to find Lizzie had retired to bed, so late did he arrive home. The house was certainly quiet, but she was dozing by the stove in the kitchen. The table had been cleared, making room for an artist's sketch pad.

"Oh, Sam!" She awoke with a start and made to close it up. "You're late, but there's something I've kept warm for you."

They embraced, and Lizzie would have pursued the matter of food.

"May I see? I didn't know you were an artist."

"It's not finished."

Sam wasn't to be put off. "Have you something that is?"

Reluctantly an earlier page was opened to reveal a charcoal drawing of a baby asleep. In the flickering gaslight little Mary had an air of contentment.

"Lizzie, that's beautiful. I didn't know…"

She busied herself with the food, then, "I used to draw before I married Albert, but…"

"When did you start again?"

A plate of something hot arrived, but Sam's interest was elsewhere.

"It was after Mary's death. I realised the child would have no idea what her mother looked like. I tried, but I couldn't get her onto the paper, then somehow, the daughter appeared." That was it. Lizzie closed up the pad with a half-promise to "…show it when it's finished. Now, tell me about your day."

By midnight he was getting toward the end. "The Figgis woman was more than put out when she realised how much Downes knew, and in the end filled in all the gaps. She and her husband were housekeeper and gardener and got into a scrape. Able got wind of it and made them a proposition they couldn't decline."

"So how was Delilah Arthurs' cousin involved?" Lizzie was intrigued. She knew he'd been set on by Downes but was shocked to find that he'd tried to extort money once he had his hands on the ledgers.

"That's where Archbold comes in. He and Able must have been acquainted; Freemasonry, gentlemen's club, gambling parties – who knows? In his position he must have come across some characters from the wrong side of the law and sent Spatcher to do any dirty work."

"So, what about the two young railwaymen?"

"I did what I should have done earlier: called on the stationmaster. He'd employed them in the first place."

Sam produced two yellowing documents covered in railway jargon. Each reference was signed in the same hand. Lizzie looked, but in the gaslight they were indecipherable.

"Archbold. That links him to Fewster." Sam had seen them in the daylight. "Fewster must have thought up the *Free Spirits in the Peak* but needed help from inside the railway. I don't know what led him to Archbold, but the two of them were in it together."

"But both lads knew Spatcher. He found them lodgings and made the landlady take them back after they'd taken fright and disappeared."

"It's guesswork, Lizzie, but they must have known each other from the London underworld."

"So Betsy knew about Fewster's activities first hand and threatened to blow the gaff when she couldn't get Mikey back, and was killed for her trouble. Fewster had done as Downes wanted but used the evidence in the ledgers to blackmail Mrs Figgis and her porter. In return, Spatcher murdered him."

And so to bed… except little Mary was awake and bawling.

PART 3

TWENTY

Late May 1877

THERE WAS A RISK, IT'S TRUE, BUT HE'D TAKEN STEPS TO avoid suspicion. From his investigations, as Commissioner of the Metropolitan Police, he was in a position to arrange such things; on the appointed day Archbold had a rendezvous elsewhere. Should there be any trouble the nature of that appointment would soon damp it down.

Just in case things went wrong he'd booked a private room for the meal and signed the visitors' book in advance. As a consequence, Richard Moon Esquire was shown into the presence of Lieutenant Colonel Edmund Henderson by a flunkey. It was an unusual arrangement; generally guests in a gentlemen's club were greeted at the entrance in person and signed in by the member. Moon was a busy man, as might be expected of the chairman of the largest joint stock company in the world, and as a rule declined luncheon invitations as a waste of time, but Henderson had hinted that a matter of importance affecting the railway was at stake.

"Now, Henderson," Moon had declined a preprandial Scotch, and they were spooning brown Windsor soup, "what's all this secrecy?"

"It's a delicate matter in which there is little prospect of conviction but the reputation of the LNWR would be damaged."

A harrumph.

"I wonder if you might prefer an alternative course. Could I suggest you meet with…?"

Richard Moon Esquire's habit was to take a growler at the end of his working day. It was an expense to have one waiting no matter the time of his departure, but the company paid. On this occasion the cabbie had instructions to pick up a fare from Scotland Yard before arriving at his usual stand in Euston Station.

By the time the great man embarked there were two others already aboard.

"Evening, Wayland." The two had met on a previous occasion.

Superintendent Wayland introduced the other man. "Detective Chief Inspector Downes of Scotland Yard, sir."

Hands were shaken. "Now then, you two, what's this about? Henderson gave me an outline but said you have the details."

The question was directed to Wayland – he was, after all, the senior – but Downes replied. It all took some time and in the end the growler was kept waiting at its destination.

"So there you have it, sir. Montague Archbold attempted to thwart the investigation into an unsavoury affair involving the unauthorised use of railway property for immoral purposes. Furthermore, there is evidence that he was involved in the enterprise," the two testimonials had already been produced, "and should he contest the allegations, Scotland Yard has evidence of unrelated indecent behaviour."

"And the rest?" Moon wanted the whole picture.

Wayland found an opening at last. "We think Golightly's death was an accident and the coroner will agree. Piggin's murderer is dead, and Spatcher is in the hands of the Metropolitan Police."

"No, no, I understand all that." He turned to Downes. "But what about Able?"

"We have a mind to let him run awhile. The losses at the Home Office can't all be accounted for by the Buxton affair. Money is leaking elsewhere. All credit to your Railway Constabulary. You must realise, sir, that without the work of Sergeant Spray—"

"Him again?"

"...Constable Archer and," Downes turned to Wayland, "the superintendent here, we would still be in the dark. Now, we know where to look."

He was a man at ease with himself when, the next morning, a knock on his door announced an unexpected visitor. Duty had been done; wrongs, if not yet righted, had passed into more powerful hands. True, it was unclear to him how news of the arrests in Buxton had arrived so promptly in the *London Times*; the article was attributed to a special correspondent, name of Snape. He was trying to place him as the door opened.

"Wasn't expecting you, Sergeant. Things in the north gone a bit dull, have they?" Jocularity didn't come naturally to the Whale.

"As you say, sir; quiet. Under the circumstances I'd like a little time away."

"Away… away from work? Ah! A trip to Blackpool for Mrs Spray and the child, that sort of thing?"

"No, sir. Mrs Spray is much taken up with her charitable activities at present. I thought… er… some weeks ago, you asked me to…"

How the letter had slipped his mind Wayland couldn't say. It had been so overwhelming at the time. Perhaps it was the excitement of detecting, or the difficult matter of bringing his senior officer to book, or even the gratification at being received by Richard Moon Esquire and the praise bestowed by that august personage, but he'd not thought of Beatrice Appleton these last days. Without self-awareness it did not occur to him that these diversions constituted a refuge. Now, as he basked in success, she had reappeared to trouble him.

"Quite so. I… er… we've been busy since…" There was a long pause. "Very well, Sergeant, you'd better carry on. Shall we say a week? Archer will manage, no doubt."

Nothing had been said about the expense of such an enterprise. Though hardly official business, the company pass served as far as Northwich, but on to Knutsford was out of Sam's pocket. From then on he walked the four miles or so to his destination. Not as simple as he'd imagined.

Before leaving Crewe there'd been the delicate matter of the letter. Nothing could be more personal than news of impending motherhood on the part of the sender, or indeed fatherhood for the recipient. Its impact might have diminished over the intervening fifty years, but the Whale had been moved when presented with it earlier. Sam had stepped carefully, and reluctantly, it had been passed to him.

"If you must, Spray..." Even in the handing over there was a reluctance to let go.

"It's the hand, sir. I may well have to compare Miss... the sender's, with others in my investigation."

In addition the letter had an address of sorts and Sam determined to start there. Peover was near to Knutsford and its railway station, but then things became more confused. A clergyman he asked was clear.

"Peover Superior? St Lawrence's is down there and turn..."

Sam hadn't asked for Superior anything, and when, still lost, he'd asked a labourer, he'd been directed to Over Peover. By the time he arrived, tired and thirsty, at the Crown Inn, he'd covered Little and Lower; been assured, with a knowing look, of the excellent fishing in the Peover Eye ("It's Mainwaring's water"); and to questions of Catholic families in the district was told several times that there were "None o' they sort round these parts."

Even with the letter in his hand, Sam had felt the need for discretion, but he must know.

"Sir, the *Faith* that is *such a cruel master*; what faith would that be?"

"Romish."

Sam had waited but Wayland had said nothing further, so he was confined to asking after families of the name Appleton. At the Crown, the man who served him knew no more than the villagers. He was young, slow and had the drooping shoulders of one without hope, and he directed Sam toward a far corner of the room.

"She'm in charge; me mam."

Beady black eyes, sunken cheeks and a grubby white bonnet faced him across the table when he sat down.

"What y' after, young man?" No greeting given, or received.

Sam stated his business.

"'S awful long time past. I were nobbut a lass but I were in service up at the Hall." She brightened. "I were lady's maid to the mistress."

Thinking he was in for a life history, Sam took a pull on his ale. Remarkably good ale, he thought, and said so. The old woman looked at his jug meaningfully, and he fetched her a pint.

"Now I see where the wind blows… I were bound to keep quiet back then."

"But it was a long time ago."

"'Tis true, Sir Henry died years ago and his wife must've by now…" Her pint had disappeared and further progress depended on a refill. "It were the governess, see. She were a Miss Appleton. Tidy body, she was, and got on wi' the mistress just fine. Her little sister came to visit times. She were allowed to stay a night or two, then home. Went on a few years, it did, and she grew into a right comely wench."

"Have you the given names?"

"The younger was Bea, everyone called her that. Suppose it was Beatrice really. Then all of a sudden the governess went and little sister with her."

"There'd be gossip, no doubt?"

"Ooh aye, there was that."

Gossip called for more ale. The bar was filling up and it took a little time.

"So what was being said?"

"That she were carrying…"

"The governess?"

"No, no, mister, not the governess, the little sister. What's more, it were the master's… 'cept it weren't."

"How d'ye mean?"

"They packed the little hussy off somewhere out of the way, but when we heard about the brat we did the sums. She weren't at the Hall when she should ha' been."

"Did the gossip extend to a name?"

"Charles… p'raps…"

"So the child was called Charles Appleton. Do you know where 'out of the way' might have been?"

Sam had squeezed the old woman dry and there was nothing more to be had. He desperately wanted to know where the child had been born.

"They say there's a lot of them sort in Warrington, but 'tis a difficult place."

The 'difficulty', as Sam found out the next day, turned out to be a journey with a change of train necessitating a walk across Altrincham. Back on the LNWR, he arrived, at no further expense, in Warrington and started asking questions.

Much of Sam's day was spent in the village of Appleton Thorn. It sounded hopeful, but no family was to be found reflecting the village's name. Back in the centre of town, he went in search of a Catholic church.

"'Tis a terrible mess they're making in Buttermarket Street. You'd think they'd realise." The man didn't think much to the Papists and their doings, and he was right that the new construction was certainly disruptive.

"You want Bewsey Street, sir. St Alban's has been there as long as I've lived in Warrington… not that I attend myself." A more tolerant response, but even so Rome was still 'the other'.

A man was tending the graveyard when Sam arrived and seemed anything than 'other'. "Afternoon, sir. Not from these parts, I'd hazard. Can I be of assistance?" Just the verger happy to stop work and spend a few moments chatting.

Sam stated his business only to be disappointed.

"There ain't no nuns in Warrington. There be talk of some by the new church they're building…" He paused and looked round conspiratorially. "They'm runnin out o' money, so it's said."

Sam turned to go.

"There be some over by… by…"

Recalling the name took time, and any notion of where the place was turned out to be even more protracted.

"No, don't know about that…" This in shocked tones to an enquiry of Sam's about the care of unwed mothers and their children. "We don't have nothin' to do wi' fallen women and their bastards here."

Whether he meant Warrington or the Church it wasn't clear as the verger found it expedient to return to his labours. Sam too had work to do.

Armed with no more than the name of an obscure Cheshire village, he repaired to the station.

"No, Sergeant, there ain't no railway there. Never 'eard of it. Try Parcels, they'll know."

Sam's dilemma was whether to incur more expense by returning to Knutsford and walk the final miles, or travel forty miles by rail on his pass and then walk a shorter distance from Chelford. He made the wrong decision. The lush grass and dairy cows that defined the county of Cheshire depended on the weather. As he set out the next day on the ten-mile walk from Knutsford it was raining;

heavy drops that found their way down his neck and, after he had been going half an hour, started seeping through his topcoat.

By the time he arrived at the modest black-and-white building that housed the Sisters of Mercy he was forlorn and soaking, much as the grounds through which he passed to reach the front door. Looking round as he waited, there was neglect everywhere. Weeds populated flower beds, paint peeled from woodwork, and the porch beneath which he sheltered leaked.

A small opening appeared with an eye on the other side. Nothing passed between them, but before it closed he heard, "There's a man at the door. I don't know what to do." The unsteady voice was full of apprehension.

"Well?" The opening had reappeared. "Who are you and what are you about?" A younger, stronger voice now.

Sam stated his business, or as much of it as would pass through a spyhole in stout woodwork.

"How many are you?"

His honesty and good intent must have permeated to the interior. The door opened as far as a safety chain would allow. After a period of appraisal it was removed altogether and he was permitted to enter.

"No further, Mr Spray. This is a house of chastity."

He was in a stone-flagged vestibule, sparse and uninviting, unless a tortured man, nailed to a cross, offered comfort. The crucifix dominated.

"Now, Mr Spray, you're asking after something that happened fifty years ago. The consequence of depravity on the part of a fallen woman and the licentious behaviour of an unprincipled man."

Sam did his best. "She was only sixteen and in love" cut no ice. "Their families were opposed" made things worse. "He left not knowing the circumstances" got a sniff; whether of disapproval he wasn't sure. The story of the letter's fifty-year journey finally sparked interest.

"So this only came to light just now?"

"About four weeks ago, Reverend Mother." Sam was talking to the head of the convent. "The man involved was posted to India and many other places around the Empire. He was a soldier."

"Was?"

"He is a senior policeman now and I am one of his officers."

The Mother Superior eyed his overcoat, dripping onto her scrubbed flags. "I see no sign of rank."

"I am not here on constabulary business." Sam had come dressed in civilian clothes. "But I have a warrant card."

A firm white hand took it, damp now, even from an inside pocket.

"Sergeant Spray… you'd better take that coat off and hang it in the porch. There'll be a flood in here else."

With the ice broken, Sam was escorted a little further into the convent. Here was an antechamber, less stark, with an ornate door leading to a chapel. Sam glimpsed its interior as an anonymous sister emerged with dustpan and brushes. Daily chores went on in a house of God as everywhere else, he mused.

"Now, Sergeant, before we proceed further you must tell me why the man himself is not making these enquiries and what his intentions are?"

The 'why' was easy enough; Sam could avoid the fact that the Whale was a hopeless detective by stressing his infirmity. "He has an injured leg and has difficulty getting about."

"Were you with him at the time?"

Sam was surprised at the gleam of interest. When he said, "Yes, we were in the Crimea together" there was a long silence.

"My brother was lost in the Siege of Sevastopol. No one has told me what happened but I have prayed for him every day since."

"I'm sorry; many fine men were lost."

The matter of intention had exercised his mind ever since he'd been instructed to 'investigate it'. "I think he wishes to see what he might do to set matters right."

"This senior policeman, one-time army officer…" The Reverend Mother was searching for a name and reached to look again at the letter.

"Wayland; Charles Wayland, and the young woman is—"

"Beatrice Appleton." The voice, thready with age and quavering with emotion, came as if from nowhere. The nun who'd been first to the door had remained, silent and unobtrusive. No longer.

The Mother Superior was first to respond. "How do you know that?" Her voice sharp and questioning. The doings of the real world were not expected to make themselves known in the secluded life of a convent.

"She was my younger sister."

Sam had no need to question. The floodgates were open and whether the Reverend Mother wanted to suppress it or not, the truth gushed forth in all its distressing detail. The nun's calling was a hindrance – not as to the subject matter, that would out whatever – but in the search for words fit for the mouth of one who has taken vows.

Mary Appleton had been governess to the children of a baronet at a big house near Knutsford. Sam itched to confirm the family name but kept his peace.

"They let me bring little Beatrice to the house times. She was only a child… but later on…"

In the pause the Mother Superior might have stepped in to restore her authority, but instead she let the opportunity pass.

"The master would show little kindnesses; a box of sweetmeats, or perhaps a ride in the carriage. I never quite knew whether they were for me or Beatrice… but we shared anyway."

Then, when she could conceal it no longer, there had come the thunderclap of pregnancy.

"She wouldn't say who… who… Our father assumed…" The words wouldn't come. "We both had to return home and then to the convent. Father arranged it. There was money…"

It struck Sam that it was acceptable to talk openly about a bribe offered by a grown man and accepted by a religious order, but not about the misfortune of a vulnerable girl.

"Then after Charlie was born Beatrice took ill. The baby thrived but Bea became fevered and delirious. I sat with her before she died. She told me then…" The old nun paused to wipe away a tear before continuing. "I'd met Charlie Wayland at the big house. He was more Bea's age than mine. I thought they were like a pair of puppies playing. How wrong I was…"

"Was it you who wrote this?" Sam had the envelope in his hand and pointed to the note scribbled on the back: *Charles Appleton, b. 1st August.*

"Yes, it was. Bea wanted to but she was so ill. Her intention was to get it sent once she'd recovered but then she gave it to me at the end. When she died I just kept it until…"

"Until what, Sister?" Sam assumed that with the convent's reputation already beyond repair, the Reverend Mother felt free to indulge her curiosity and chase after the compelling story.

"Little Charles was sent to a workhouse when he was five." She was addressing the Mother Superior directly now. "It was your arrival that provoked his departure. You were the first novice since the… the terrible things. Everyone here at the time knew what had happened, but Reverend Mother felt your coming heralded a fresh start so the matter has been closed ever since."

"What happened to the letter?"

"It went with him."

"And you never heard of him again?"

The answer to Sam's question came from the Mother Superior. "It was him, the gardener's boy; he came back for a while. I always wondered why the older sisters were allowed to make such a fuss of him." She was much taken with her own detective skills. "Then a girl in the village with child…"

"He went off to the Crimea and never came back, like your brother, Reverend Mother."

For a while all three stood in silence; perhaps in meditation on the part of the nuns. Sam was on tenterhooks. To be so close…

He didn't relish putting on a sodden coat. It was made all the less alluring by the weather, but there was nothing else for it. Information, having gushed forth almost unbidden, dried up when Sam had enquired after the woman left behind by Charlie Appleton. The older nun might have helped, left to herself, but authority had been restored to its proper place and Sam was out in the rain.

The hamlet, when he found it, with no help from the convent, who'd declined to offer directions, was a sorry affair. A single muddy track through two lines of labourers' cottages, and a public house barely bigger than the dwellings of its customers. Inside the smell of smoke and stale beer dominated. Furniture was sparse; the most prominent item a trestle with two scotches keeping a firkin from rolling.

"Anybody about?" Sam shouted across the empty room.

For a moment he didn't recognise the response. "My mam's out the back." A ragged child of perhaps six or seven stood looking at him without curiosity. "Never no customers this time o' day."

It wasn't clear to Sam if he was to follow the retreating figure, but he did anyway.

"She'm in there tendin' the beer." The boy pointed to an open doorway across the yard. "Mam, there's a man."

Outside, the fetid air of the bar gave way to an altogether fresher aroma of beer in active fermentation. The rear view of a young woman, bent to her task, filled the doorway. Standing, she turned.

"What can I do for you, sir?" Stocky, but not fat, she was businesslike and polite.

They recrossed the yard.

"At last, it's stopped." A glint of sun had appeared.

"You get used to it in these parts, Mr…?"

Sam gave his name and asked for beer. "Will you have one with me?"

They sat on a bench together. "Now, Mr Spray, you want something; you wouldn't have bought this else."

"What can you tell me about Charlie Appleton?"

She was startled, no doubt about it. But Sam watched other emotions cross her face too. Anger mostly, but concern as well.

"Why him? He's long gone…"

"It's what he left behind that interests me."

Sam had to explain himself before she would say anything.

"So you're here asking questions on behalf of Charlie's father. Bit late in the day, isn't it? What's he up to?"

The same question as before; the same answer.

"So this letter took fifty years…"

Sam showed it to her. What the Whale would have made of this most intimate fragment of his life being shown to others Sam could only surmise, but it certainly unlocked secrets.

"Him and my aunt got together. There weren't the money to marry, but… They say it goes on in them big cities, but not out here… Anyways, they did, an' he got her with child. Then that recruiting sergeant came round."

"Couldn't resist the King's shilling?"

"Dunno 'bout that, I was only a child back then, but Aunty and the baby lived with us for a time. Got very crowded and she went in the end and my ma looked after the little 'un. Well, she was family, and that matters, doesn't it?"

"And then?"

"Aunty came back for the child. I must have been eight or nine then. My, she looked different. Lace at her neck, velvet dress, cape with fur collar... Didn't stop long, took her gloves off, though... no ring."

"Have you heard anything since?"

"My mam had letters times, but she never told an' she's dead now. I don't think things went well. She'd have said else. Aunty Anne were in Manchester, I do know that. Is there a place called Crumps...? Something like that?"

"One last thing." The beer mugs were empty. "What was your name before you married?"

Her answer shook him.

The weather had fined up by the time Sam arrived at Chelford Station. He'd been away for three nights, and until a few months ago it wouldn't have signified. Away from what would have been an empty question. Now he ached for home, for little Mary, for tea at the kitchen table, even for young Jimmy and his dog, but above all for Lizzie. For her warmth, for her intelligence, for... for her.

What he'd learnt in the last days had revealed a lot but the last revelation of all threw up as many questions as it answered.

"So you see, Lizzie, I think I need to go there."

He was home at last. They had kissed with a passion that he barely recognised in himself, and then he'd cradled little Mary. By the time tea was over and the household was at peace again after the perturbation of his return, Sam and Lizzie could sit and talk.

"I'm sure Crumpsall was the place she meant, and you've visited the workhouse there. Would you... would you come with me? I need your... your common sense."

"But just because she thought her aunt was in Manchester, why do you want to go to Crumpsall Workhouse?" Lizzie had been engrossed in Sam's unfolding story.

"The woman was obviously living a life of affluence but had no wedding ring…"

"You mean she was a kept woman. A child by a previous liaison wouldn't be welcome in such a relationship…" Lizzie seemed unruffled by such impropriety, and Sam was grateful for it. "She was taking a risk by going back for her daughter."

"And that might have led her in the direction of destitution, either for them both or just for the child."

"So you think the letter had somehow gone with Charles to his… his…" Lizzie settled on "woman, and then from her to her daughter, who left it with a child at the workhouse."

"It was probably part of a package with something of value, sentimental or religious value, in it. That would make it worth preserving but not worth trying to sell. Some desperately poor people must have wished otherwise."

Lizzie detached herself from the romance of Sam's theory and dragged him back to reality.

"It all sounds very unlikely."

"It's all I've got, and I'm going to follow where it leads. If that turns out to be nowhere, then at least I've tried.

It took some organising. Elsie'd already had little Mary once in the week, and, willing though she was, it was a very contrite Lizzie who asked for a further indulgence.

"Of course, my dear, one more doesn't make much difference. I'll look in on that lad you have at home, too."

So it was that Sam and Lizzie repeated the journey she had made a few days before. There was no hailing of cabs this time and they walked together in pleasurable companionship. It struck Sam that his marriage had thus far provided precious little opportunity for shared idleness. Had he thought about it in advance he might have feared it, but side by side in the spring sunshine he could think of nothing finer. Their hands found each other for some of the way, but by the time they arrived at the intimidating pile that was Crumpsall Workhouse gravitas had been restored, and it was a respectable married couple that enquired after Mrs Pincher.

"If anyone knows it'll be her. She was very kind when I visited with Miss Arthurs."

It was a familiar atmosphere that enveloped the couple as they waited in the entrance hall. Lizzie had first experienced it only recently, but for Sam it aroused childhood memories he'd abandoned long ago. He wondered why he hadn't felt the same during his visit to the school in Buxton, but on that occasion it had been a matter of constabulary business. Lizzie had taught him that there was life beyond work, and now they were in that world, together.

"Mrs Spray, a pleasure to meet you again. You were here recently with Lady Pinkstone, I recall."

They shook hands.

"This is my husband, Sergeant Spray."

Social niceties completed, the matter in hand was addressed. The much-travelled envelope received an unexpected reaction.

"Oh yes, I sent it, but I rather wish I hadn't… it was the diphtheria, you see. It carried the little girl off with most of the others." Mrs Pincher crossed herself perfunctorily, more to impress her visitors, thought Sam, than for her own comfort.

"So the child was a baby girl? Did she have a name?"

"Oh yes. She'd been born here and Betsy Piggin called her Beatrice. She always said she was Mrs, but we knew better. Betsy's mother was in and out of here before she died, and she was a Piggin."

"So Betsy went off without her baby?"

"She's not supposed to do that. She'll never be allowed in here again. She did take the boy with her, though."

"Betsy Piggin won't be seeking admission here or at any other workhouse; she was murdered a few weeks back."

The shocked silence was broken when Mrs Pincher asked after Betsy's older child.

"Mikey's being taken care of." It was Lizzie's first foray into the conversation and she kept it brief.

"The letter was in a package with a rosary. I don't know why I kept it… it's difficult to throw such a thing away. Would you give it to him?"

"I know someone else who will value it more than an eight-year-old boy."

By now they were in Mrs Pincher's office, and she was rummaging around in a drawer. Brown paper tied up with ribbon, faded now but once red, was unwrapped to expose purplish-brown beads strung together with a simple cross.

"Of course, I'll leave it to your discretion."

He'd received them before, letters from headquarters in Euston, but this was different. The envelope had an embossed flap and on closer inspection he discovered it came from the office of the chairman of directors, and it seemed from the address that he'd reverted to Lieutenant Colonel Wayland.

It instructed him to attend on Mr Richard Moon the next day at the convenient hour of half past two of the afternoon. By the time it had arrived he'd already given his blessing for his sergeant's furlough, and it did cross his mind that the unofficial business Sam Spray was about might be frowned on by higher authority.

Presenting himself promptly at the appointed hour, it struck him that he was being treated, if not with servility, then at least with a greater respect than had been the case on his visit some months before.

"Ah, Wayland… we meet again. Rather more comfortable than the growler I should say…"

Tumblers of Scotch were being handed round, except on this occasion the silver salver came with a decanter and it remained on the chairman's desk when the flunkey departed.

"See here, we're in something of a spot. Previous man departed under a bit of a cloud, don't you know."

Charles Wayland certainly knew, having been involved only a few days past in the creation of the cloud in question, and having brought it, along with Ernest Downes, to the chairman's attention. It appeared that the unseemly matter was not to be referred to again.

"Done rather well down there in Crewe; credit to the constabulary and to the company. The Midland have been sniffing round; wouldn't be surprised if they don't try the same thing. Count on your loyalty…?"

It occurred to Wayland that he was about to be offered some pecuniary reward for doing his duty.

"Of course, sir, but I must draw your attention to the work of Sergeant—"

"Yes, yes, Wayland, we'll come to him in a minute... It's you I'm talking about just now." Then, after a portentous pause, "Would you accept the post of chief of the Railway Constabulary? I can assure you the remuneration will be to your satisfaction."

The startled silence might have discomfited a lesser man than Moon. The Whale, who of course knew of his soubriquet, couldn't keep it out of his mind in these moments of humility, and was temporarily at a loss. Finally, "It would be an honour, sir; I'm happy to accept."

"Very good, let's drink to that."

Moon downed the remains of his glass in one and the Whale, who had been nursing his tumbler untouched, did the same.

Things had become more relaxed by the time the two men parted. The newly appointed chief of the Railway Constabulary left knowing that he had a free hand in the appointing of staff, that constabulary operations were to extend northward beyond Manchester, and that if he wished, his headquarters could be established at Crewe.

"Sent a directive to the stationmaster about accommodation this morning."

It struck Wayland that such a directive had rather pre-empted his acceptance, but after a while his reservation was lost in a haze of alcohol. As he was being assisted by a flunkey, thoughtfully summoned by Moon, back to his train, there was one instruction that belied the free hand he'd been given.

"Do not lose sight of the man Spray. Keep him close."

TWENTY-ONE

Late May 1877

TWO LETTERS CROSSED ON THEIR OVERNIGHT JOURNEYS to and from Crewe. Both had taken serious thought before pen was put to paper, and both had the potential to change lives. The one going south originated in Whaley Bridge.

"You are sure, aren't you, Sam? It would be a terrible thing to get the wrong of it."

Lizzie was right of course, and Sam knew they mustn't make a mistake, but he *was* sure. Betsy Piggin had been the Whale's granddaughter and young Mikey, in bed upstairs, was his great-grandson.

"I am certain, my dear, but goodness knows what he'll make of it."

That being settled, there remained the matter of how to present the situation.

"You've been involved all along, Lizzie, and it would benefit from a woman's touch."

"If you're sure."

They sent the letter to the Whale's home, as befitted such a personal matter, and both appended their signatures.

The other letter, travelling north from Crewe, was destined for the Stockport office of the Railway Constabulary. It was couched in official terms and directed Sergeant Spray and Constable Archer to present themselves to their senior officer on the next working day after receipt of same. Both arrived on Saturday morning. Constable Archer considered that incoming mail was his sergeant's prerogative, and in his absence the summons from above remained unopened.

At Hall House, Charles Wayland handled his letter as if it was a hot coal. He knew it had to do with Sam's special assignment. It was his writing, and why else had it been addressed to his home? Now the moment had come he wished desperately to know the contents, whilst equally fearing what they might be. It had been placed at the breakfast table by his housekeeper and he sat, his porridge cooling, whilst he picked it up and put it down repeatedly.

Finally, courage gathered up, he tore open the envelope, only to read:

Sir,
I have to report that the investigation with which you recently charged me is now complete. It became necessary to involve Mrs Spray. She has been crucial in bringing matters to their present state.

If you would kindly determine a meeting place acceptable to you we would be happy to report in person.

Yours faithfully…

Whatever he'd expected it wasn't to be stalled like this, and he, Charles Wayland, wasn't going to put up with it. He'd barely entered the office before leaving to catch the next train north to Stockport.

Getting from home to the office wasn't a problem – he had a regular cab, and he limped across to the Buxton platform on Edgeley Station – but in Whaley Bridge, Mill End was beyond him. It was not the sort of place to have cabs for hire, and it was only by the good offices of a porter, and a large tip, that he arrived at Number 37 behind a sweating horse aboard a carter's dray.

He failed to notice the two lads and a dog heading downhill.

"Look, Mikey," Jimmy tapped the other on the shoulder. "That's Superintendent Something-or-Other. He's above Mr Spray."

They passed on for their ramble along the cut.

Returning to ground level took some time and not a little noisy discourse. By the end of it the carter felt he and his horse had earned their money. The disturbance in the street was sufficient to alert the household, so that by the time Wayland had reached the front door it was open and Lizzie was on hand to ensure he didn't trip over the threshold.

"What a pleasure, sir." Coat and stick were being disposed of. "I'm sure my husband didn't mean you to come all the way out here." His hat was joining his gloves on the hall dresser. "Have you had a good journey?"

By now they'd repaired the parlour and were joined by Sam.

"Thought I'd better come and attend to this right away." The morning's letter was waved about. "Don't say much, do it?"

"Sir, perhaps you would like to sit?"

Wayland was beginning to sway; whether from tiredness or emotion it wasn't clear. He sank into Lizzie's button-back, looking relieved, and accepted her offer of tea.

"See here, Spray, what's all this about?"

Sam wasn't to be hurried and insisted on waiting for Lizzie's return and the proffering of teacups.

"Well, sir, there are two strands to this investigation that come together—"

"Get on with it, man, don't beat about the bush."

"I started at Peover since that was the address on the letter…"

The Whale was a sombre man by the time Sam's story reached the outbreak of diphtheria.

"So you say this murdered woman was my granddaughter and her little girl is dead too? So there's an end of it."

"Not quite, sir. You may wish to see this." Sam produced the rosary. "It was given to me by the matron at Crumpsall. It accompanied the letter that was left with the child."

"Here, give me that." Charles Wayland, military man, senior policeman and leader of men, snatched the string of beads as a spoilt child might a sweetmeat. He cradled it in his hands and raised it to his lips. Tears welled up; embarrassing tears, unbecoming of such a man.

Lizzie busied herself clearing the tea things, and Sam helped her to carry them to the kitchen. They talked quietly.

"Best not say more for now. He's so upset already."

Sam agreed, and with Jimmy and Mikey clattering about in the scullery after Benjy's dinner, the conversation lapsed.

Later, the senior officer in him having reasserted itself, Charles Wayland made his way to the kitchen. The room was a busy place. Lizzie was preparing pap for little Mary, who was making her presence felt in the way only a hungry baby can. Jimmy was attending to the contents of the meat safe.

"It's a good big one, missus."

Mikey was out at the back. Benjy had been his first friend; after all, it was the dog who found the child, cold and starving. The trust between them had helped the boy come to believe in the adults around him. They were playing together with a ball which Mikey threw and Benjy would return to him; the resulting tussle being resolved with a counter-attraction of a scrap of dead rabbit cut from the carcass Jimmy had just skinned.

The old man had contained himself since the gentlemen's convenience on Edgeley Station, but that had been some time past, and Lizzie's tea had proved the last straw. Charles Wayland was on his way to the privy. Sam had divined his superior's intention and, without the need for embarrassing words, nodded in the direction of the yard.

Outbound, Wayland had only one thing on his mind – matters were becoming desperate – but on his return it was different. Feeling much relieved, he could take his time.

"What's your dog called, young man?

"Benjy, sir. He's Jimmy's, not mine." Mikey was shy and spoke to his feet, then, looking up, "But we're all friends."

"And what's your name?"

"Mikey, sir." He was back to addressing his feet.

"Very good, Mikey." Conversation was exhausted. "Carry on."

Back in the kitchen, the one-time ensign in an India cavalry regiment, and latterly holder of a number of more senior positions, enquired after the antecedents of a destitute orphan, born out of wedlock.

"Mrs Spray, who's the boy Mikey out there in the yard?"

End Piece

"I'M HOME!" SAM HAD MUCH TO TELL AFTER THIS, HIS FIRST day back at work. "Would you believe it, the Whale's for London and in charge of everything, I'm to be inspector..." he'd taken off his coat and was following Lizzie to the kitchen, "and William's to be sergeant."

After their initial kiss he'd been talking to the back of her head. Now she turned, but even then he missed the gleam in her eye.

"And I'm to be in charge at Crewe."

Her arms were round his neck. "Sam, I have news too." She was laughing and serious at the same time. "I'm with child... we're going to have a baby of our own."

GLOSSARY

Away: In prison.

Bobby: Signalman.

Cab ride: Much-prized trip in the cab of a locomotive by a non-footplate individual.

Cast: As of a sheep: lying on its back, unable to right itself.

Cess: Part of the track bed outside the two rails of a rail line.

Clough: Ravine or narrow valley.

Common p.: Abbreviation; common prostitute.

Congreve: Match with head containing white phosphorus and necessitating airtight storage.

Clinker: Impurities in coal that collect in the bottom of an engine's firebox, requiring regular removal to permit the free flow of air.

CRC:	Chief of the Railway Constabulary (Montague Archbold).
Diagram:	Plan of movement for rail stock.
Da:	Daddy.
Dd:	Abbreviation; discharge dead.
District school:	For the education of children in the care of the workhouse.
Dolly:	Signal set close to the ground for controlling shunting movements.
Fenian (brotherhood):	Violent Irish republican movement
Ground frame:	Mechanism for operating points from ground level.
GPI:	General paralysis of the insane; a late complication of syphilis.
Gassing up:	Replenishing the gas reservoir of a coach.
Gralloch:	To disembowel a shot deer.
Growler:	Horse-drawn, four-wheeled, closed cab for hire.
Gruel:	Mixture of oatmeal and water.
Harping on:	Talking mindlessly.
In irons:	Of a sailing ship; immobilised head to wind whilst failing to tack successfully.
Issue:	Children or other linear descendants
Jack:	A policeman, usually of the detective sort.
Jakes:	Urinal
Jannock:	Genuine.
Jimmy riddle:	To pass urine.

Lady's disease:	Syphilis.
Lengthman:	Man responsible for the maintenance of a specific length of rail track (also used of canal workers).
Lag:	Former prisoner.
Lorgnette:	Pair of eyeglasses with a handle.
Mash:	A brew of tea.
Middling:	Not very well.
Midland:	The Midland Railway, rival of the LNWR.
MPD:	Motive power department, responsible for the maintenance and provision of locomotives.
Purchase:	Of army commissions; prevalent in fashionable regiments until it was abolished in 1871.
Paup.:	Abbreviation; pauper.
Points:	Devices that direct rail traffic from one track onto another.
Rake:	Of coaches; group coupled together.
Reform school:	Set up on a national basis as a place of correction for wrongdoers below the age of criminal responsibility.
Road:	Route.
Rootle:	To search in the undergrowth (as would a pig).
Sawbones:	Medical man.
Sen:	Self.

Six foot: The space between two sets of rail track.

Spike: Slang for workhouse.

Terrier crop: Short, bristly haircut, as imposed on prisoners.

Traffic: Department responsible for transport operations.

Up (and down): In railway parlance, toward and away from London.

Valentine's Gallop: A piece scored for brass band and published in *Distin's Brass Band Journal*.

Wagoner: Man in charge of a train of wagons on the Peak Forest Tramway.

Wicket (gate): Small gate for pedestrian access, set in a larger one.

Yer sen: Yourself.

Yow: Vernacular for a female sheep.